CLEAVED

BY

Sue Coletta

Tirgearr Publishing

Published by Tirgearr Publishing
Ireland
www.tirgearrpublishing.com

ISBN 978-1-910234-28-0

A CIP catalogue record for this book is
available from the British Library.

10 9 8 7 6 5 4 3 2 1

DEDICATION

To my husband and best friend, Bob; without your love and support none of this would be possible. You're my everything.

To Bobby, Kathy, Dad, Berlyn, Scarlet, and the new baby who'll be joining us soon…love you to the moon, 'round the world, and back again.

ACKNOWLEDGMENTS

A special thank you to all the men and women in law enforcement, especially those who helped with my research. First, to my detective friends who mean the world to me: my Partner in Crime Kimberly McGath aka "Scoobs", Garry Rodgers, and Joe Broadmeadow. Thank you for always being there. Love you guys. A nod toward Adam, too, who also goes out of his way to help. Thanks, buddy.

Next, to Lt. Crystal McLain from NH State Police/NH Marine Patrol for taking time out of your busy schedule to help Sheriff Niko Quintano work with Marine Patrol, so my story would ring true; Kristin Harmon from NH Fish & Game for all the information on waterways in the state; Cheryl Hutchinson, Communications Supervisor II for NH Marine Patrol/NH State Police for the information on interagency cooperation; the Grafton County Medical Examiner for taking the time to chat with me about the floating patterns of a corpse in fresh water vs. salt water; and Alexandria Taxidermy for the plethora of information about deer antlers. You all went out of your way, and I'm so grateful. I spoke with other members of NH Fish & Game, too. You know who you are…thank you for dealing with a crazy crime writer who forgot to mention the deceased was, in fact, fictional when calling in a report of a body in the marsh. That situation could've gone a total different way!

A quick shout-out to my faithful readers, blog followers, and the writing community. You're so special to me. And to God, for blessing my life in unimaginable ways.

Prologue

March 24, 2008

Bloodied and battered, suspended between this world and hell, I could barely catch my breath. Cool air struck my face and my eyelids fluttered open. Pure blackness enveloped my body, stuffed inside a steel drum. Metal scraped my bare back. Sharp pain shot to my knees, ankles, and neck, bent at such an angle moving was not an option. No longer did I control my breathing, my chest heaving much faster than I could regulate. Within this sinister trap, the oxygen thinned with every *patter, patter, patter* of my heart.

Animals shrieked outside the barrel. A throaty rattle shuffled in the trees. Croaks and crickets. A far off screech owl's predatory cry increased the blood coursing through my veins.

Where am I?

A throb pulsed at my forehead. I reached to assess the damage, but pulled back. Part of me didn't dare. With a deep inhale—not too deep or I'd deplete what little oxygen I had left—I allowed my fingertips to brush my eyebrow, now flopped over one eye. The bridge of my nose seemed off-kilter, shoved over to the right. Tiny bits of bone swam under my cheekbone and my lips swelled to the size of the wax candy Chloe and I played with as children.

With an open hand, I banged the metal wall. A *clang* from my wedding band echoed in return. "Help." My voice coiled against the steel. Water lapped against my unforgiving grave—rocking, swaying me from side to side. "Help," I called out, louder this time, tears flooding my throat. I couldn't die like this, trapped, no one to discover my remains. If I couldn't escape, I'd never see my

1

family again. Our thirteen-month-old son hadn't matured enough to understand death. He'd grow up without a mother, without a crucial piece of his life. Niko would starve. During our nineteen-year marriage, all he ever made were reservations.

Above all else, I must survive. If not for me, then for my family.

Tears warmed my frigid cheeks. Colt and Ruger would never understand why I didn't come home. Who'd walk them? Who'd keep their coats silky smooth? Did my family know—inherently grasp, deep in their soul—how much I loved them? They're my whole world, my everything. Their unconditional devotion enhanced the very breath I breathed.

Had I prepared them for the day I stopped walking through the door? No. I'd taken my life for granted, maybe theirs too. How many "I love you's" did it take to last a lifetime?

Dear God, don't let me die this way.

With my last unbroken fingernail, I picked at the curved metal walls, clawed at the lid, and scratched the bottom of the steel drum that trapped me from my life, death, or whatever cruel cosmic joke. Nothing worked.

How did I get here? The memory blurred.

A woman's whispering shriek sliced the crisp evening air. "Help me!"

Hope soared like an unexpected burst of energy on a never-ending hike. "Hello? Can you hear me?"

She pleaded with me to free her.

"You're trapped too? Do you know where we are? Who did this to us?" I fired off questions faster than bullets left a fully automatic pistol.

She said, "The man."

Water trickled on my bare shoulder, and my gaze shot to the right. A streak of moonlight lasered through a tiny crack, metal shavings shimmying onto my bent knees. Little by little, inch by inch, I peeled back the layers while my chest constricted like a boa firmed his grasp.

"Are you still there?"

"Yes." *Where else would I be?*

"I'm Lisa."

"Sage, Sage Quintano."

"The author?"

"Yes, but we need to conserve oxygen." As much as I adored my fans, talking about my books was the last thing we should do. "Can you find a way out?"

Think, Sage, think. If an average oil drum held fifty-five gallons, then I had about seven-point-three-five cubic feet of air, but with each expelled breath I traded one molecule of oxygen for one of carbon dioxide. I didn't have long before the confined space won this battle. If only I could widen the crack. Or maybe, if I wedged my fingers under the lid, I might be able to pop it loose. That is, if the metal bung wasn't secured.

With the back of my head and flat hands against the cold steel, I thrust against the lid, and it moved. Not much, but enough to define my chances of survival. Fortunately, whoever trapped me forgot to lock the clasp. Perhaps he intended for me to escape. Did he lurk outside, ready to ambush me?

"Sage?"

"Yes?"

"I wanna go home," she cried, her words laced with panic. "I'm so scared."

"I know. Me too."

"The man said he'd be back."

"Man?" For a moment, I stopped fighting to free myself. "Did you see his face?"

"Not really. He wore some sort of mask. I only caught a quick peek before he blindfolded me."

"Did you say mask?"

"Yeah. Why?"

"Oh. My. God. Where's Noah?"

"Who's Noah?"

Had I taken him with me? "The last thing I remember, I was loading groceries into my SUV. The rest is fuzzy." Oxygen-deprivation disoriented me. Tingles numbed my legs and feet, with the exception of pain—sharp, intense, a stabbing sensation burrowed bone-deep.

"Who's Noah? Aren't you married to the sheriff?"

"Noah's our son." The air grew thick. No matter how hard I tried, I could not catch my breath. Did Niko have Noah?

"I need to get out of here." I coughed, choked, my lungs betraying me faster than I anticipated. "Tell me everything you remember."

A sob broke from somewhere deep inside her. "When he comes back, he'll kill us. That's what he told me."

"Okay, shhh… I've got an idea." With my face smashed against the lid, I squared my bare feet and tried to straighten. Grunting, I threw my weight behind the force.

The lid moved about a quarter inch.

I tried again.

It still refused to budge.

One last time I thrust my bare feet into the steel bottom and straightened, my body releasing an animalistic cry. The lid popped loose and splashed into the water. I wiggled out the barrel, into an icy marsh, a film of green riding the ripples.

"Are you free?" asked Lisa.

Pressure still weighted my lungs as I gulped the arctic air. "Yes, but…" Five other oil drums floated in the water, each at different depths, some almost submerged. "Ah…did the man mention anyone else?"

"What? Why?"

"Umm…no reason. Bang on the side of the barrel so I can find you."

"Find me? I'm inside of it. Hurry. He'll be back soon."

A silhouette streaked across the tree line, and I ducked. Neck-deep in the chilled water, I paddled toward the first drum, hushed, "Lisa?"

No answer.

Gaze volleying back and forth, I scanned the darkened forest. Twigs cracked under someone's feet; thick brush obscured my view. Hidden behind barrel number two, I whispered, "Lisa, if you're in

4

there, don't speak. Someone's here."

All movement stopped in the forest. Silence overshadowed the area, except for wood frogs chirping back and forth as if discussing the danger nearby. The full moon, big and bright, acted as a beacon to our exact location.

Was my abductor trying to lure me into a false sense of security?

Chapter One

Sheriff Niko Quintano raced through the country backroads on the way to the site of the latest murder. Two canoers had found the body of a female at Quincy Bog in Rumney, New Hampshire, a location desolate enough not to arouse suspicion. Hundred-foot-tall white pines edged the water, creating the perfect cover for sinister deeds.

Some days in late March, the scenery demanded Niko's full attention. Early morning hues of scarlet and lavender brushed the dawn sky like an organic Norman Rockwell painting. The only downfall was the unpredictable weather. One day it could be sixty-five degrees with a scorching sun. And the next, two feet of snow could fall. In New England, Jack Frost had quite the sense of humor. Especially in the Lakes Region of New Hampshire, where the hills and valleys of Alexandria mimicked the weather in the White Mountains. In fact, the first year he and Sage lived here, they'd fired up the woodstove in June, as crazy as it sounds.

In the passenger seat, Deputy Frankie Campanelli had a death grip on the dash, her chestnut hair wafting with the breeze from the open window. "Slow down. I'd rather not die on the way to a homicide."

Niko eased off the gas. "Sorry. I'm aggravated. Ever since the first murder, even though it was outside our jurisdiction, Sage's been a wreck. She's talking crazy, convinced she's the one this killer's after. And no matter how hard I try to convince her otherwise, she won't believe me."

"Can you blame her? Not for nothin', Niko, after what happened to her sister, I'd probably be paranoid, too."

"Still, she's been married to a cop for nearly twenty years. You'd think she'd be used to it by now." Niko banged a right down a dirt trail that led through a wooded lot. About a mile in, the road ended. He slid the shifter into park. "C'mon. We're here."

"We are?" Frankie twisted to peer out the back windshield. "Where's the crime scene?"

Niko pointed into the forest. "Up there. We need to hoof it the rest of the way." His gaze ran down Frankie's denim-clad legs to her five-inch heels. "Maybe one of these days you'll listen to me and dress accordingly."

Shoving open the door, she muttered, "If I ruin these boots, you're springin' for a new pair." She slammed the door.

Lord, give me strength.

Halfway down the dirt trail, and still no crime scene tape. "Why isn't this path cordoned off?" He didn't expect a response. Good thing too, because Frankie just shrugged. Classic. Unless something directly affected her or she was responsible in some way, she showed no reaction. Hence, part of the reason why she remained a deputy while more eager officers scored promotions.

When Niko and Frankie reached the crime scene, confusion rocked his senses. A tiny bog, surrounded by tall pines and wiry brush, held one lone oil drum on its shore. Deputy Ben Mathews was tagging evidence, his uniform pressed to perfection, his shoes polished to a glossy shine.

Niko approached, and Ben snapped to attention. With his military background, his posture and close-cropped hair aligned with an active serviceman. "Where's the body?"

"In the barrel, sir."

Before Niko had a chance to turn around, Frankie remarked, "That sick, twisted sonofabitch. Come look at this."

Inside the steel drum a woman's corpse lay fetal-style, the top half of her nude body spilling onto the sand, her left hand severed at the wrist. Blood coated her fair skin in crimson. Long, blonde hair with blood-soaked strands matted to the sides of her face.

Blowflies gorged on her protruding eyeballs, consumed the inside of her gaping mouth and both nostrils. Maggots packed every orifice. The stench of rotting flesh clawed through Niko's sinuses. No matter how many years he investigated the dead—thirty at Boston PD; five as Sheriff of Grafton County—the rankness of death brought back every unsolved case.

He hooked an arm at Ben. "C'mon. You're with me. While we wait for Gaines, this gives us the perfect opportunity to learn about entomology."

As usual, Frankie couldn't control the urge to zing a comment Ben's way. "Go ahead, Benny boy. Have fun playing with maggots."

Gagging, Ben neared the decomposing corpse, and Frankie snickered. "Watch out, Niko. He may blow."

"All right, that's enough." Niko tossed her a pointed glare. "Don't you have evidence to collect?"

Ben shuffled his feet backward. "Uh, I'm cool with collecting evidence. Why don't you do this part with Frankie?"

"Ben," he warned. "If you can't get used to being around corpses, why am I wasting my time?" Even though Frankie was his right-hand, Niko could never groom her for sheriff. With her gruff exterior and obvious allergy to authority she'd last about two days before telling the judge, mayor, or anyone else in the power chair, where to stick it. "Closer." He rolled his finger. "They're more interested in the vic than they are in you."

A hand cupping his mouth and nose, Ben inched toward the drum like Niko had ordered him to line up for the firing squad. "Oh, my God. He took her hand."

"Excellent observation skills, Deputy Mathews. You just noticed that now?"

"Well, I...uh...only saw her for a second earlier."

"Uh-ha." Not surprising that Ben didn't examine the corpse. He and Niko had travelled down this particular road before. Nonetheless, if he even had a shot of retiring one day, he needed to prepare Ben no matter how uncomfortable it made him.

Niko pointed to the congregation of maggots in the victim's mouth. "Entomology is a fascinating field. As a death investigator, you should at least know the basics. Ready to begin?"

Ben mumbled, "No" but Niko ignored it.

"Blowflies, which these are, flock to a corpse left in the open. Even indoor crime scenes are loaded with them, but it takes the flies roughly three days to find their way inside. By examining the victim, tell me which part of the body attracts the most flies."

Ben barely glanced at the corpse. "Umm, the eyes?"

"Yes and no. Blowflies attack any and all open wounds. That includes any entry into the body, like the eyes, mouth, nose, etcetera. You with me so far?"

Ben nodded in agreement.

"The flies lay eggs right away, and they hatch anywhere from almost immediately up to thirty-six hours, depending on the weather. Warmer temps, like we've been having lately, increase the life cycle speed." His gaze ran up and down Ben's body, and he paused. "Why aren't you writing this down?"

"Oops." He offered Niko an awkward grin. "Sorry, boss." Ben withdrew his notepad from his chest pocket, flipped to a fresh page, and dabbed the tip of his pen on his tongue. "Immediately to thirty-six hours. Got it."

Bent over the body, Niko focused on the victim's face. What was left of it, anyway. "Larvae, aka maggots, stay active from five to ten days. See them wiggling? It's almost as if the vic's moving her tongue." When he glanced over his shoulder, the coloring in his deputy's face washed away like shoeprints in melting snow.

"Don't fall apart on me." Niko rooted around in his jacket pocket, withdrew Vick's Vapor Rub* and passed it to him. "Here. Pack your nostrils with this. It'll weaken the smell."

Deputy Preston Bradley hung on the outskirts of the scene, the farthest point from the victim, cordoning off the area. Even though Bradley had been on the force for a few years now, he was still very green. Violent crime rarely occurred in and around Alexandria, New Hampshire and when it did, Bradley didn't have the stomach for it. For that matter, neither did Ben.

Two years ago, Frankie took it upon herself to mentor Bradley. Because Ben shadowed Niko, it gave her someone to boss around.

With a long whistle, she got her protégé's attention, then waved him closer. "That looks good. C'mon back."

As he neared, cupped hands flew to his mouth, his head shaking ever so slightly, cheeks puffed like a squirrel with a mouthful of nuts. Within a minute, two max, he spun on heels and bolted toward the exit.

Niko couldn't resist. "He looks good, Frankie. You've done well with him."

"Ha, ha." Her lips twisted into a sarcastic smirk. "At least his face doesn't match the swamp water, unlike someone else we know." She coughed Ben's name.

"Hey." Shoulders pinned back, Ben stuck out his chest.

Niko patted his arm, not unlike the way he'd pet a stray dog. "Don't let her rattle you. Let's get back to it." He squatted to examine the victim's injuries more closely. "Where was I?"

Ben checked his notes. "The eggs hatch up to thirty-six hours."

"Very good."

Niko enjoyed teaching. When the day came for him to hang up his badge, he'd dreamed of teaching classes at the academy. Sage was the only obstacle. She wanted him home with her and Noah, their thirteen-month-old toddler who completed their near-perfect life. Perfect until recently, that is.

Clearing his throat, he refocused on the vic. "Larvae stay active from five to ten days, then transform into pupa. When this happens, they leave behind casings aka pupa shells."

Eyes in a squint, Ben scratched his cheek, repeated, "Pupa shells?"

"Similar to cocoons."

Nodding deeply like a student prepping for a big exam, he jotted the information in his notepad.

"Oh." Niko waited for Ben to look up. "I should point out that before the pupa stage, the maggots crawl away from the body, which is where you'll find the largest ones. The pupa stage lasts about a week before the blowfly emerges from its cocoon. The new blowfly will then lay eggs, and the cycle repeats. Any questions?"

"Nope." Clearly thrilled that the lesson was over, Ben slammed his notepad closed and slid his pen into its spiral binder. "I think I've got it." He turned halfway, and Niko grabbed his arm.

"We're not done here." With a sweep of his hand toward the corpse, he gestured for Ben to squat beside him. "Take a good, hard look at her face this time."

To say Ben had a difficult time would be an understatement. Eyes slitted as if trying to filter the gruesomeness, he did as instructed, his face scrunched like an adolescent forced to eat cauliflower.

For now, Niko ignored it. "Knowing the length of each cycle, tell me this. Roughly how long has this victim been dead? Gimme your best guess. Gaines will need to determine TOD, but I want you to get a feel for how to estimate."

Unlike major cities where crime ran rampant, his team needed to be familiar with all aspects of investigation. Entomologists weren't readily available around here. The area offered breathtaking views and friendly townsfolk, but gaining access to experts wasn't an easy task.

Panic registered on Ben's face, eyes wide, his body board-stiff like he'd been tasered, causing a massive shock to the system. "I dunno. I'm not even sure where the flies begin and the maggots end." He gagged. "I really think Frankie should do this. She's way better at this stuff."

"That's why I'm takin' this time with you. Relax. I've given you all the tools you need."

Ben leaned in and studied every inch, checked his notes, then re-examined the victim, his gaze ping-ponging between the two for what felt like twenty years. Finally, he straightened. A befuddled expression crossed his face, but he took a shot anyway. "A week?"

"That a question?"

"One week," he said, his words steeped in conviction.

"And you're basing that on…?"

"The pupa shells. Sorry. Casings."

Not even remotely close to the right answer. With a heavy sigh, he resisted shaking his head in disappointment. "On the low scale, let's say the blowflies laid eggs immediately. And let's even assume the maggots were active for only five days because the warm stretch tends to speed up the process. Are you telling me the pupa shed its casings in two days?"

"Yeah. No. Wait. Umm…" Ben flipped back a few pages in his notes.

Hovering nearby, Frankie butted in. "Hey, golden boy, five plus two is seven, so how could it only be one week?"

His shoulders dropped in defeat. "See? I told you she's better at this stuff."

Niko laid a supportive hand on his shoulder. "Look closely. See those shell-like structures? Those are the pupa casings. But there's still plenty of maggots. That tells us the cycle continued, right? Otherwise, there'd be no maggots."

Ben agreed.

"Okay. But we also see only one set of pupa casings, which indicates one full cycle. In other words, they're not scattered everywhere. Still with me?"

His gaze clouded over like he was someplace else. "I think so."

"So if one full cycle occurred, and the new blowflies laid eggs, which already hatched into maggots, yet haven't transformed into pupa, how many days have passed?" Nothing, not even a spark of acknowledgment from Ben. "A safe assumption would be around twelve to fourteen days, give or take. Make sense?"

Neck turtled in his shoulders, Ben shook his head in a circular motion, neither confirming nor denying.

Frankie burst out laughing. "He looks good, Niko. You've done well with him."

"Thank you, Deputy Campanelli. That's enough." A puff of Aramis struck him in the face. Without turning around, he remarked, "We'll get back to this later. Gaines is here."

As Niko's gaze roamed the wooded lot, he couldn't help but notice the serenity. A brutal killer dumped his victim in this desolate swamp, surrounded by the sultry songs of nature. Birds whistled serenades, trees soughed, their limbs gently swaying in the morning breeze, the sun cascading through the leaves, spreading warmth and glow over this wondrous land. And yet, a serial killer stalked the streets. He preyed on the most vulnerable, the unsuspecting, the trusting, and the innocent.

In a brief moment of clarity, Niko understood Sage's fears. What if she'd crossed this killer's path?

Chapter Two

March 22, 2008, Friday, 1:15 p.m.

"It was then that the voice uttered the words that haunted me. 'Do you want to live forever?'" As if on cue, the audience in the Minot-Sleeper Library all gasped at once. "Thank you for having me today. If you'd like a signed copy of *Scarred*, I'd be happy to personalize it for you."

A crowd formed a single line in front of my table. No matter how many book signings I attended, nerves fluttered my belly as though I was standing naked for all to judge. I'd poured my very being into *Scarred*. Beside the personal connection and the tragedy that followed, I'd labored over every word to strike the right chord at the perfect moment to elicit the strongest reaction in my reader. Whether folks realized it or not, authors bared their souls in their books. Nothing quite compared to the intimacy shared between writers and readers, however subconscious it may be.

"Hi, name please?" I asked a woman about sixty whose twinkling eyes and bright smile warmed my heart.

"I loved *Hurt* so much, and I can hardly wait to read *Scarred*. You're my favorite author." She palmed her cheek. "I can't believe I'm meeting you in person."

Warmth swept up my face. "Thank you." No matter how many times someone complimented my writing, I never quite got used to the gushing. In private, I wrote for hours on end, struggled for years to get published, so when my mysteries finally hit the shelves, I wasn't prepared for what awaited me. Still wasn't after years of writing story after story.

Pen at the ready on the inside of the first page, I offered my standard warm smile while the middle-aged woman rambled on and on about *Hurt*, a true story I'd rather forget. When she finally took a breath, I asked for her name.

"Kathryn Fontaine." With one hand shielding her mouth, she tittered. "The way you read that chapter gave me goose bumps everywhere. Will there be an audio version? If so, you should narrate it." She yanked up her sleeve. "Look. I'm getting them right now just thinking about it."

"That's so nice of you to say." Over the years, I'd been blessed with such an amazing and loyal audience.

"I'm your biggest fan. I tell all the ladies in my book club how wonderful you are."

"Thank you." A flush crossed my cheekbones. "You have no idea how much that means to me." I scrawled my signature and a quick note.

To Kathryn, my biggest fan.
Love your enthusiasm and support.
xo,
Sage Quintano

When I passed her the novel, she read what I wrote, and a wide grin brightened her ruddy cheeks. "I'll never forget this day." Clutching my novel to her chest, she shuffled away and a brawny man with a knit hat pulled low to his soulless eyes and straggly beard, stepped into her spot.

I chanced a peek at Noah in his stroller, sound asleep by my side. "Hi, name please?"

"John."

As I personalized the page, I asked, "Just John, or would you like me to include a last name?"

"Doe."

The room whirled, and my pen slid across the page. I fumbled to grab another book from the pile and scrawled a quick signature. When I handed him the novel his thumb caressed my finger—slow, intentional, deliberate—as if to make his presence known.

I yanked my hand away, but his murderous glare lasered right through me.

Swallowing hard, I scanned the library for Niko, but couldn't find him anywhere. "Did you say Doe? As in, John Doe?"

"Dunn. Two Ns."

A tightness fisted in my chest when I passed him the autographed paperback of *Scarred*. "Well, have a great day, John Dunn."

He didn't leave. "Cute kid."

I waved over the next person in line.

John leaned over the table, his fingertips balanced on my books. "I said, cute kid."

Gulp. "Thank you?"

With a grunt of approval, he strode away. Even though every bone in my body screamed for me to run, I couldn't disappoint everyone else in line. They'd taken time out of their busy schedule to come meet me—a gesture I still could barely wrap my head around. Townsfolk in our sleepy community treated local authors like celebrities.

Ice crackled against the thermal sides of my travel mug, filled with water and lemon wedges, when I set my dry lips on the rim and chugged half in the hopes of settling my stomach. Frosty tingles trickled down my esophagus, then churned with the acids in my gut. My confident front ebbed more and more the longer I stayed, signing book after book, hungering for the moment I could escape into the SUV.

An introvert by nature, crowds and public speaking jittered my nerves on a good day. After meeting such a bizarre and suspicious individual, this event propelled my darkest fears to the forefront of my mind. Authors did not have the option of staying home year-round. Those who chose not to mingle with fans, limited their audience. A catch-22 on steroids under the best circumstances. Today, it compared more to diving off the Brooklyn Bridge and hoping to land in the kiddy pool below.

When the line at my table whittled a bit I peeked around a twenty-something-year-old girl. Hands stuffed in his jacket pockets, John leaned against the wall at the far end of the library, a cold stare in my direction.

Niko said, "Babe?"

I flinched.

"Everything all right?"

"Hi there." Offering an elderly woman a warm smile, I dragged another book from the pile, the pen juddering in my hand. "Name please?"

"Grace Howard."

Niko set his hand on my shoulder, and I startled. "Could you give us a sec, Grace? I need to steal my wife." He bundled Noah in his arms and jabbed his head toward the corner. I followed.

"What happened? You look like you've seen a ghost."

Scorching heat jagged up my chest. "Where were you? I thought you went to the restroom, but you've been gone twenty minutes."

"Frankie called."

"And?"

"And I told her to start without me."

"Start what?"

"Maybe we should discuss this on the way home."

An old, thick scar tugged at my skin as the chords in my neck protruded. "There's been another murder, hasn't there?"

His gaze sidled. My husband couldn't lie his way out of jury duty while wearing his sheriff's uniform. "Your fans are getting restless."

Head librarian Judy Cohen marched over, arms scissoring by her side, a scowl in my direction. "Your fans came to speak with you. Please do not keep them waiting."

"Sorry, Judy. I'll be right there." For most, that comment would signal them to leave. Not Judy. She never took a hint.

By the arm, I dragged Niko a few feet away. "This conversation isn't over." I caressed Noah's head in the palm of my hand, leaned in, and pressed my lips to his silky-soft cheek, murmured, "Mommy's almost done." I straightened, and thinned my eyes. "Look, I have to get back, but I will expect the full story on the way home, rather than your edited version."

Niko agreed faster than he should. Beneath his pinched smile lay a secret, something he was all too keen not to share, but with Judy sneering on the sidelines I didn't have time to press him for details.

Back at my table, I personalized Grace's novel. "Thanks for coming." Peering around her full figure, I searched for John Dunn.

Did he leave? Or was he waiting outside to ambush me?

For over an hour, I greeted each patron and pretended to be upbeat while a torrential downpour of dread washed over me.

Once my family settled inside the Land Rover, I swiveled toward Niko. "Are you ready to tell me the whole truth?"

"You drew quite the crowd today. If I haven't told you lately, I'm so proud of you."

Classic Niko. Avoid the question with a compliment. Folding my arms on my chest, I faced front. "Some things never change."

"That's not fair."

I shrugged one shoulder. "If the shoe fits."

"Fine." He exhaled as though I was prying into his personal business.

Maybe I was, but I could not risk him keeping me in the dark. No way would I put my child or myself in jeopardy because my husband believed I couldn't handle the truth about the recent murder spree, rocking our quaint, rural town.

"It's nothing you haven't heard before." As usual, he minimalized the news. "A young couple found a body in the woods."

"In Alexandria?"

"Babe, we've been over this. Murder happens everywhere, even places as beautiful as this."

So he wouldn't evade my question a second time, I firmed my tone. "Did they find the body in Alexandria?"

"Yes, but—"

"Oh. My. God. It's happening again. That's why you don't want to tell me."

He patted my knee. "Don't read too much into it. Like I said, crime happens everywhere. After all these years, you should know that."

I craned my neck around the seat. Noah's tiny tongue darted through wet, puckered lips. "Are you willing to bet your son's life on whether this has anything to do with what happened before?"

"Babe—"

"Don't babe me. Answer the question."

Hands wringing the steering wheel, he lifted his shoulders. "How can I answer that? I haven't even seen the crime scene yet."

"My point exactly." The way that man touched my hand sent a spine-tingling chill through my bones. This was not the time to doubt my intuition, which hollered that John Dunn was involved in the tragedy two years ago, as well as the recent murder spree.

Only one question lingered. When would he make his move?

Chapter Three

After Niko dropped his family at home and tried to calm his wife's fears, he jumped into his Ford Interceptor SUV, hit the lights, and sped down the country backroads toward Mulberry Lane. Overnight, an unexpected snowstorm hit the area, dropping two feet of snow, coating the world in sparkly white. The tires hit frost heaves in the asphalt, and he jounced in his seat. Regardless of how long he lived here, he'd never get used to the hills and valleys in Alexandria. Half the town flat, the other half compared to driving up Mt. Washington.

Outside her house, Frankie Campanelli waved him over to the curb.

When he coasted to a stop, she hopped in the passenger seat and blew into cupped hands. "Man, it's colder than a witch's tit out there. Keep going straight about a half-mile till you see my sled."

"You memorialized the crime scene, right?"

Similar to a charging bull, she exhaled through her nostrils. "Does Moby Dick have a wet—?"

"All right." He flashed a flat hand. "I get it."

"What? I was gonna say belly."

"Uh-ha. Run the case for me."

Frankie flipped open her notepad. "Nude woman about forty braced to a tree by buck antlers."

"Buck antlers? Through her body?"

"Yeah. I can't describe it. We're here, anyway." She gestured toward the right side of the road, where her jet-black Arctic Cat gleamed in the afternoon sun.

20

Niko killed the engine, and then swiped the leather bag, stuffed with camera equipment, off the backseat. By the time he approached the snowmobile, Frankie was already on the seat, scooting forward. "Hop on. I'll give ya a lift."

"I'll drive."

Her head bobbed like a turkey at Thanksgiving. "The hell you will. I just got this puppy."

"The Sheriff of Grafton County doesn't ride bitch."

She smirked a cat's grin. "He does if he wants a ride."

"Seriously, scoot back."

Hand cupped around her ear, she revved the engine. "What?"

Dammit. No use arguing with her. She never listened to a word he said anyway. Niko swung his leg over the seat. His hands hovered over her slim hips, a flush assaulting his cheeks. Without warning, Frankie gunned the gas. To keep from sliding off the back, he hooked his fingers in her belt loops.

Why didn't he take the four-wheeler?

They barreled through the snow-lined trails to a clearing the size of a double-wide casket. Frankie's fur-lined heeled boots crunched the snow as they plodded to the corpse. Buck antlers impaled the woman's bare chest and stomach, braced her halfway up the side of the thick birch tree. Blood had leaked from the wounds—frozen—snaking red lines down both legs, scarlet drips off the toes. A bluish fog blurred the victim's eyes, splayed open as though she'd seen the final blow coming and with it an unimaginable death at the hands of a psycho with a cinematic fondness.

Similar to the victim found at Quincy Bog—later ID'd as Amy St. John, thirty-seven-year-old high school English teacher and part-time camp counselor—this woman also had a missing left hand.

Did the change in weather force the killer to change his MO?

Beneath the body the snow slurped the blood like a leech, reddening the crystals, with two opposing angles etched in the ice. The birch tree's paper-thin bark crimsoned, the antler tips jammed through the body to the animal's bare skull.

"Someone's been reading too much King," said Frankie. "It takes a seriously twisted individual to do this to another human being."

Eyes widening as he approached the body, Niko's jaw slacked. "It also takes a great deal of strength." He passed Frankie a pair of black surgical gloves then finally got the joke. "Too much Stephen King." He chuckled. "I'm assuming you photographed the scene."

Frankie wiggled her cell. "Yup. Got it right here."

The cameras in cell phones were nowhere near as good as digital cameras, but it would do for now. "Video too?"

"Err…"

"Frankie," he warned.

"I know, I know. Sorry, but I needed to get Chance outta here. If we weren't out snowmobiling when the call came in, I would've never brought him to a crime scene. Can't we do it now?"

He dabbed his head to the side. "Camera's in the bag."

"Cool, but first, check around back. He left us another calling card."

"Do the antlers go straight through?"

"See for yourself."

With one eye on Frankie he chanced a peek around the birch tree. "What the hell?" He pulled back. "So we've got a woman with no clear cause of death, other than being impaled by deer antlers with her left-hand severed and a King of Hearts playing card. Perfect." Sarcasm tainted his tone. "Anything else I should know?"

Frankie's shoulders sprang to her ears. "I only got a quick peek before Chance turned white." Dr. Chance Rocco was a well-respected veterinarian, and the only man to ever pierce the outer layer of Frankie Campanelli's heart. How he dealt with her remained one of life's unsolved mysteries.

Niko scrutinized the remains. Without making eye contact, he said, "I'm assuming you didn't find the hand."

"Nope. Like before, the sick sonofabitch took it with him."

"What about Gaines, you call him?"

"No. Just you."

"Uh…Frankie? Notice anything else missing?"

"No. Why?" She followed Niko's finger to the woman's chest.

"Now might be a good time to grab the camera."

Frankie didn't budge. "Oh, you mean now? Right." She followed her own footprints, careful not to create new ones, and swiped the video camera from the bag.

Once she'd focused on the corpse, he continued. "Tell me if you're seeing the same thing I am. To me, it looks like this side of her chest has more damage than the other, like maybe he sliced her open before impaling her. By the way, he used a spike to nail her to the tree. See the head?"

Frankie zoomed in. "That looks like a log cabin spike. Y'know, what they use to hold the logs together."

"If you say so." What'd he know? Unlike rural New Hampshire, there weren't many log cabins in Boston. "Check out this area."

"Aw, shit. You don't think…"

"Yup. I bet he took the heart this time. My guess, that's why he left the card. King of Hearts. Meaning, him. Call Gaines. Now."

Frankie called the Medical Examiner's office and reported the homicide. She slid her phone into her jacket pocket. "Gaines said to give him ten minutes. He's leaving now."

"Let's get Ben here, too. And Bradley. Tell them to bring my four-wheeler. Garage is unlocked. Key's in it. We need to scour these woods for evidence. In the meantime, I'll cordon off the area. We'll finish documenting the injuries once the scene is secure."

"I'm on it."

While Frankie called the station, ordering Ben and Bradley to the scene, Niko twined crime scene tape around a thick ash tree, several yards back. He hooked a young beech tree and unfurled the tape to stretch around a wide rock maple, perpendicular to the first tree. Working his way around six trees, he created a sixty-foot-octagon around the victim, an enormous area that would take hours to search.

Ten minutes later, Dr. Gaines and Ben arrived on scene, with Bradley perched on the back of Niko's four-wheeler. Frankie waved them over.

When Gaines first spotted the victim all he said was, "Wow."

Niko stepped out of the way to allow him to exam the remains. Bradley turned an interesting shade of green, his cheeks stretched to capacity.

Frankie urged, "Go. Do it in the woods this time." At full speed, Bradley took off in the opposite direction. "Deep in the woods! Past the tape!"

Bradley plodded through two feet of snow, then fell to one knee when he ducked under the police tape.

"Yup. He's a fine deputy, indeed." Niko suppressed a chuckle. "You must be so proud. The added training really shows."

She biffed his arm. "Very funny." Her gaze traced Ben's body—back ramrod straight, flawless pressed uniform, a military stance. "We can't all have perfect little soldiers."

Gaines interrupted. "We will have to take the tree, too, Sheriff."

"That's what I figured." Niko turned to Ben. "There's a chainsaw in the four-wheeler. Go get it, please."

"Am I missing something?" asked Frankie. "How're we supposed to bring the friggin' tree? Can't we just take her down from there?"

Before Niko could answer, Gaines said, "In layman's terms, we need the tree so I can examine how she was impaled. Meaning, if we compromise the evidence by dismantling her, it could cause further damage to the remains. Then we will not know what caused the injuries, us or the perpetrator."

Chainsaw in hand, Ben jogged back from the four-wheeler. Niko didn't have much experience in this area, but he wasn't about to let down his crew. They looked to him for direction. Leaders led. Period. "Ben, you wanna support the body while I cut?" He wasn't really asking. Rather, he clung to the hope that Ben would be eager to assist with a victim. Sadly, that didn't happen.

"Me?" Ben's voice raised three octaves.

Bradley returned from the woods, wiping his mouth on his sleeve.

Ben jabbed his head toward Bradley. "What about him?"

"Be serious. He can't even look at her, never mind touch her."

Right on cue, Frankie razzed Ben. "You don't think you can handle it, Benny boy?"

Arms curled, Ben puffed his chest like a tom turkey during mating season. "Of course, I can handle it." His gloved hands hovered over the dead woman's breasts, slid down to her pubic area, then back up to her shoulders. Eyes wide, he glanced over his shoulder at Niko and then at Gaines, as if praying for direction.

"Put one hand on the buck skull and one on her forehead," said Frankie. Her gaze met Niko's. "You're doin' the top cut first, right?"

"Uh, right." Did it matter? He didn't dare ask.

"Yeah, so I'd think that's the best way, then."

Hesitantly, Ben laid his gloved hands where Frankie suggested.

Niko fired up the chainsaw. "Ready?"

As the chainsaw was about to bite into the tree Frankie shouted, "Wait!"

Niko shut down the saw.

"You need a come-along so the tree doesn't topple over. *Minga*. Am I the only one who knows anything about felling a tree?"

Niko shrugged. "Hey, don't look at me. I'm a city boy, remember? Where do we get one of these come-along thingies?"

Frankie turned to Ben. "In my garage on the back wall. Don't forget the cables, chain, and rope." Ben jogged toward the four-wheeler. "Take Bradley with you. And hurry up!" When she turned back toward Niko a smile broke across his face. "What?"

"Nice job, Deputy Campanelli."

"Yeah, yeah. Don't go all mushy on me."

Indeed, he had a fine group deputies under his command. Still, catching this elusive killer wouldn't be an easy task. The change in MO could mean a number of things. Without more to go on, the murderer had the advantage. Where he'd strike next was anyone's guess.

Chapter Four

As much as I adored my husband, he tended to downplay my fears. Granted, I might have been a bit overly paranoid lately, but not without reason. Ever since the book signing at Innisfree Books two weeks ago, I'd swear someone was following me… just out of reach, lurking in the shadows to hide his identity. The signing at the Minot-Sleeper Library only intensified my suspicions.

Over the years, I'd learned to trust my intuition. As of yet, it'd never failed me.

With Noah on my hip, I poured hot water over the tea bag in my favorite mug. Chamomile, spearmint, lemongrass, and orange blossoms steeped from the scalding heat. It was getting late, and Niko still wasn't home. I should be writing, but instead, I flipped on the TV and snuggled with Noah on the sofa.

About halfway through a Lifetime movie my eyelids grew more and more weighted, so I gave in and drifted to a celestial place, where I twirled on a tire swing in an open field of tiger lilies. Above me, the most majestic sunset drew my attention. Hot pink, violet, and an incredible sea-green swirled across the aqua sky. Serene, beautiful, the twilight tickled my skin.

I leaned way back, my hair tumbling beneath me, and pumped my legs, my fingers curled around the rope. Kick after kick, I swung higher than I'd ever been before, and I shrieked. Pure joy. It was as if I possessed the soul of a five-year-old, a blissful center where no darkness could penetrate.

A female voice said, "I've missed you so much." Then Chloe,

my twin sister, materialized in a swing next to mine, our legs pumping in unison.

Tears rose in my chest. "Is that really you, Chlo?"

"In the flesh." Smiling, her inner light shining brighter than ever, she soared even higher. So we could talk, I reached for the rope to slow her down, but she maneuvered away from my grasp. "Noah's beautiful. I watch over him while he sleeps."

The words wouldn't come. For months, I'd longed to speak with her. Now that I had the chance, I had no idea where to start. "Am I in danger? Is that why you came now, and not before?"

"Colt and Ruger are as adorable as ever. What was it that you call them?"

My legs lunged to meet hers. "My puppy loves."

"That's it."

"Or the kids."

"Right." She giggled. "The kids."

"How are you? Stupid question. I'm sorry. I don't know what to say."

"Then don't say anything. Let's just swing."

And so, we did.

"Hold on tight," she said, but by the time I worked up the nerve to ask a serious question, she jumped to the ground.

I leaped after her. "Please don't go."

She flipped her long sable locks over one shoulder. "It's time."

"But we haven't had a chance to talk yet. Nor have I thanked you for what you did for me. I'm so sorry, Chlo. If I'd known—"

"Shhh…it doesn't matter now. I never blamed you. How could I? You're my baby sister."

"By two minutes."

"Still makes me older." She razzed me the way she did in high school. "I love you, Sage. I wouldn't change a second of our lives together."

The tears bubbled over the rims of my eyes and streamed down both cheeks. "Love you to the moon, 'round the world, and back again."

As if God had waved a magic wand, Chloe disappeared. A soft

whisper rode the gentle wind, "Hold on tight, little sis."

I jolted awake. Hold on tight? The first time she said it, I figured she meant the swing, but now I wasn't so sure.

Sound asleep, Noah's tiny lips suckling so sweetly, I scooped him into my arms and tiptoed into the nursery, where I tucked him in his crib.

Odd. Ruger never missed the nightly ritual. Normally he curled into his usual spot on the carpet in front of the crib, his massive chocolate paws crossed in front of him.

"Rugey, honey, Noah's going night-night." When he didn't respond, I called for his brother. "Colt?" He didn't respond, either.

I headed for the door, but a disembodied voice crippled my stride. "Rock-a-bye baby...on the treetop."

Every muscle in my body tensed, and I whirled toward the baby monitor on the changing table.

"When the tree blows, the cradle will rock."

I glanced at Noah, then at the monitor, my gaze darting back and forth between the two.

"When the bough breaks, the cradle will fall."

I swept Noah into my arms and held him tight against my chest, protected him from the danger that loomed outside.

"And down will come baby, cradle and all." A maniacal laugh coiled through the nursery.

I padded to the window overlooking the main drag. With two fingers, I separated the blinds. Darkness cloaked the area, the waning moon barely brightening the road.

"Rock-a-bye baby, on the tree top."

Against my will, my jaw fell open. I whirled toward the monitor.

"When the wind blows, the cradle will rock."

In survival mode, I dropped to my knees, crawled with one arm, Noah in my other, to get to the cordless phone in my bedroom without being seen. For all I knew, he could be in a tree, spying on us through a telephoto lens. Or, God forbid, a rifle's scope.

"When the bough breaks, the cradle will fall."

I dialed Niko's cell phone. It rang and rang. Which wasn't unusual around here. On country backroads signals went in and out at will.

"And down will come baby, cradle and all."

Niko's voicemail picked up.

"Get home now," I whispered. "There's someone outside the house."

But where? In a car out front? Parked next door? I slapped a hand over my mouth and held back screams, refusing to upset my child. What if he's inside the house?

Slow, sideways, my back pressed to the knotty pine wall, I crept down the stairs. Niko kept a spare gun in the safe, but the safe was in the living room. I could be dead before I reached it, never mind taking the time to dial in the combination. What was the combination?

On the bottom tread, I leaned over the railing, searching for Colt and Ruger.

I couldn't find them anywhere. Did the intruder lock them outside like my attacker had that night in Boston?

"Colt," I hushed.

Silence.

"Colt." Louder this time, but still barely above a whisper.

Boots hit the ceramic kitchen tiles.

I tucked Noah even tighter to my chest and slipped inside the coat closet, huddling in the corner behind my and Niko's full-length leather jackets. My heartbeat thundered, panic thrashed at my ears, dire scenarios flitting through my mind— Niko investigating my death, my body abandoned in the woods, dumped like broken snowmobile parts.

Gazing at my precious boy, tears trickled down my cheeks. No matter what I had to endure, I would never let anything happen to him. In order to get to Noah, he'd have to kill me first. Slinking to the floor, I tried to summon the strength to face the stranger who'd invaded our home.

One eye squeezed shut, I spied through the keyhole.

Navy-clad legs stood on the other side. Startled, I fell back against the wall. When Niko was in uniform he wore tan chinos with a chocolate stripe down the seam. Noah wailed, and my heart nearly catapulted from my chest. Even though silence equaled survival, I refused to cover his mouth. He was too young to understand, and I never wanted him to fear repercussions if he cried. Instead, I rose and bounced him on my hip.

Come on, Niko. Where are you?

Chapter Five

6:30 p.m.

Frankie startled when the guys returned with the come-along. In that time, she and Niko had searched the immediate area around the tree, collected stray fibers off the body, and found a soda can in the snow, lipstick on the rim.

Once she demonstrated how to hook the cable around the birch tree and attach the come-along, she marched thirty-feet away and tossed a weighted rope over the high branch of an oak tree, then tugged to noose it in place. Lastly, she connected a cable from the oak to the other end of the come-along. "Ben, after Niko notches out the first side and starts sawing into the backside, crank the come-along till you see the tree falling, then run like hell."

His eye popped wide. "What? Why?"

"So you don't get hit, genius. This birch is a good seventy-feet tall. It could kill you." She turned her gaze to Niko. "The first cut should be at an angle. You're creating a wedge. Got it?" She didn't wait for an answer. "Doc, you may wanna stand back here with me." Boy, her country upbringing was really coming in handy today.

The chainsaw blade sawed into the bark, and the body vibrated against the tree. Cringing, Frankie prayed the woman's chest didn't rip down the middle, or Niko would have her badge. Maybe acting cocky wasn't the smartest move. Eh, whatever. It wasn't her fault they couldn't grasp basic survival techniques.

After Niko wedged one side of the tree, he sliced into the backside. Frankie signaled to Ben to crank the handle. When the birch gave way, he hauled ass, zigzagging through the trees like he was on a frickin' military combat mission. Moron.

A loud *crack* echoed through the forest. The massive birch took out two young saplings on its way down—a reverberating crash that shook the ground beneath Frankie's fur-lined boots.

Regrouping at the body, she said, "Since Benny boy is probably in Bristol by now and Bradley's as useless as tits on a bull, I'll hold the top half of the body while Dr. Gaines, you grab her legs. Niko, saw about a foot below the card. That way we don't have to bring that much of the tree. Sound like a plan, everyone?" Meaning, Niko and Gaines. Bradley's opinion was irrelevant.

The sheriff and the ME exchanged an amenable glance. Imitating Niko, Frankie clapped once. "Great. Let's do this."

After restarting the chainsaw, Niko waited until Frankie had a firm grip on the body and antlers before sawing into the tree. Gaines' glasses fell off-kilter, his nose wiggling to keep them from falling.

When the body and stump broke free, Frankie whistled for Bradley. "Little help here?"

Even though he kept his face to the side—unable to view the corpse—he managed to help her lay the victim and stump on the snow, body-side up.

The Medical Examiner asked, "How do you propose we get her back to the van?"

All eyes turned to Frankie. "What, I'm the expert now? Fine. How 'bout Ben and Bradley sit on the back of the four-wheeler with the stump over their laps?" She figured saying stump, not body, might work better to convince them.

Niko agreed. "Works for me."

Breath labored, Ben jogged out of the woods. "I found something. Come quick. You're never gonna believe this."

Frankie, Niko, and Bradley followed Ben while Gaines stayed behind with the remains. They trekked through icy streams, over rocks, through heavy brush, and around massive conifers, until they came to a clearing about a half-mile away from the crime scene.

"Ben, when I told you to run, I didn't mean a marathon.

It's gonna be dark soon. Where the hell are you taking—?" She stopped dead in her tracks. "Oh, my effin' head."

Chapter Six

7:00 p.m.

Niko could barely believe his eyes. Another nude woman had an antler rack impaling her chest, bracing her body to a silver birch tree, her feet dangling a foot above the snow. One was bad enough. Two was the makings of an uncatchable serial killer, especially if Amy St. John's murder was connected. He had a hunch it was. Or did they have two psychopaths stalking their sleepy community? Nah. The chances of two killers lobbing off the left hand must be astronomical.

Blood still leaked down the victim's bare stomach and legs, crimson fluid dripping off her feet and severed wrist, puddling in the reddened snow below. Grayish-blue lips, her skin cold to the touch. Unlike the last victim, however, she had her eyelids closed, icy tears frozen on thick, dark lashes.

"Before anyone moves," he said, "let's document the scene. This time, we're doin' it right." He glimpsed the gold watch Sage bought him for their wedding anniversary last year, signed with love from Noah and the kids. "It's seven o'clock. Bradley, make a note of it, then memorialize the scene. Don't forget to include all exit and entrance routes. Ben, you run the video. Also, when we return to the station, get me a rundown on the availability of log cabin spikes, where to buy them, how accessible they are, as well as where to find deer antlers. Without hunting the actual animal, I'm guessing they're not easily attainable. We might get lucky if the mutt left a paper trail."

"You got it, boss."

"Oh, and remember to keep the chain of evidence intact.

34

Frankie, you're with me. Is everyone clear on what they need to do?"

All three mumbled under their breath, something like, "Yeah," but no one moved.

"Let's go. Move it. And Bradley, make sure you use numbered markers to measure height, distance, and radius. Because these crime scenes are outside, it's even more imperative that we show scaled images. Understood?"

"Yes, sir."

Even though Niko had a great bunch of deputies under his command, they needed a bit of hand-holding. With the exception of a serial homicide case a couple years ago, Frankie was the only one on his team who'd dealt with the dead, and even then, she mainly handled suicides, motor vehicle accidents, and domestic squabbles that escalated to murder. No one ever promised him the sheriff's job would be easy, but some days it was all he could do not to dream about retirement.

Niko chanced a peek around the back of the birch tree. The King of Hearts—same calling card as before. "This didn't happen that long ago," he said, then kicked himself for stating the obvious.

Right on cue, Frankie remarked, "No shit, Sherlock," as she stepped closer, her emerald eyes squinting at the dead woman's chest. "Ya think she still has her heart?"

The woman gasped, and Frankie jumped backward, landing ass-first in the snow. Lips folded around his teeth, Niko stifled a laugh. When she scrambled to her feet, she rushed the woman, pressed two gloved fingers to the side of her neck. "She's got a pulse."

Though it wasn't easy, Niko resisted the urge to toss her snarky line back at her, "No shit, Sherlock." The woman took a breath. Of course, she had a pulse. Albeit, probably not for long.

"I've got this." He switched places with Frankie and pressed his middle and forefinger to her carotid artery, next to the windpipe. "Call a bus. Get Gaines over here, too." Staring at his watch, he counted the number of beats in a ten-second period. If he multiplied the beats by six, he could calculate her heart rate per minute.

The victim's pulse was fading fast.

To warm her, he wrangled out of his jacket and draped the material over the animal skull. "Can you speak?"

She let out a pained moan.

"What's your name? Do you know who did this to you?"

With the exception of her right hand opening and closing as if trying to communicate, the poor woman could barely move, the antlers entrapping the majority of her torso.

"Sorry, but I don't understand. Let's try this another way. Can you blink your eyes?"

The victim blinked.

"Blink once for yes, twice for no. Understand?"

She blinked once.

"Very good. Do you know who did this to you? What I mean is, did you know him personally, before he assaulted you?"

Her mouth opened and closed, but no words escaped. Probably in shock, and who could blame her?

At this point, words were meaningless. Nonetheless, he did his best to soothe her. "Don't worry. Help is on the way."

Dr. Gaines jogged toward the victim. "We need to warm her. Do you have a blanket in the four-wheeler, Sheriff?"

Without answering, Niko took off, sprinting toward the trail to retrieve an army blanket. He always kept one handy for Sage and Noah. On beautiful days, they took leisurely rides through the woods, drinking in the scenery, enjoying each other's company. They weren't much for off-roading, especially with their son in the vehicle. Niko left that for the younger crowd. However, time away from the hustle of daily living turned into a vigorous escape.

After all, once they moved from Boston to New Hampshire, he'd vowed to concentrate on his marriage. When Noah blessed their lives, that promise increased twofold. Until recently, he'd made it home for supper almost every night. Juggling the safety of Grafton County residents with a set schedule wasn't an easy task

Within minutes, he returned to the victim and wrapped the blanket around her shoulders and the tree, antlers and all. "Shouldn't we get her down from here, Doc?"

Gaines gestured for Niko to step out of the victim's earshot. When he followed the medical examiner far enough away, the doctor lowered his voice. "If I remove the spike, I am afraid she will exsanguinate. Right now, the spike as well as the antlers are acting as a plug for the holes in her chest. Though I suspect her lung, or lungs, have already collapsed. Which can cause pneumothorax, sepsis, ARDS—"

"ARDS? I thought that only occurs days after a lung injury?"

"Yes. That is true, but we do not know how long she has been out here. The body has self-protection mechanisms that aid in prolonging life, especially with the abrupt drop in temperature. My thinking is, her body shutdown to sustain life. If I am correct, she could only have a matter of minutes left to live."

"Well, then, we better make 'em count." Niko returned to the victim, impaled by an enormous antler rank. With any luck, she could tell him something that might help them narrow the suspect list. "Did your assailant have brown hair like mine? Blink once for yes, two for no."

She blinked once.

"What about his eyes? Were they brown like mine?" He opened his eyes wide so she could take a good look.

Two blinks.

"No? Okay. How 'bout blue?"

One blink.

"Excellent. How tall was he? Sorry. Was he taller than me? I'm about six feet."

One blink.

His adrenaline pumped harder. Unbelievable. This was actually working. "All right. Let's do weight. Was he—? Scratch that. Did he have a similar build to mine?"

Two blinks, and Niko let out a guffaw. "Maybe I should rephrase. I know he's probably not an old bastard like me, but as far as overall build goes, are we similar?"

One blink.

"Okay." Excitement building in his chest, he rubbed his palms together. "Now we're getting somewhere. Let's try age."

Scanning the woods, he called out, "Ben, front and center," then turned back to the woman and explained his choice of words. "He's a marine."

Ben hustled over.

"I need to use you for my model."

Hands clasped behind his back, Ben set his legs slightly apart, shoulders squared, chest out.

"I don't mean for *Soldier of Fortune Magazine*. Relax."

Shaking out his arms, Ben rolled the bones in his neck, and Niko resisted the urge to biff him upside the head. "Ben, here, is about—" He raised his chin to Ben. "How old are you?"

"Twenty-five, sir."

Niko furrowed his brow. "Really? That's it? My God, you're a baby." He swatted his comment away. "Anyway, Ben is twenty-five. Was your assailant roughly the same age?"

Two blinks.

"Hmm." He turned back to Ben. "Go get Bradley for me please."

Within seconds, Bradley moved in to Ben's spot.

"How old are you?"

"Twenty-nine, boss. I'll be thirty next month."

Niko's gaze traced him up and down. Facing the victim, he jabbed his head toward Bradley. "Was he about his age? Let's say, thirtyish."

The woman blinked once.

Searching for a second blink, Niko leaned in. When her eyes didn't move, he slapped his knee. "Excellent. You're doing really well. This is gr—" He caught himself. Great for him maybe, not so much for the woman braced to a tree by buck antlers, a spike drilled into her chest.

A flash of familiarity shone in her eyes. Lowering his voice, he hated to ask, "Do we know each other?"

One blink.

Niko jerked away. "We do?" While he stared into the saddest eyes he'd ever seen, he reviewed each encounter he'd had since moving to the area. He really should be questioning her, but that last blink, the blink that confirmed they knew each other, threw his mind into a tailspin.

A gut-wrenching realization hit him hard. "Do you know my wife, Sage?"

The woman gulped the air, her head rolling side to side, the fingers on her right hand curling in desperation, like she needed to tell him something important, like she used every ounce of energy she had left to give him a message.

What was it?

So much had changed since Boston, where a masked man attacked Sage in their living room. The details of which, he discovered three years too late, causing a rift in their marriage. Niko hadn't handled the news well. In fact, he acted like a total ass. Shame still kept him up nights, and he prayed Noah would grow to be a better man than he. The assailant not only torpedoed Sage's life but Niko's, too, damaged him in ways he never thought possible. He couldn't handle another psycho after his wife. Not again.

Blood chilled from the look in the woman's eyes, and his whole body stiffened. "Did the assailant mention my wife?" he asked, a hesitation to his tone.

One blink.

Heart in his throat, he held his breath. A flutter of the lids gave him hope, but uncertainty hung in the air. "Was that a second blink?"

She didn't respond.

"Did you blink once or twice? I don't understand. Please, I'll ask again. Did he mention my wife?"

The woman's gaze locked—a hollow, vacant stare that blasted right past him.

"Please. I need to know. Please, ma'am. Did he mention Sage? Did he say he's coming after her?"

Nothing. No response.

If only he could shake her, force her to reveal if his wife was in danger. But he couldn't. She'd already experienced enough horror. "I know you're scared." His voice quavered, his whole body pleading for answers.

The woman's breath grew more and more ragged.

"Stay with me." He ached for confirmation of Sage's safety. "Help is on the way. Did he mention my wife? Did he say he'd come after her?"

A few more staccato breaths and the victim fell silent, her gaze fixed on Niko's pleading eyes.

"Ma'am? Ma'am?" He pressed two fingers to her neck. "No," he shrilled, his arms curling around his head, burying the devastation on his face. Tears wet his lashes as he strode deeper into the woods.

After stumbling through the snow to find solace among a thicket of trees away from his team, he dropped to his knees, hands held in prayer. "Dear God, tell me this isn't happening. I can't bear the thought of someone harming my family. Not again. Not now." In an attempt to absorb this devastating uncertainty, he fell back on the snow-covered earth, his chinos drinking the moisture, and hugged his bent knees.

Moments later, Frankie appeared out of nowhere. "Niko, you all right? What'd she say? Did she give you a description?"

The unknown strangled his words, his Adam's apple rising and falling. "Sage. She mentioned Sage. But then, she died. And now, I have no friggin' clue if my wife's in danger." Choking back tears, he ground his jaw.

"Aw, shit." Frankie squatted beside him. "Listen. We'll find the guy. Nothing's gonna happen to her. We won't let it."

He dragged his fingers down his cheeks. "If you remember correctly, that's exactly what you said last time. Look how well that turned out."

Bradley called, "Uh, guys?"

"Dammit. What now?" Niko jumped to his feet, brushed snow off the seat of his pants. "C'mon. Let's see what happened now."

By the time Niko and Frankie reached Bradley, they found him pointing at a third victim, braced to a birch tree. A rack of antlers impaled her chest, the left hand severed at the wrist.

Niko waved his arms. "Spread out and search these woods. We need to know how many victims we're dealing with." He turned back to Gaines. "Cancel the bus, please."

"Already done."

While Niko checked the vic for signs of life, his team scattered like ants over rotted food, swarming the woods without caring where they stepped or what evidence they trampled over in the process. On his way to the trail, a tension headache pulsed above his right eye as he plodded through the snow.

In the driver's seat of the four-wheeler, he breathed in…out…in…out…tried to steady his nerves enough to radio dispatch. Between his fingertips he massaged his forehead, then cued up the mic. When Doris answered, he announced himself. "First, contact the state police to switch channels. Then connect me with Lt. McLain from State Police, Major Crimes Division, please."

"Major Crimes?" repeated Doris. "Ooh, must be serious. Right away, Sheriff."

When Lt. McLain came on the line, Niko explained the urgency for reinforcements.

"No problem," said Kimberly McLain, a brilliant investigator he'd worked with in the past. "I'll need the coordinates in order to inform my men."

"Sure." Niko clicked the compass app on his cell phone. "Four three point six six seven zero degrees north. Seven one eight seven zero four degrees west. We're on the right-side, deep in the forest. You can't miss my four-wheeler, blocking the trail."

"Copy that. Consider them en route."

"Ten-four. Thanks for the assist." Next, he re-radioed dispatch. "Send Deputy Childs to my house please, Doris. Wellness check. He reports directly to me."

"Copy that, sir."

"Under no circumstances is he to leave. In fact, send local patrol too."

"Copy that."

Niko returned the radio to his hip and flipped open his cell phone. No signal bars. Crap. He couldn't warn Sage.

With a strong whistle he called for his team. Arms crossed, he leaned against the four-wheeler, waiting for Frankie, Ben, and Bradley to slog through the snow. "Since none of you called me over, I'm assuming there are no other victims." Silently they confirmed—the shaking of three heads, eager stares looking for direction. "Okay, listen up. Because this is an outdoors crime scene—I'm collectively calling it one scene because it's clearly the killer's dumping ground—we need to do a grid search. Do any of you know what that is?"

Frankie spoke up first. "Yeah. It's when we walk shoulder-to-shoulder through the woods, searching for evidence."

Niko's eyebrows lifted in amazement. "Very good. State Police is coming to assist. Until then, let's get started." He lined everyone in a row, a few yards apart. "Because we're few in numbers, we'll conduct the search this way for now. Walk in a straight line and swish the snow with your boots. If you see something, mark it and call me over. We've got a lot of ground to cover and not much time. In about an hour it'll be dark. He smacked his hand together. "Let's get moving, people. Time's a wastin'."

While the others searched the grounds, Niko called CSU. Headquarters was a good hour away, and there was no guarantee they'd arrive anytime soon. In this part of the state, police and sheriff departments shared crime scene investigators with two other counties.

Forty-five minutes later, the tangerine sun dipped its head into the evening sky as four State Police officers and his team worked together. Hues of lilac, pink, and violet painted the vastness, spreading majestic colors past cottony white clouds. Minutes turned into hours. If they didn't find a lead soon, they'd be out here all night.

He trekked toward Frankie, elbow-deep in the snow, squatting next to a mound. "Find somethin'?"

"I think so." She tugged on denim-like material. "This sucker's buried deep."

"What is it?"

"How the hell should I know? It looks like some sorta— Aw,

shit, Niko. Smell that?"

"Don't tell me it's another vic."

"Dammit." She squared her feet on either side of the suspicious evidence, tugging, fighting to raise it to the surface. With one final pull, she fell backward. Snow piled around her thin frame.

Niko extended a hand to help her up. At the last second, he yanked his hand away. "Don't move."

"Why?" Chin tucked, she stared down the front of her Sheriff's Department jacket. "What is it? What's on me?"

Slipping his fingers into fresh latex gloves to avoid cross-contamination, he squatted beside her. The wretched package sat on her chest.

"What is it? You're freakin' me out. I'm not kidding. Tell me what it is."

Wrapped several times around the decaying lump, Niko unfurled the material. A few layers down, blood stained the denim. He hesitated. Maybe he should view this in private.

"Stop messin' around and tell me."

Ravens circled overhead. More blackbirds joined the hungry mob, squawking about dinner below.

"Oh, great. You know they're eyeing me, right?" She slapped the snow. "Dammit, Niko. Why won't you answer me? Am I'm gonna need a frickin' tetanus shot?"

Without a word, he glanced at her hands. Gloved, thankfully. He lifted the package off her chest and set it on the snow, denim-side down, where he peeled back the last layer.

Frankie blinked. Blinked again, and again. "Is that what I think it is?"

"I dunno. Whaddaya think it is?"

She biffed his arm. "Very funny. Seriously, get outta the way."

If he moved, she'd go berserk and his headache would escalate to a migraine, especially if she screamed. No, that wasn't the smart play here. Instead, he maneuvered to block her even more.

Frankie crawled closer.

Shielding the object, Niko turned his back. If only he could bag and tag this without her around. "It's nothin'. I'm just messin' with ya. Why don't you continue searching with the guys. We're runnin' outta daylight."

With a furrowed brow she held his gaze, and Niko tried his best not to blink. A full minute passed before she looked away.

"Okay," she said, but Niko didn't buy it. Frankie brushed the snow off her skin-tight jeans, her sight transfixed over his shoulder. "Before I go, do you need help bagging the evidence?"

"Nope. I've got it, thanks."

She invaded his personal space. "If it's nothing, then why aren't you processing it? I mean, if it's *really nothing*."

Frankie was no dummy. And, unfortunately, she'd been riding with him long enough to know when he was hiding something. "I will," he said, but his voice betrayed him.

"Lemme see it then. I'm serious. You can't lie to save your ass."

He deepened his voice, kept it even, firm. "Go finish the search. That's an order, Deputy."

Her hands flung to her hips. "You're ordering me? Now I really know something's up. You might as well tell me because I'm not goin' anywhere till you do."

"Dammit, Frankie. Why can't you ever just do what I ask?"

"I'm not kidding. You're pissing me off."

If she were anyone else, he'd write her up for insubordination and call it a day, but Frankie was his right hand. Not to mention his best friend, besides Sage.

Two objects bundled together inside the denim. Cupping the smaller of the two, he unfolded the top layer.

Frankie leaned in. "Is that a dead cat?"

"Yup. Looks that way."

"What's the big deal? Why wouldn't you want me to see a dead cat?"

His nails bit into his palm as he gripped the smaller object tighter. "I didn't want to upset you."

"Whaddaya got there?" She jabbed her chin toward his right hand.

"Nothin'." Dammit. His voice pitched like an adolescent girl.

"Nice try." She swiped at his hand, but he swung his arm behind his back. With a running leap, she tackled him in the snow, pinned him to the ground, and uncurled his fingers one by one. "It's a scalpel. Probably the murder weapon. I don't get it. What's the big deal?"

Niko flipped the scalpel over to show her the engraved handle. It read, *Chance Rocco, DVM.*

Stunned, her jaw slacked.

"Mind if I borrow your sled? I promised Sage I'd run an errand for her."

She tossed him the key. "You know this is a mistake, right? There's no way Chance is involved in this."

"We'll talk about it later. I need to go."

"You warning Sage about what the vic said?"

"No. Yes. I dunno."

"Then why are you leaving? Is it about the guy at the book signing?"

"No. Nothing like that."

"Hey, what about that guy? Is he the one we're looking for?"

Clever. Reposition the spotlight away from Chance. "Nah. Why would the killer attend a book signing? I've got an errand to run, and then I'm swinging by the house. I'm sure it's nothing, but I'd feel better if I checked on her and Noah. You've got this, right?" Meaning the crime scene.

"Does Raggedy Andy have cotton balls?"

"Good Lord, I hope not, but I'll take that as a yes. Make sure to bag and tag that scalpel, too." Niko jogged toward the snowmobile. Halfway there, Frankie called his name. "For shits and giggles, maybe we should run Dunn's name."

"Great idea. Lemme know what you find."

Niko swung his leg over the seat and turned the ignition key. The engine roared. With a glance back at Frankie, endless possibilities consumed his mind. Chance couldn't be the killer they're hunting. Could he?

Chapter Seven

8:30 p.m.

Nestled between the coats, a sinister voice whispered outside the closet door.

"Rock-a-bye baby on the tree top. When the wind blows, the cradle will rock. When the bough breaks, the cradle will fall. And down will come baby…cradle and all."

Footsteps quickened toward the back door. A *click* confirmed he was gone.

Why did he let us live? Why didn't he make his move? He'd have to be deaf to miss Noah's cry.

When I turned the doorknob several minutes later, paws skittered into the living room.

"Colt?" I hushed through a crack in the door. "Rugey, honey, tell Mommy it's safe to come out." Colt stuck his black, wet nose through the opening. "You sure it's safe?" Unsteady on my feet, I crept out the closet.

"Babe, I'm home." Niko strolled into the living room. "What's wrong?" He folded me and Noah into his strong chest. "My God, you're shaking. Talk to me. What happened?"

I didn't answer. I couldn't. Instead, I sobbed on his shoulder.

He pulled me away from his chest. "What's goin' on? Is Noah all right?" With the back of his fingers, he stroked our precious son's cheek. "Hey, little man. Are you not feeling well?"

"Didn't you get my message? Someone was in the house."

"I know. I sent Childs to check on you. A local patrol officer is outside too. I've asked him to hang around so you'll feel safe."

"Childs?" Ruger snuggled against my leg, and I tousled his

fur. "Good boy. Why'd you send him and not come yourself?

"Because I had to go to the vet. Don't you remember asking me to pick up the kids? Clean bill of health for both, by the way. Well, Ruger's arthritis is worsening, but we expected that."

"Was that tonight?"

"You didn't notice they weren't home all afternoon? Honestly, Sage, you really need to get some rest. You've been so wound up lately. It's not healthy for you or Noah. Kids can sense that sorta thing, y'know."

I passed Noah to Niko and slumped into the sofa. "This voice came over the baby monitor." I told him about the nursery rhyme and ducking into the coat closet to protect us.

Dismissing what happened as the overactive imagination of a crime writer, Niko swatted his hand. Typical. "Those things pick up every baby monitor for miles. We sometimes hear mothers on the squad radios. You probably overheard some father tucking his child in bed."

"And the legs I saw through the keyhole? How do you explain that?"

"I told you, I sent Childs here. If you weren't hiding inside the closet, maybe you would've seen him." Across from me in his Lay-Z-Boy, he bounced Noah on his knee. In a squeaky voice he said, "You and Mommy had an exciting day, huh, little man?"

"Exciting?" I rolled my lips. "Aren't you hearing me? Childs wouldn't whisper nursery rhymes outside the door."

"Babe, when people get frightened, they can imagine all sorts of things. You already said the voice came from the baby monitor. Maybe it just sounded closer."

Flames jagged up my chest. "Don't you dare patronize me. I know what I saw."

He didn't respond, but I could swear he rolled his eyes.

"Tell me the details of the murders. You promised we wouldn't keep secrets anymore."

After hesitating for what felt like ten years, he agreed to tell me about the homicides, but as usual, he first cautioned me against it. "Are you sure you wanna hear this? Maybe now's not the time."

I raked my fingers through my hair. "I don't think I have a choice anymore."

"Fine." His expanded cheeks released an exaggerated exhale. "Frankie and Chance found the vic off the snowmobile trails."

"Where, exactly?"

"You mean like GPS coordinates?"

I tsked my tongue. "Of course not. GPS location…" I shook my head in disgust. "Was she stabbed, shot, strangled, raped, strung up in abandoned buildings like before? You know exactly what I mean."

"What makes you think the vic was female?"

"Don't play games with me, Niko." It took all my energy to slow the surge of adrenaline. "We both know females are the easiest prey."

Staring at Noah, bouncing on his knee, he held a tight smile. Upbeat, he said, "Nude woman in her forties braced to a tree with a log cabin spike, her left-hand severed at the wrist. Buck antlers were then shoved over the spike, under the woman's armpits, to make it look like she was impaled by the rack."

I shot to my feet. "What kind of tree?"

"Birch. Why?"

"Oh. My. God." I zipped over to my laptop, on the desk in the corner. In the search engine, I typed "Rock-A-Bye Baby." Pages and pages of hidden meanings filled the screen. Years ago, I'd written a murder mystery that involved several hours of research, like they so often did. During that time, I'd stumbled across the history of nursery rhymes; I'd never forget the horror of learning how these charming little ditties came to be. But before I told Niko, I needed proof.

When I clicked the first link a fierce shudder swept through me. I was right. This nursery rhyme stemmed from early Native Americans, who swaddled their infants in birch trees while they worked in the fields so feral animals would not eat them. The wind would rock them asleep, but if a fierce gust swept through the area, the baby and cradle would crash to the ground. The killer Niko was hunting…the sociopath who stalked our quiet streets…

the animal slaughtering innocent lives…wasn't some lunatic who killed without purpose. He was after me and Noah.

I showed Niko what I'd found.

"Babe, you're reading into this too much." Even though he uttered those words, he winced, his expression betraying his confident front. Call it intuition, instinct, or knowing someone as well as yourself, a wife can tell when her husband fears the worse.

There was something he wasn't telling me. Whatever it was might be the key to stopping this. If only he kept me informed, maybe I could help track this psychopath and prevent whatever was coming. As usual, however, Niko shielded me from the truth the way he did the last time a serial killer stalked our country roads.

I gave it a shot anyway. "Maybe we could play our game. It might help you catch this sicko." Niko and I role-played—one acted as victim, one as killer—to re-enact especially gruesome homicides. By doing so, we could determine the trajectory of the wounds and how the killer was able to create such macabre crime scenes. Over the years, we'd solved many high-profile cases this way.

He rubbed my upper arms. "Not this time, okay? You've been under a lot of stress lately."

"I'm stressed because you're keeping me in the dark. And when I do share how I feel, you dismiss it as nonsense."

"That's not fair."

I scrubbed a hand over my face. "How can you say that? You just did it ten seconds ago."

"It's late. Why don't you go to bed, and we'll talk about this later."

"Fine, but Noah's sleeping with us." I wedged my hands around our son and lifted him out of Niko's grasp. "I refuse to let anything happen to him because of your failure to accept what's really going on."

"About that…" He tugged on his ear.

"Don't even tell me you're going back out."

Siding my face in his palms, he kissed my forehead. "Don't

be like that. You know I'd stay if I could, but we're not done processing the scene yet."

"I hate this. I really hate this. You promised me you'd put us first from now on."

"I know. I'm sorry. The faster I catch this guy, the faster we'll get back to normal. I promise." Tucking me into his chest, he wrapped his strong arms around me and kissed the top of my head. "I won't be too late, okay?"

With my face buried in the crook of his arm, I nodded.

"I love you."

"Love you too, pup." I raised my head and smiled warmly, but all that went through my mind was, what if the stranger returned?

Chapter Eight

Midnight

Frankie set up the last light around the edge of the cordoned-off area so they could continue the search. How did Chance's scalpel get buried with a mutilated cat? He loved animals. There must be a logical explanation.

Around the base of the birch tree, where the mutt impaled the third victim, she sifted through the snow. Niko had designated each tree with letters. The victim closest to the trail was scene A. The woman who survived briefly was scene B and scene C was the body Bradley found in the woods.

No matter what killers believed, it was almost impossible to commit the perfect crime, especially nowadays. When a suspect came in contact with something else, be it another person or object, they transferred microscopic skin cells and other trace evidence. Unless the mutt wore protective gear and gloves, law enforcement could uncover their sins. Frankie held on to Locard's Exchange Principle—the aforementioned forensics dogma—as her saving grace to clear Chance.

Without Gaines' autopsy reports they had no way to determine if the killer bled on his victims' clothes, and that's why he'd stripped them naked. Or if the vics had been sexually assaulted. The mere fact that all three women were nude didn't prove a thing. The mutt could've done it to humiliate them. Even if he disrobed them after death, it wasn't unusual for sickos to want to shock law enforcement, as well as the poor schlub who discovered the remains. Basically, without an autopsy and supporting evidence, why he targeted these specific women remained unclear.

"Frankie." Ben called her from the woods beyond scene C. "I think I found something."

She glanced back at Niko, on the trail with his cell to his ear, and then quickened her pace toward Ben. In the palm of his gloved-hand he held a surgical instrument, glimmering under the spotlights. "What is it?"

"Forceps."

Please don't let them belong to Chance. "Lemme see it." She snatched the instrument from his grasp and examined the handle. The ends had the same gold leafing but no engraving. "I bet he used this to grab the heart from the vic over there." She gestured toward scene A.

"Then why leave it behind?"

"No idea."

Ben extended his hand for the forceps. "Should I just bag it, or show it to Niko first?"

"I'll take care of it. Listen, Niko's dealing with a personal issue right now, so don't bother him. Once he sorts it out, I'll show him myself. Got it?"

Head cocked, Ben's forehead wrinkled in confusion. "But he said—"

"No shit, Sherlock. I'm not tellin' you to lie. I'm just sayin' to give him a little time."

He lifted his shoulders. "Okay. I guess I can do that. But I still don't—"

"Doesn't matter. Finish searching the area. We've got a lot of ground to cover." When Ben turned to leave, Frankie hooked his arm. "If you find anything else, call me, not Niko."

He offered her a lame half-shrug. "Okay, I guess."

She patted his shoulder, similar to petting a rock. "Niko would be proud."

Before his smile widened and turned her stomach, she strode to scene B, her fingers gripping the forceps so tightly she almost tore the latex glove. Once out of eyeshot, she examined the forceps. Gold handles, smooth silver shaft and tips. Nothing distinguishable, except the design. Forceps normally came in all silver. Only custom sets had different handles. Like Chance's set, for example.

Niko startled her when he crept up behind her. "Whaddaya got there?"

Contrite, she swung her hand behind her back. "Nothin'."

"I'm not blind. Lemme see it."

With no other choice, she brought her hand forward. "Forceps. Ben found it over there." She waved her hand toward scene C. "They probably weren't even used in the commission of the crimes. So, how's Sage?"

Eyebrows clenched, Niko studied her expression like a suspect in the box. "She's fine, thank you. And so is Noah. Is there anything you wanna tell me?"

Frankie tried to keep her voice even. "Like what?"

"I think we need to talk about Chance."

"What? Why?"

"Frankie, I wouldn't be doing my job if I ignored the evidence. You know that as well as I do. I'm not sayin' we need to involve the state police yet, but maybe I should talk to him, feel him out."

Cringing, her heart sank to her feet. "Talk to him about what, exactly?"

"You let me worry about that."

She swallowed hard. "Now? But it's after midnight. Can't this wait?"

"Sure, it could, but if the state police catches wind of this evidence, don't you think it'd be better if we had answers?"

Frankie stared at her boots. "I guess."

"I won't be long." He patted her shoulder. "Keep everyone in line while I'm gone."

Jogging to keep up with Niko's fast strides, she begged him to reconsider. "Maybe I should talk to him first. Y'know, lessen the blow." She kicked the snow. "Dammit, Niko. Will you talk to me for sec? For chrissakes, this is my fiancé we're talkin' about."

Slowly he rotated toward her. "I don't think that's a good idea."

"But—"

He flashed a flat hand. "This is happening whether you like it or not, so you better get your head in the game."

As Niko soldiered toward the four-wheeler, blood rushed like rapids in Frankie's ears, muffling the world around her. What if Chance really was guilty?

If she could beat Niko home, maybe she could get some answers to satisfy her curiosity and with any luck, stop the inevitable. On the trail, she swung her leg over the seat of her skimobile.

Niko hollered over the engine of his four-wheeler. "What're you doin'?"

Veering around him, she gunned the gas. No way could his half-assed four-wheeler outrun her new sled. In the glow of her headlight, slicing a flaxen cylinder over the dark trail, her mind spun with every possible scenario. Maybe someone was trying to set him up to take the fall. Although, as far as she could tell, everyone liked Chance. He didn't have enemies.

The brisk March air chapped her face, watered her eyes, and left frozen tears on her cheeks. At her house, she let her thumb off the throttle and coasted into the garage.

Careful not to make a sound, she twisted the doorknob to the kitchen, then poked her head inside. Darkness overshadowed the interior. No lights, except for the dim utility bulb over the stove. Chance must be asleep. Maybe she had time to prove Niko's absurd theory was, in fact, insane. A brilliant detective in her own right, she'd know if she slept next to a murderer night after night. This whole situation had to be one big mistake. No question.

Two strides inside and the light blazed on. Scowling, Chance rolled his fingers on the kitchen table. "Where the hell have you been? It's almost one o'clock in the morning."

She darted to his side. "Listen to me. Niko's on his way over. We found something at—"

The door swung open.

Shaking his head like a disappointed father who came home to find his teenage daughter in the throes of lust, Niko shot her a cutting glare.

Frankie parted her lips to speak.

"Take a seat, Deputy Campanelli. You're on very thin ice as it is." At the table, Niko pulled out a chair and sat across from her and Chance, leaned forward, and folded his hands in front of him. Parting his lips to speak, he tossed one last spiteful glare her way.

Crap. If she didn't lose her badge over this, it'd be a miracle. What was she thinking? Dammit. For the first time, she'd let her emotions obstruct an investigation. Admittedly, this wasn't the finest moment of her career.

"As you know," he said in a matter-of-fact tone, "three women lost their lives in the woods behind your house."

Hands in surrender, Chance quailed back in his seat. "Whoa. Three?"

"Save it." A lackluster expression crossed Niko's face, eyes closed as though he'd heard every imaginable excuse for why someone claimed innocence. "We found your scalpel at the scene."

"Pardon me?"

A sarcastic smirk toyed with the corners of his lips. "You didn't understand my statement? Or you'd like me to be more specific?"

"I have no idea what you're talking about."

"Uh-ha."

Head swiveling between Niko and Frankie, Chance raised splayed fingers to his chest. "You think *I* had something to do with this?"

"That would be why I'm here in the middle of the night, yes."

"That's crazy. First of all, if I murdered these women, why would I go with Frankie to the crime scene? How stupid do you think I am? I mean, come on. If I planned to kill someone, I certainly wouldn't let my fiancé witness my reaction when she discovered the body. And I sure as hell wouldn't leave my custom-made scalpel behind."

"What makes you think we found a custom-made scalpel? I didn't mention what it looked like."

Good question. The tongue of suspicion licked up Frankie's spine. Everything about Chance screamed guilty—the way he crossed his arms firmly over his chest, closed off, unwilling to listen, his downturned gaze and defensive attitude. Not that his attitude surprised her. Lately, Chance had an answer for everything, which usually turned into a shit comment directed at her.

Even so, she tried to hasten the aggression between the two. "What Niko means is, how do you know which scalpel we found? Did it get stolen or something?"

"Frankie," scolded Niko, "you know better than that."

She did know better than to ask a suspect a leading question, but she couldn't help herself. If it turned out she'd been engaged to a murderer, she'd never live it down. "Niko, you don't know beyond a shadow of a doubt. I mean, really know. Maybe his scalpel was stolen, and maybe, someone planted it at the crime scene to set him up."

"Deputy, you're crossing so many lines, you might never recover."

Chance swiveled to face her—paused, as if considering his options—and said, "They *were* stolen."

Aw, shit. Why didn't she keep her mouth shut? Now she might never learn the truth.

Eyes slitted, Niko curled his upper lip. "Did you file a police report for this alleged burglary?"

Comparable to a cornered animal, Chance shifted in his chair, crossing and uncrossing his legs. "Actually, I told *you* about the break-in at the clinic. Remember, babe? You said you'd take care of filing the report."

Her heart somersaulted in her chest. No matter how much she cared, she couldn't perjure herself. In her world, that'd be akin to burning the American flag. Rather, she tap-danced around the subject. "You might've. Especially if you told me when I had that stomach flu. That whole week's a blur."

Niko wasn't amused, evident by his sneer through gritted teeth. "When was this alleged burglary, exactly?"

"Like I said, I'm not really sure. You remember how sick I was."

Judging by the expression on his face, he was this close to strangling her with his bare hands. "I wasn't asking *you*, Deputy."

"Right." Zings ricocheted through her body like the metal ball in a pinball machine. Shamefaced, she hung her head. "Sorry."

"I'd have to check my records at the clinic. Can I get back to you, Niko?"

"No. You can't get back to me, Mr. Rocco." The way he addressed Chance had a bite of indignation. "By rights, we should be having this conversation at the station. I think I'm being more than generous here, and I don't appreciate you lying to my face."

"Since when does the law say I have to prove my innocence?" said her pain-in-the-ass fiancé, who'd dug himself a deeper grave. His constant denial and unwillingness to clear his name worked to escalate the situation.

Chance, shut the hell up already.

"Your job is to prove my guilt, not the other way around."

Frankie winced. That last comment wouldn't go over well, either.

"Fine. Maybe your clinic did get burglarized, but you two are making that really difficult to believe." When he rose from the table his handcuffs jingled, and sent dread through Frankie's system. "I'm done playing games." He gestured for Chance to stand. "Let's continue this conversation at the station."

Instinct took over, and Frankie latched onto Chance's arm. "Wait. Niko, please. He said he'd get you the records."

"Remove your hand, Deputy. Either he proves his instruments were stolen, or he's taking a ride downtown. It's that simple. You shouldn't even be here, so stay out of it before you find yourself in even more trouble. In fact, as of now you're suspended. I can't have you working this case. That's obvious."

Praying hands held to her chin, she begged him to reconsider. "Please don't do this. You and I both know he couldn't've killed anyone. Please, Niko. The job is all I have."

"I'm sorry. I truly am. But you need time to remember why you became a cop."

Tonight she crossed the thin blue line, shattered the blue wall of silence into tiny bits. Cops didn't cover for criminals, especially murderers. It didn't matter if they were in love with them or not.

57

Damn you, Chance, for forcing her to go against everything she believed in. If they proved his guilt, she'd lock his ass away herself.

If, such a powerful word. It was precisely that "if" that blackened her blue blood. She released Chance's arm. "Take him."

Chapter Nine

March 23, 2008, 1:15 a.m.

A loud crash jostled me awake, and I bolted upright in bed. Pitch blackness eclipsed the loft. Even the moon didn't dare shine. I never intended to sleep so soundly. When Noah slept with us, the soft whistles from his nose, or the faint suckle of his lips—two of the most angelic timbres on earth—oriented me to his presence at all times.

Niko said I had "mother's ears," a gift I'd developed when Colt and Ruger were still puppies. When Noah blessed our lives, the natural instinct increased. Lately, though, I'd been so exhausted, likely due to the rheumatoid arthritis wreaking havoc in my joints. With RA, a body could feel normal one moment and utterly wiped the next. While breastfeeding, I didn't dare inject the monthly shot or take the medication to fight pain.

Careful not to wake Noah, I reached for him. When my hand didn't connect with his tiny frame, I ran my palms over the silk sheets. Breath trapped in my chest, and I sprang to my knees, waving both arms across the bed, searching from headboard to footboard.

Did he roll off the side?

With the sheets and quilt stripped, I flicked on the bedside lamp, and my gaze shot to the empty bed. I crawled to Niko's side and peered over the edge. Also empty.

Oh. My. God. Where'd he go? Did Niko move him to the crib?

After checking the nursery, I sprinted down the stairs. "Noah!" I zoomed in and out of every room. "Noah!" Praying hands to my

59

chin, I fell to my knees, cried, "Dear God, no. Don't let this be true." Stunned silent, I clutched my heart. Where were the kids?

Cupped hands around my mouth, I shouted, "Colt!"

Silence.

"Ruger!"

Silence.

In spite of how hard I concentrated, I failed to process the savageness of the situation. How could I admit someone kidnapped our child while I slept a foot away? In all my years, I never pictured myself as a careless mother. How did I let this happen?

Outside, in the stillness of evening hours, a car engine revved. Dual exhaust pipes tightened the tendons in my neck.

A switch clicked in my head, and I jolted to my bare feet, careened out the kitchen door. A dark sedan idled in the driveway. In my nightshirt, I barreled up the walkway. The moment I crested the top, the car took off down the hill.

Waving my arms, I chased the sedan. "Please, come back!" Halfway down the mountain road, I slipped in the icy slush. My legs split apart, and I fell face-first, sliding faster and faster, my hands groping for a way to stop. Toward the bottom, my head smashed against a loose rock from the stone wall around our property.

Half-dazed, I glanced up at the dark sedan, idling at the end of our road—waiting, taunting me, daring me to follow. I crawled to my feet. Arms outstretched, I staggered down the mountain, begging the stranger to stop. "Please...take me instead!" I cried, my mouth barely able to form words.

The second my hand slapped the bumper the interior light flicked on to torture me, Noah's frightened face illuminated in the back windshield. The car banged a left and sped down the icy road, its headlights casting tunnels of light, which bounced off neighboring houses, bare trees, illuminated "Moose Crossing" and weight limit signs. With a tightness in my chest, I charged against the cold night air, the soles of my feet frozen in the slush, my arms pumping to increase momentum.

When I finally slapped the trunk, I refused to let go. As the stranger revved the car engine I clung to the bumper. Jogging to keep up, I pulled myself to the back passenger door.

Noah screamed, a shrill that sliced my heart in two.

The car launched into high gear, with my fingers vice-gripped around the door handle. One tiny hand pressed against the glass. Bawling, Noah's chest heaved in, out, in, out, fear rising in his voice. Tears washed his delicate cheeks, and I banged on the glass.

"Stop! Take me instead! Please...don't do this!"

The car swerved left, then right. My legs gave way, the sedan dragging my knees across the road. Sweat loosened my grip on the door handle; I couldn't hang on much longer. With one final jerk of the wheel, the stranger bucked me off the door and my body spiraled across the road, into a ditch. Gritty slush from the plow trucks coated my skin, soaked from head to toe.

Cherry-red taillights faded into the blackness.

"Come back!" I raked my fingers through my wet hair. "No, no, no, no, no..." My heart gutted from my chest. How did I let this happen? I could never return to a childless life. Not now. Not after loving him for so long.

Lines of tears saturated both cheeks, my insides twisting in desperation. The day I had Noah, my life took on new meaning. Who was I without him? For seventeen years, Niko and the kids filled me with love. Even so, I ached for the baby I'd lost in Boston.

When God blessed our lives with Noah Phillip Quintano, a heavenly halo enhanced the world around me. Colors became more vibrant. Nature sang sweet lullabies. Without Noah, the day to day wasn't worth living. I couldn't experience another loss. I'd already lost so much. No way would I survive if I didn't see him again, hold him again, kiss him again.

Why, Lord? Please tell me this is a nightmare that I'll wake from. Please...I can't bear this pain.

Sobbing incoherently, my breath ragged, hot tears doused my frigid cheeks, the warmth unable to penetrate my agony. I crawled to my feet, my nightshirt soaked, legs frozen from the cruel New England weather. I dragged myself up the mountain road when every fragment of my being longed to chase that car.

"Noah," I called into the darkness, my soul shattered beyond repair. If only I'd held him while I slept. How could I let this happen? If only God would grant me one wish. I'd snuggle him in my arms and never let him go. Maybe this punishment I'd brought on myself, my incompetence as a mother. "I'm so sorry I failed you, baby," I cried out, my hands clutching my empty womb, my body aching for the child I carried.

When I slogged through the opened kitchen door, Noah's panicked cries coiled through the empty house. A twinge of hope seeped into my soul, and I double-stepped it up the stairs to the nursery. Blood seeped from my road-rashed knees, palms, and feet. Stains trailed my path.

Through the baby monitor my son screamed, his words spiked with terror.

I swiped the baby monitor off the dresser and cradled it against my breast, cooed, "Mommy's here, baby. I'm coming for you." Pain edged my tone, revealing my desperation. "Hang on, baby. Hang on."

A man's eerily raspy voice sang, "Rock-A-Bye Baby." His maniacal laugh amplified through the speaker. "Call this number, Mommy." He rattled off the digits.

Hands juddering, I swiped the cordless handset off the nightstand and dialed. He answered on the first ring. Before I had time to get a hold of my emotions, scorching heat assaulted every fiber of my soul. "Give me back my son, you prick!"

"My, my." Cold and harsh, he sniggered. "Haven't we gotten brave."

"What do you want? Name your price."

"It's not money I desire, Mommy. Just a few moments of your time, is all. You see, we share a mutual acquaintance."

"What?" My mind spiraled back in time, shuffling through memories like playing cards. "Who?"

"Does the name John Doe ring a bell?"

The room whirled. Against my will my knees buckled, and I latched onto the bars of the crib to stop my imminent collapse.

"You're listening now, aren't you, Mommy?"

"Yes. *Please* don't do this." My whole body pleaded for him to reconsider. "Please don't hurt my child. He's innocent in all this. I'll do anything you want."

"I know you will, Mommy. Stay by the phone. I'll call with further instructions. Oh, and no police. I see one cop car, and your son is dead. You hear me?" A shuffle came over the line as though he was about to hang up.

"No... Wait."

"Yes, Mommy?"

"Tell me now. Whatever it is, I'll do it."

"Now, what fun would that be?"

"Please let Noah go." At that moment, I would have done anything he asked. "Please, mister." Begging wasn't working. I needed a new tactic. "How 'bout we meet?" I used a soft and sensual tone. "Afterward, I'll bring Noah home and no one needs to ever know what transpired between us." Vomit lurched up my throat from the very thought of my proposal. I didn't care. In a heartbeat, I'd endure the harshest committal if it meant Noah could come home, unharmed. Even if the stranger stole my life, my son could flourish into a man someday. Without question, without hesitation, I'd do anything to ensure his future no matter how painful or reckless.

"Stay by the phone, Mommy."

A dial tone flat-lined.'

As I settled into denial, the cordless phone still gripped in my hand, Chloe's warning flitted through my mind. "Hold on tight, little sis." This whole time, I figured she'd prophesized about me, but she meant Noah.

I dialed Niko's cell phone.

"The person you are trying to reach is unavailable. Please try your call again later."

Chapter Ten

1:15 a.m.

Frankie stared out the window as Niko's taillights faded into the darkness, with Chance in the backseat of the Sheriff's SUV. It wasn't as if Niko didn't know Chance. They went to the movies with the Quintanos, out to eat, and occasionally for Saturday night drinks when they managed to convince Sage to get a babysitter. They barbecued while Noah and the dogs played in the backyard. Niko and Chance had man-to-man talks, Sage and Frankie in the kitchen with the food. He wasn't a stranger to Niko, and he sure as hell wasn't a murderer.

She dashed upstairs and tore through every drawer in Chance's bureau, searched under the bed, between the mattresses, in the closet, and in the shoeboxes on the top shelf.

Found nothing.

She fished in coat pockets, in the pockets of his work coat.

Found nothing.

Downstairs, she darted into Chance's home office and rifled through his desk drawers.

No incriminating evidence anywhere.

"This is crazy." When she reached to switch off the desk lamp, the edge of a key drew her attention. Hmm…why would he stash a key?

Stuffing the key in her pocket, she rushed out the back door.

Ten minutes later, she pulled curbside down the street from Rocco Animal Clinic. The Grafton County Sheriff SUV idled in the parking lot. A few moments later, it drove out the exit, and she snuck to the clinic door. With an erect finger, she punched in the alarm code. The green light announced safe entry.

Meows bellowed from the back room, instantly sending a cold crackle down her spine, the image of the mutilated cat still fresh in her mind.

"Get a grip," she told herself, her flashlight levelled in front of her. In the back room, she found three adult cats in cages: a tabby, an orange tiger, and a calico. "Hey, kitties." She stuck her fingers through the bars and scratched the tabby cat's forehead. "You're a little sweetheart. What's your name?" She lowered the light to a white card on the front of the crate. "Queenie. It fits you."

She moved on to the orange tiger cat and brightened his nameplate. "Hi, Jack."

After a quick pat, she read the nameplate on the third kennel door, and a gazillion scenarios flitted through her mind.

She scuttled into the surgical suite. As she unfurled Chance's instrument case, she brushed her fingertips across three different sized scalpels, then an empty space, scissors, another space, and then four other surgical tools. How Chance used them or for what purpose she had no idea, but they all had gold-leafed handles. Studying the imprint of forceps in the purple velvet, she leaned in.

Niko must've seen these. Though if he had, then why didn't he bag them as evidence? Did Chance talk his way out of it?

A faint knocking from the closet in Chance's office drew her attention, and she slid her service weapon from the holster. Triangling it out in front of her, her left hand supporting her right, she crept toward the closet. "Come out with your hands on your head."

No response.

"Sheriff's Department. Show yourself."

All movement stopped.

Careful to stay out of the line of fire, she pressed her back against the wall, reached around the doorjamb, and twisted open the door.

She chanced a quick peek.

Odd. The closet sat empty, except for Chance's white lab coats and a change of clothes. Shoving the hangers aside, she searched left, right, high, low.

Get a hold of yourself, Campanelli.

She holstered her weapon. Maybe Chance had a sick dog in one of the exam rooms.

A quick scan with the flashlight cleared all three rooms.

On her way to the front door, she spun on her heels and changed direction, bustling toward the back room to snap a photo of the instruments. Sometimes, the smallest detail could break a case wide-open. Though in this case, hopefully it wouldn't.

To be safe, she left through the back. Halfway down the narrow hallway, she tripped over a lump in the oriental runner and went sailing through the air, landing face-down on the floor.

A gunshot rang out.

What the fuck was that? Jumping to her feet, nerves pinged like hot oil in a cast iron skillet.

Someone moaned. Groaned. Then shuffled.

Hands trembling with adrenaline, she aimed the flashlight to the area where she fell. "Aw, shit." Squirming on the floor, Niko's hands were cuffed behind his back, ankles zip-tied, a white cloth pulled tight between his teeth. Blood haloed his head. A brass cube lay beside him, blood on the squared edge. On the ivory-painted wall, crimson dots speckled an arch—castoff spray from more than one strike.

Niko mumbled something like, "Untie me."

How was this possible? She saw him leave the parking lot. Was Chance behind the wheel? If so, who was the silhouette in the backseat?

Moaning so loudly he was practically screaming, Niko thrashed from side to side.

"Sorry." She lowered his gag. "You all right?"

He spit out a thread. "No, I'm not all right. Your fiancé attacked me." He raised his arms, still cuffed behind his back. "Tell me you have your key 'cause he took mine."

Smirking, she raised the handcuff key in the air. "Never leave home without it." As she un-cuffed him, she tried to reason with him. "Let's think about this. You got knocked on the back of the head, right? I saw the blood spatter on the wall."

He massaged the deep imprints in his wrists. "Excellent observation, Deputy. Yes, I got slammed in the head. What do you think, I stopped for a nap?"

"Then how do you know it was Chance?"

His lips smoothed to a straight line.

"I'm not making excuses for him, but did you actually see him hit you?"

Niko grimaced. "If I saw him, he'd be dead right now. I know you don't wanna believe it, but I've never lied to you."

"But—" She paused, rephrased. "I'm just sayin', if you got jumped from behind, how do you know it was Chance? You can't really *know*. Maybe someone else was hiding out, and *they* hit you and kidnapped Chance."

Niko released an aggravated exhale.

"Hold that thought." She dashed to the kitchenette, grabbed two ice-cold beers from the fridge, and then returned. "Here."

"Does this look like party time to you?"

"It's for your head, genius."

"What's that one for, then?"

"Me." She chugged half the can and let out a loud burp. "Ahh...I needed that."

"I hate to interrupt your celebratory drink, but we've got a serious problem here. Where would Chance go? I know he's an outdoorsmen, so does he have somewhere special he goes to think?"

"We don't even know Chance did this and already you're convicting him."

"I'm not gonna—" He stopped to eye her up and down, probably wondering if she'd stolen evidence from the clinic. "Why are you here?"

"I...uh..."

"Deputy Campanelli," he warned.

"Okay, okay. I came to have a look around." The cats in the back room mewled, and churned the beer in her stomach. "I need to show you something. But before I do, you need to promise me you'll keep an open mind."

"During a murder investigation, the Sheriff of Grafton County doesn't *need* to promise anything."

"Please, Niko. It's probably a coincidence, anyway. For just a minute, can't you at least entertain the possibility that Chance is innocent, and someone's doing a damn fine job of making him look guilty?"

"I don't have tunnel vision, if that's what you're asking."

She slammed a fist against her thigh. "Promise me you'll keep an open mind."

"Fine. I promise."

"That's not very convincing. Promise me, or I'm not showing you shit. If we find evidence that backs your theory, fine. But it sure as hell won't be me who hammers the last nail in his coffin."

With two fingers Niko crossed his heart. "I promise."

"C'mon." She led him toward the back room. With any luck, he'd see things her way. Chance could be in real trouble and need their help. "Remember your promise." She shined the flashlight on the calico cat's nameplate.

It read, "King."

* * *

2:15 a.m.

While Niko drove her SUV, Frankie remained silent. Whether they drove in his vehicle or hers, he insisted on driving. As much as it irked her, she didn't dare protest. Not this time, anyway, with her badge on the line.

"Over here on the left." Guilt chewed her insides as Niko pulled down a dirt trail, into a wooded lot, where Chance often went to clear his head. Passed down from generation to generation, his grandfather's land had been in his family for decades. A tiny log cabin sat back off the road. Weather-beaten exterior, sagging tin roof, and a front porch with no railing.

Flashlight clenched between her teeth, Frankie searched her keyring to unlock the front door. Why Chance even bothered to lock it turned into a running joke. With two missing windows, plastic stapled over the holes to keep out the critters, anyone with half a brain could crawl into the cabin.

Inside, Niko skimmed the interior with his flashlight. "This place have power?"

Frankie flipped on the light switch. A dome light flickered, dimmed, and then blew. "Dammit. Hang on. There's another light somewhere over here." With a twist of the switch a desk lamp blazed on. "Shit. What's in here, a hundred-watt bulb?"

When she leaned over the top of the shade to check the wattage, Niko called her name. He swung his arm toward the wall, where three animal busts hung—moose, deer, and an elk from his hunting trip in Alaska, last year.

"That doesn't mean a thing. Lots of people hunt."

"My first instinct was correct. You can't be objective. You're way too close to this." His tone softened. "It only means you're human, Frankie. Why don't I drive you home and come back alone. You've been through enough today...yesterday...the days are blending together at this point."

Heat rose from her chest and swept up her neck. "First of all, I can be objective. I showed you the frickin' cats, didn't I? Secondly, you're forgetting we took my vehicle. I'm not lettin' you leave me without wheels."

"Be reasonable about this. Your fiancé is a murder suspect. Never mind the repercussions your being here could cause. By presence alone, any evidence we find could be called into question, and rightfully so."

"How 'bout this? If we find supporting evidence that Chance is guilty, I'll back you one hundred percent. No one has to ever know I was here. But if we find something that fits my theory, I'm off suspension and back on the case. Deal?"

"Deal. Up or down?" Meaning, did Frankie want to search the first or second level.

"Up." Most people hid secrets in their bedroom.

The cabin consisted of a great room, sectioned into a kitchenette, dining area, and living room, with a full bath off the kitchen. Upstairs held the master bedroom. The loft walls masked hidden passageways that ran the length of the cabin.

Frankie flipped the mattress, searched under the box spring. Other than a *Playboy* magazine from 1999, she found no incriminating evidence. Doing her due diligence, she swung open the closet door, shoved the empty hangers aside. A half-door hid against the back wall. Flashlight leveled, she ducked under the doorjamb, into the creepy space. Cobwebs hung from the low unfinished ceiling. Blackness loomed in the narrow opening as if cloaked by dark magic. Mildew and dust climbed through her nasal passages and down her throat, and she coughed to clear her lungs.

Up ahead, something scratched the plywood walls, and stopped Frankie cold.

Out of nowhere a mouse scurried through the beam of light and ducked into a hole.

A shiver shimmied down her back. She snarled. Whatever their purpose in life, they should do it somewhere else. Where one showed up, others weren't far away. To frighten the filthy varmints into staying hidden, she stomped her heel into the wooden floorboards.

"You okay up there?"

"Mice," she called out.

The flashlight caught the edge of tan canvas. The outline of a man slumped in the corner. With one step closer, she hushed, "Chance?"

No response.

Another step, and she whispered again. "Chance, is that you?" Head rolled forward, the caramel-colored Carhart jacket covered his back, huddled in a ball as if to warm himself. With a gloved hand, Frankie clamped down on his shoulder.

The male corpse fell backward, grazed her legs on the way down, and she jumped, striking her head against the low ceiling. Wetness seeped through her cut scalp, but she couldn't tear her gaze away from the body in Chance's storage area.

The male vic looked about twenty years old at the time of death, dressed in a dark suit, Chance's Carhart dragged over his broad shoulders. No visible injuries. Manner and cause of death unknown. Perfectly preserved, had he been embalmed?

With the tip of a number two pencil she'd found on the floor, she raised the left sleeve to check for defensive wounds. Thick caked-on makeup blanketed the skin as though a funeral director had prepared this body for viewing.

Why stash him here? A gazillion questions whirled in her mind—the usual who, what, where, and how. If she shared this find, the chances of convincing Niko of Chance's innocence dwindled to nil. Even Frankie seriously questioned it now. If he had no part in the murder spree, then why stash a corpse inside his own hunting cabin? Unless he needed time to bury the body.

Niko called from the bottom of the stairs, "Frankie?"

"Be right down." She raced through the storage area to meet him at the top landing. Out of breath, she held a tight smile and focused on not allowing her chest to heave. "Hmm?"

"You all right? You seem…I dunno…different."

Frankie swatted her shaky hand.

"Okay, cool. You need to come see this."

While Niko waited at the bottom tread, she stepped down the stairs. If only she could clear her lungs with a deep cleansing breath, but if she took the chance, Niko would drill her with questions. Too risky. He had twice her experience. If anyone could sniff out deception, it was Niko. The only way to save Chance was to get one-step ahead of him. If she found proof of her fiancé's guilt, she'd lock his ass away, but if her theory panned out, and she could prove Chance's innocence, she needed Niko on her side. The way she saw it, this left her with one option. Crack this case on her own.

Hooking an arm at Frankie, Niko prompted her to follow him into the kitchenette, where he'd laid out four decks of playing cards. "Tell me what's missing."

"Lemme guess. King of Hearts?"

"I know you don't wanna believe it, but this proves my theory."

"Before crucifying him over a deck a cards, gimme a friggin' second to think."

He patted her shoulder. "You take all the time you need. Just don't touch anything." He dropped each deck into separate evidence bags, bundled them in one hand, and strode through the great room. When he swung open the front door, he glanced over his shoulder. "I really am sorry. I'll wait for you in the truck." He closed the door behind him.

Tears welled in her eyes. Either she'd been blinded by the man she loved, the one person to ever share her bed, or someone had used him as their patsy.

Shit. Her makeup must be a mess

Searching for travel tissues, she fished in the open drawer where Niko'd found the damning evidence. Way in the back, her gloved fingers brushed another box of playing cards. The SUV's headlights streamed through the sheer curtains as she shuffled through the deck. No King of Hearts.

Four victims. Five missing kings.

Chapter Eleven

3:00 a.m.

After dropping off Frankie, Niko took his time getting home. Contrary to what she believed, he derived no pleasure from being right. In the peacefulness of desolate streets, his mind journeyed back to when he and Sage first bought the house in Alexandria. Sage planted a peach tree to signify the first year at their new home. Over time the tree blossomed into an impressive specimen.

Last spring, Sage showed him buds on nearly every branch. When they sprouted into full, round, juicy peaches she insisted they needed one more day to fully ripen. The next morning, as Niko left for work, he glanced at the tree, his mouth watering in anticipation.

No peaches.

When he strolled over to investigate, pits and bear prints littered the soft soil, like Mr. Bear had a grand ol' time for himself. Niko was surprised he hadn't found a furry black blob snoring beneath the tree with a belly full of fruit. Damn bears.

Tonight, as he turned into his driveway, a light flickered in the backyard, bounced to the rhythm of someone's stride. He unholstered his service weapon. As quietly as possible he pressed the car door shut. Down the walkway he crept, hugging the sides, out of the stranger's sight, and around the side of their country contemporary.

The light streaked from tree to tree, pausing briefly at each one. Niko flattened against the cedar siding and inched toward the corner of the house. With a quick jab of the head, he glimpsed the intruder and then fell back into position. Weapon at the ready, trigger finger along the gun's slide, his adrenaline spiked, his mind alert and aware. No one would get past him tonight. Before he allowed some animal near his family, they'd have to kill him.

Snow-covered bushes shook like someone had separated the gnarled branches to peer through. Niko scurried to Sage's peach tree, not far from the stranger.

The slivered moon offered a feeble attempt at brightening the backyard, the landscape hauntingly quiet. Even the squirrels that lived one tree over in a burrowed-out knot didn't move. Evergreen and burning firewood enveloped the area as the silhouette of a man in a black-and-red-plaid coat fiddled behind a tree.

Niko closed the gap between. Ten feet separated him from the stranger. The light beam bounced up and down with jerky movements.

Peeping Tom? "Hey," he called out, and the man froze. "Slowly come around the tree with your fingers laced on top of your head."

The suspect didn't budge.

"Don't make me tell you twice. You're trespassing on private property. I can, and will, shoot if you refuse to comply."

The flashlight dropped on the ice-coated snow, and a tinny crash coiled through the darkness.

Hands raised, the suspect slithered around the tree. "Don't shoot. I'm unarmed."

"Whaddaya think you're doin' in my yard?"

The strange man lowered his hands to shoulder-level.

"I didn't tell you to move." He gestured with the gun. "Get 'em up. Keep 'em up. Answer the question."

"I was just—" He jabbed his chin at the flashlight. "Can I show you?"

"Use your words. I understand the English language quite well, thank you."

"It's March, you see, and I work eighty hours a week."

Niko's eyebrows drew together. "What does that have to do with why you're in my yard?"

"Well, if I could just—" Again he lowered his arms.

"If I have to tell you one more time to keep your damn hands up…"

"But I could show you—"

"That's it." Niko spun him around, threw him face-first into the bark, and cuffed the suspect's hands behind his back. When he refaced him, Niko prompted, "Well?"

"My little girl loves pancakes, you see. And her birthday is the day after tomorrow. I can't let her wake up without her favorite breakfast, now can I?"

An eyebrow cocked in bewilderment, Niko held a stone-cold expression. "You a little slow? I asked you what you're doin' in my yard and you give me some cockamamie story about pancakes?"

The man had the nerve to smirk.

"Did I say something to amuse you?" Ah, now he was beginning to get the picture. "Walk a straight line for me, heel to toe."

"You think I'm drunk?"

He gestured for him to comply. "Heel to toe. Let's go."

The man did as instructed, walked a stick-straight line with only a slight wobble at the end. Niko shined light in his eyes to check the suspect's pupils. Both contracted and expanded as normal. He flipped open his notepad. "Name?"

"Craig J. Pamms, Jr."

The name registered with Niko. "As in, the Pamms who live next door?"

"Yep. Been in my family for decades. My pa built the cabin with his own two hands. Sure, I've done some renovations to the place here and there, but always tried to keep Pa's original work. Amazing handyman, ol' Pa was."

"Fascinating, really, but you still haven't told me why you're in my yard."

Craig chuckled. "It's all very innocent, I assure you."

"I'll be the judge of that, thank you."

"Well, years ago we had a hurricane sweep through the area. Really nailed our trees, too."

Fire burned in his gut. "Enough of the family history. Make your point."

"When we lost our trees, I wasn't able to make maple syrup anymore. And as I said, my daughter loves pancakes. What kind of father would I be if I let her wake on her birthday without homemade syrup for her pancakes?"

"I'm still not following."

"I tapped a few of your trees. Sorry. The previous owners never minded."

"You make maple syrup from the sap in our trees?" Niko's stomach grumbled as he unlocked the handcuffs. "I'll tell ya what. Toss a jug my way, and you can tap all the trees you'd like. My son loves pancakes, too."

Mr. Pamms stuck out his hand. "You've got yourself a deal, Sheriff."

"Do me a favor and conduct your business in the daylight so you don't scare my wife. With the homicides recently, she's a little jumpy."

"Understandable. Again, I'm truly sorry for the confusion."

"No worries. Better you than—" Perhaps he shouldn't finish that sentence.

Chapter Twelve

3:40 a.m.

When Niko came up the stairs, I was still pacing the floors. "Hi, babe. What're you doin' up so late?"

Through burning, puffy eyes I shot him a look to pay attention. "He's gone! I told you I wasn't imagining things."

"Who?"

"Noah. He took him from our bed. I chased the car but..." I dropped my face in my hands. "Dear God, it's worse than last time. Our little boy, he's so frightened. I'll never forget the panic in his voice."

Always the cool detective, Niko tucked me into his chest. "Okay, shhh...go slow and tell me everything you remember. The model of car, license plate number, no matter how tiny the detail, I wanna know about it. Don't worry. We'll find him."

I squirmed out of his clutches. "How can you promise something like that?"

"Sage," he used a conciliatory tone, "tell me exactly what happened."

"I woke up and he was gone—abducted from our bed!"

"Okay, okay, breathe... You're no good to anyone this hysterical."

After several minutes, tears catching in my breath, I managed to slow the raging fury coursing through my mind, body, and spirit. "Dark sedan."

"What?"

"He drove a dark sedan. Wait." I raced into the nursery, grabbed the cordless phone and returned to Niko. "I called him.

Maybe you can press redial and trace his location." I palmed my forehead. "Why didn't I write down the number? Stupid, stupid, stupid."

"Don't blame yourself. You did nothing wrong. Great idea about the number. I'll get IT on it." He unclasped my fingers from the cordless phone. On his cell phone, he dialed the station. As it rang, he covered the mouthpiece. "Babe, where are Colt and Ruger?"

"What?" I scanned left, right. "Colt!" I bolted down the stairs. "Ruger!" I zipped in and out of the kitchen and living room. "They're gone! Sweet Jesus, he took them too!"

Niko rushed down the stairs. "Backup's on the way. I called in local and state police. Tom Rainhorse is tracing the call. Now, whaddaya mean, he took them too? No one in their right mind would abduct a full-grown Rottweiler and English mastiff while kidnapping a toddler. Hang on." Flashlight in hand, he scuttled out the kitchen door.

I chased after him.

In the backyard, Colt and Ruger lay on the snow, motionless, their tongues flopped out their mouths. "No, no, no, no, no…" Beside their bodies, I fell to my knees. "This can't be happening. Please tell me this isn't real. Maybe this is a nightmare. Or I'm having a nervous breakdown and Noah's abduction and…and…this…are figments of my imagination. Yes, that must be it." I jumped to my feet, crumpled Niko's shirt in balled fists. "Things like this don't happen to good people, right? None of this is real. It's all in my head, right? Right?"

The world spun, blackened, and then…*thud.*

When I came to I was on the sofa, Colt's slobbery tongue kissing one cheek while Ruger nudged my arm, trying to wake me. Uniformed officers swarmed the house, some dusting for fingerprints, lifting shoe impressions off the hardwood, Niko directing another officer up the stairs to the scene of the crime.

How long had I been out? Then it dawned on me. "My babies, thank God you're all right." The pain of losing Noah burrowed deep into my soul. If only he could be beside me, too. Oh, no. What if his abductor saw these officers? He specifically said not to call the police. Dear Lord, don't let him kill our son.

Chapter Thirteen

4:45 a.m.

As much as I hated to go behind Niko's back, his reinforcements worked nowhere near fast enough for me. Anything could be happening to Noah. I had no way to keep tabs. So, as nonchalantly as possible, I slipped the baby monitor into my jacket pocket and told Niko I needed fresh air, that I might go for a ride to clear my head.

"Be careful, babe. I'd rather you wait for me."

"I know, but I can't. I need to get out of here."

"All right, but call me every fifteen minutes. Okay?"

"I will." Out the door I fled and up the walkway. With any luck the baby monitor would still work away from the house. I drove to Niko's office. Obviously, he was hiding something about these murders plaguing our small town.

Curbside in front of the Grafton County Sheriff's Department, I checked my rear and side mirrors to ensure no one had followed me, then hurried into the building, up the stairs, and jimmied the lock on Niko's office door. If one of Niko's deputies discovered the victims' names, I might have a starting point for who had Noah. That is, if the murders and the kidnapping were connected. The timing struck me as too coincidental not to be related.

A quick scan of Niko's desk with my flashlight illuminated the murder book for the victim he told me about. Prints came back to Mary Anne Goodman, twenty-seven years old, unmarried, no kids. Mary Anne worked as an ER nurse at Franklin General Hospital, located a few towns over from Alexandria. The state board of nursing required all licensees to complete a background check with the FBI. Hence, why her prints were on file.

Dr. Gaines ID'd the first victim, which Niko conveniently neglected to mention. Amy St. John, a thirty-five-year-old high school English teacher and part-time camp counselor, found inside a barrel at Quincy Bog, married to Carlton St. John. They had a ten-year-old son named Carlton Jr. Victim number three, Wendy Laurent, also found in the woods, filed for divorce two weeks prior to her death. She had an eight-year-old son named Milo, who now lived with the soon-to-be ex, Milton Laurent.

Notes said Ben wasn't able to ID the other woman in the woods—marked as Jane Doe 21—until they could track her through missing persons' records, if a family member reported her disappearance.

How many victims did they have? Damn you, Niko.

In the silence of the office, a deep, raspy voice sounded outside the door. "Stand watch. I'll be in and out."

I twisted the lock in the doorknob, and then tiptoed to the desk, crawled underneath, and rolled the chair to block my body.

Metal jangled, scratched at the door. Someone was breaking into the office. With the murder books clutched close to my chest, I held my breath as the intruder's heavy strides circled the desk. Above my head, papers shuffled.

What was he looking for? I glanced at the case files in my arms. Did he want to see what evidence they had? Oh, my God. Did he have Noah? Wait. He spoke to a partner. Someone else stood watch. How many killers were there?

A musical trill emanated from his cell phone. "Yeah," he answered. "Then knock 'im out. Just don't kill 'im...yet. We might need 'im later."

Knock him out? Perhaps I should show myself. Maybe he'd take me instead and leave my son alone. But what if he then viewed Noah as a nuisance, an inconvenience he needed out of the way?

I couldn't risk it. Better to find out where he was holding him.

"Don't even say her name," he said. "I told you, I'll deal with her later."

Gulp.

Without warning, the desk chair slid from under the desk, and I scooted back out of view. I held my breath a second time, as if that would make a damn bit of difference now.

Denim-clad legs sat in Niko's chair—a similar navy blue to the ones I'd seen outside the closet door.

This guy was as brazen as they come. Not only did he kidnap the Sheriff's son, but breaking into his office, sitting at his desk, took brass balls. Why wasn't he the least bit concerned that he'd get caught? My shoulders curled around the case files. How could I go toe-to-toe with a serial killer? If only I could catch a glimpse of his face. Then maybe I could ask Frankie to help me ID him, because Niko would never allow me to get involved. Not now.

Careful not to get too close, I craned my neck around his legs.

Blackness shrouded the office, except for one beam of light from the man's flashlight, which bounced off the desktop and kissed the brass plaque behind Niko's chair.

Perfect.

I focused on the reflection, but all I could make out was dark hair, a husky build, and some sort of scar or tattoo on his neck.

The chair slid backward, and I tucked into the darkness, my back pressed against the desk wall. The man rose, took a few steps toward the door, and then returned. He hovered above the desk, and a jolt of raw adrenaline shot through my core.

"If I were you, I'd stay hidden," he said, his voice venomous.

Both hands shielded my mouth to quell the scream that threatened to explode.

The man didn't move. Didn't speak. He just stood there, looming over me like he held all the power.

Seconds felt like days.

When he finally left, I waited several grueling minutes before I crawled out from under the desk. Head swiveling right, left, I steadied my hand long enough to notate Mary Anne Goodman's address. I ran off copies of the case notes and autopsy reports, and then snuck out of the office and locked the door.

As I turned to leave, I drew in a sharp breath. Frankie filled the doorway, a fist planted on her hip. "Sage?" She prompted me to fill in the blanks.

"What do you expect me to do? Someone kidnapped Noah." Tears blurred my vision. "Niko called in the local and state police to assist, and now, I've got cops crawling all over my house. If the man finds out they're there, he'll hurt Noah, and I can't bear it, I just can't, Frankie, tell me you understand."

"First, take a breath. You're no good to anyone this hysterical."

My upper lip twitched. "Now you sound like Niko."

"Because he's right." Staring into my eyes, she set her hands on my shoulders. "Tell me why you're really here."

"I need to find my son. Why do you think?"

"I heard the call over the radio. I'm so sorry, Sage." She hugged me the way you'd console someone at a funeral. When we broke apart, she spoke eerily calm. "Find him how, exactly?"

"I've got a plan." Studying her expression, unsure how she'd react, I waited a beat. "I could use your help."

"Is it legal? As it is I'm already on Niko's shit-list."

Neither confirming nor denying, I swung my head in a circular motion. "Yeah. Probably. I don't know. Maybe."

"Aw, shit, Sage. Your timing really sucks."

"Is that a yes?"

"Of course, I'll help. What kind of godmother would I be if I said no?"

The baby monitor crackled in my pocket.

"You're wired? Un-fuckin'-believable! I can't believe Niko would stoop this low. And you." Glowering at me, her radiant eyes darkened to forest-green. "I thought we were friends."

"What are you talking about?" I showed her the monitor. "It's Noah's. The man said he'd be in touch."

"Oh. Sorry. My bad." Her forehead rippled in confusion. "Umm…you all right?" By her tone one might think I'd been confined to a mental health facility.

Before she had me committed, I told her how the man taunted me through the baby monitor.

"Those things have a range of about six-hundred feet, not miles. You know that, right?"

"But Niko said you guys pick up interference all the time."

"Yeah, but…y'know what? Never mind. If it makes you feel better to keep it close, then do it."

I caught the insinuation of me being paranoid, but chose not to call her on it.

"C'mon. We don't have much time before Niko comes looking for me. Oh, that reminds me. I've gotta check in. Give me one sec." I bustled into the office and raised the receiver on Niko's desk phone.

Frankie charged in after me and snatched the phone from my grasp. "Caller ID, remember? Use your cell."

I withdrew my iPhone* and pressed "Home" in my contacts. With any luck, Niko's fellow investigators found evidence to locate Noah. Then Frankie and I wouldn't need to journey down this particular path, a foray my husband could never learn about.

Chapter Fourteen

4:55 a.m.

Investigators from several different departments diligently dusted for prints, lifted shoe impressions, and collected trace evidence from the bed Niko shared with his wife. When crime hit this close to home, nothing prepared you for the rollercoaster of emotions. Sure, he'd acted level-headed in front of Sage, but the truth was, he longed to curl into the fetal position and pray for Noah's safe return. He and Sage had waited a lifetime for their child. Even though they were happy for many years, something magical occurred the day of Noah's birth. They transformed from a couple to a family, and if he didn't find him soon, he and his wife might never recover.

Ben burst through the kitchen door, his breath labored as if he ran five miles to deliver a message. "Boss, troopers found your truck abandoned on Rte. 114 in Springfield."

"Copy that. Okay, let's go."

Ben didn't follow him into the mudroom. "Wait. I, umm, had it towed."

"To where?"

"Here. It's outside."

He poked his head out the door, but dim lighting and the multitude of squad cars made it impossible to tell one vehicle from another. "Has it been processed?"

"Nope. I didn't let anyone touch it."

He patted his back. "Good job, Deputy. Let's hope the suspect wasn't smart enough to wipe down the steering wheel. I still need you to show me exactly where they found it. Can you do that?"

"Absolutely."

"Great. Let's go."

With Ben leading the way, Niko quickened his pace. If Chance left on foot after ditching his SUV, they might be able to narrow in on his location.

Twenty minutes later, the blues swirling overhead, tumbling colors onto the dark road, Ben pulled curbside on Rte. 114.

Eyebrows clenched, Niko swiveled to peer out each window. "Not a lot of houses around here." He pointed to the right, where a thick tree line obscured the view. "What's down there?"

"McDaniels Marsh."

A marsh? Did Chance dump another body? "Anyone check it out?"

"I don't think so. Why?"

"Our killer likes waterways. Maybe there's a reason he abandoned my vehicle here." He opened the passenger door, then sensed Ben's apprehension. "You comin'?"

"Uh, now? Shouldn't we wait for daylight?"

A large vein in his forehead throbbed in defiance. "Is there a problem?"

"No problem. I just thought you might wanna call Frankie. Y'know, to assist."

Niko grimaced. "Did she put you up to this?"

"Huh?" Ben's tongue played with the inside of his cheek, evident by the shifting protrusion. Classic sign of guilt.

"What aren't you tellin' me?"

"Nothing. I swear."

"Then let's get a move on." He wasn't ready to share his theory about Chance, but if Frankie went behind his back to conduct her own investigation, he'd demand her resignation. From the mere thought of her betrayal, blood boiled in his arteries, heating him from the inside out.

A few yards down the road, they veered through the main gates of McDaniels Marsh. Technically, this was not his jurisdiction—State Police and New Hampshire Fish and Game governed the waterways—but he'd be remiss if he didn't investigate. In law enforcement, coincidences rarely existed. No matter how cunning, patterns followed everyone, especially killers. Whether that be a certain MO, favorite hunting ground, or some other subconscious tic. By unraveling the pattern—some puzzles much harder to crack than others—the suspect left behind a wealth of information that helped investigators zero in on his or her identity.

Flashlight in hand, Niko brightened the poorly lit marsh "Other than shoeprints in the snow everything looks copasetic. How're you doin' over there?"

Ben stood on the adjacent shoreline, scanning the icy water. "All good here too, boss."

"Okay, we did our due diligence. Let's take a closer look at where the suspect abandoned my vehicle." He marched up the slight embankment to the main drag. Ben followed on his heels. "Show me the exact location."

Ben waved toward the side opposite his SUV. "Right about there." His flashlight flooded a speed limit sign in a golden luster. "Yep. That's it. I remember wondering why he'd dump the sheriff's vehicle in such an open area."

"Any tire impressions?" He strode toward the spot, irradiated the coating of snow on the pavement. Tread marks crisscrossed. "Crap. I bet he switched vehicles, but with so many intersecting impressions we'll never be able to determine the make and model of the getaway car or truck."

No luck in finding Chance, and his son was still missing. Not much compared to how grim the future looked at this moment.

Chapter Fifteen

5:15 a.m.

Frankie swung in front of 149 Morrison Drive in Alexandria, Mary Anne Goodman's residence, and I pulled in behind her. Bare tree branches cast long shadows across the road like bony fingers grasping slices of the slivered moon's meager light. Silence encompassed the area. Neighbors tucked inside their homes, probably dreaming sweet nothings, oblivious to the dangers around them.

A quaint log cabin nestled in the woods, with pine tree cutouts in hunter-green shutters. No light revived the interior. No street lamps rejuvenated the road. Nothing but death and darkness awaited us. Coyotes howled in unison; their tonality slashed the blackness of night. Tiny hairs on the nape of my neck stood on end, and I shuddered.

With my sleeve yanked over my fingers I jiggled the handle on the front door.

Locked.

I stalked into the backyard, climbed the stairs to the deck, and jostled the nearest window frame. It didn't budge.

"Dammit."

Backing away from the house, Frankie turned her gaze to the second story, with a miniature barn door in the center. From growing up in an old farmhouse, she detected something I didn't.

"It wouldn't take much to kick in those old doors," she said. "They make great decorative pieces, but when it comes to home security, they're as useless as doorknobs on a toilet seat."

I wiggled my flashlight into my back pocket and grabbed

hold of the support beam that ran the height of the house, then scrawled a mental note to never buy a log home; they're much too easy to climb. Hand over hand, I shimmied up the back corner of the cabin until I reached the decorative door. On the count of three I threw my best karate kick.

The door busted open.

Gloom veiled the interior. From the yard the place looked impressive. Quite the opposite in here. Old varnish peeled the log walls, wads of cement slapped in between, the musty stench of an attic no one let breathe.

In the corner, a stained mattress lounged on the floor. The seamstress model of a woman with no head or limbs nearly jolted me into cardiac arrest. Backing away, my heart thundered.

Clamoring down the wooden ladder, into the living room, I skimmed the interior, my head swiveling left and right. Neat and tidy, a kitchen table seated two, dragged in front of a picture glass window, a white lace tablecloth draped over the top, a vase of cut roses in the center. Wilted. Crumbling. Dead.

If a struggle occurred, it didn't take place in the living room. Once I hit the kitchen a different story emerged.

Solid pine cabinets all open, the contents strewn across the floor. Broken dishes, spices, tea bags, canned vegetables and soups scattered everywhere. Mary Anne must have thrown anything within arm's reach at her attacker.

The flashlight beam connected with a large blood pool by the back door. A white, squared object floated beneath the surface, a scarlet layer obscuring it from view. The edges of the puddle dried, dark, crusty splotches stuck to the linoleum tiles. Clumps of hair matted in the blood, torn from the woman's scalp while she fought to stay indoors, evident by the shoe prints on both sides of the doorjamb.

When I twisted open the padlock to let Frankie inside, her eyes flashed wide. "Whoa. You might be onto something, Sage."

"What does this tell you? Do you think it's the same guy who took Noah?"

"Hmmm…" Her heeled boot almost hit the blood pool

when she leaped over the top. After strolling in and out of every room downstairs, she offered a theory. "Intruder enters through the back door while Mary Anne is…" She poked her head in the doorway of the half-bath, off the kitchen, and I followed close behind. "Where?"

A perfume atomizer lay in the sink. The medicine cabinet door wide-open, rubbing alcohol and tweezers on the bathmat, underneath.

"Okay, so she's in the bathroom tweezing her eyebrows when he busts through the back door. She spins a few moments too late and he's on her in a millisecond. With houses on either side of the property, he shut her up right away. The bruising on her right wrist could indicate he also restrained her, even though Gaines found no ligature mark. For shits and giggles, let's say gagged, too."

Deep in thought, eyes squinting at the bedlam, Frankie chewed her bottom lip. "Nope. Scratch that. Mary Anne fought back. Okay, she's in the bathroom plucking her eyebrows when she hears someone jimmying the lock on the back door. She runs into the kitchen to call for help as the suspect bursts through the door. Yup, that makes more sense. Then she whips shit at his head, trying to keep him as far away as possible." Something must have dawned on Frankie because she encircled the phone with light.

A corded phone dangled down the wall. With gloved fingers, she slapped the hook switch to disconnect, then punched in star-six-nine. Holding the receiver out in front of her allowed me to overhear the voice of the person who answered and compare it to the sinister ramblings haunting the baby monitor.

Without saying hello, the man questioned, "Who's this?" as if he knew Mary Anne couldn't be calling.

Startled, Frankie said, "Chance?"

A dial tone hummed.

"Chance?" My neck snapped back. "What does he have to do with Noah's kidnapping?"

Frankie's gaze sidled as she re-cradled the phone. Then, without a word, she scurried outside. Drilling her with questions,

I chased her around the yard while she snapped photographs of the property's wooded perimeter. Married to a death investigator longer than dirt had earthworms, her memorializing possible entry and exit routes wasn't foreign to me. "What's Chance's involvement in this?" I slapped my hand on her shoulder and spun her around. "Dammit, Frankie. Answer me. Please don't keep me in the dark like someone else we know."

During the several minutes of silence, a rustling diverted my attention, and I shined my light at a massive maple tree, its skeletal branches reaching into the backyard. Two young squirrels leaped from limb to limb, playing tag, chirping back and forth, their mother eagle-eyed from a hollowed-out knot in the trunk. Smoke billowed out neighboring chimneys, the warm aroma of firewood wafting in the brisk early-morning air.

On an ordinary day, I might appreciate the peacefulness with its majestic wonder, but today was anything but. Four women lost their lives. Maybe more. Some lunatic had my child and a serial killer stalked the streets. Nothing could erase the sense of impending doom. Nothing.

"You better start talking. I mean it, Frankie. I want answers now."

With some reluctance, she told me about Chance being a murder suspect, but remained vague about the details. "I promise you, he would never harm Noah. There's no way. But after what happened, I can see why you'd be leery."

"Niko told you?"

"Told me? I was there."

Obviously, Frankie didn't mean the nursery rhyme and its significance to birch trees. In an attempt to find out what else my husband refused to share I played along. "Right. You mean at the crime scene." Cringing, I waited to see if my intuition steered me right.

"After what happened to Chloe, I can't even imagine what went through your mind when you heard what Mary Anne said." She sighed. "Anyway, c'mon." She hooked an arm, prompting me to follow. "I don't want the neighbors to see us."

I flung out my hands. "Wait. What did Mary Anne say?"

"What? Ah, nothin'. I wouldn't worry about it."

"You just said I'd be leery after hearing about Mary Anne, so it's obviously not nothing. No matter what my husband believes I can handle the truth."

Frankie raised a splayed hand to her chest. "I said that?"

I wagged my finger in her face. "Don't you dare play games with me when my child's life is on the line."

"Honestly, Sage, I've got no frickin' clue what you're talkin' about."

"Seriously, that's your answer? Deny a conversation that took place two fuckin' seconds ago?" Rarely did I swear. Dropping the f-bomb signaled I meant business.

"I'm sorry." Shamefaced, she stared at the ground. "I haven't slept since we found Chance's instruments at the crime scene. And now, Niko thinks he killed those women."

A calmness rolled over my face, softening the tightness of my shrinking scowl, the anger melting away. "I get it, I really do, but I'm trying to save my son." In an instant, my body temperature spiked. "What instruments?"

"Niko didn't tell you." She sneered. "Damn him. All right, fine. At the killer's dumping ground, not far from two of the vics, we found a scalpel and forceps that may or may not belong to Chance."

I flared my nostrils. "You mean to tell me, your fiancé did this to us?"

"Whoa." As if warding off an attack, she flashed her palms. "How'd you make the leap to that?"

I tsked my tongue. "The nursery rhymes, obviously."

"I've got no clue what that means."

"Why didn't Niko just look into the voice over the monitor? If he'd taken the threat seriously rather than assume it was my overactive imagination or paranoia, this all might have been avoided."

"Sage, you lost me."

"Aack." I swatted my hand. "Never mind. Let's just get this over with."

Opening the back door, she cautioned me about proper procedure. "Remember to watch where you step. Actually—" she reached into the inside pocket of her jacket and withdrew a pair of crime scene booties— "put these on so we don't further contaminate the scene. Oh, and while we're here, let's look for the Suicide King."

"The King of Hearts? As in, playing cards?"

She threw her hands in the air. "Niko didn't tell you that either? For chrissakes, don't you two talk?"

"Of course we do. Though, admittedly, lately Niko hasn't been as forthcoming as he usually is."

"Uh-ha," she said, glib.

"He's only trying to protect me." Why was I making excuses for him? Old habit. No matter what transpired in my marriage, I didn't allow anyone to drag Niko's character through the mud. Except me. Even then, I often kept my comments to myself. One of the worst things a spouse could do was to air their personal grievances in public. Besides, it was no one's business what transpired in the sanctity of our home. "Regardless, what's the significance of the Suicide King?"

"No idea. One of the victims had her heart removed, so originally Niko thought the card symbolized the killer. King of Hearts, get it? But the others still had their hearts, so it kinda blows his theory to hell."

"Hmmm...must be a clue of some kind." When my gaze met the blood pool, I winced. "I don't know what I was thinking, coming here. Perhaps we *should* call Niko."

"No." She answered much too fast. "I mean, Mary Anne didn't die here or anything. When we found her, she was still alive for a few minutes."

"Oh, right." I lied so convincingly she never saw through my deceit. "That's when she mentioned me."

"It's true."

"What'd she say again?"

She studied me like a suspect opposite the interrogation table.

"Okay, fine," I conceded. "He wouldn't tell me the details.

But you will, because if you don't, I'll have no choice but to ask Niko, and then he'll wonder when we spoke."

Eyes crimped, her lips clamped together as if biting back the anger. "If I tell you, you've gotta swear not to tell Niko."

With two fingers, I crossed my heart, then raised them to shoulder-level. "Scout's honor."

Frankie held my gaze, ruminating over how much to share, or how to lessen the blow. I couldn't tell which. "When we first found Mary Anne she was— How much has he told you about the murders?"

"Enough," I lied.

"What's that mean, exactly?"

"Just say what you have to say."

"When we found Mary Anne she was barely alive, impaled like the others. Even though she was in rough shape, she was still able to communicate…sort of."

Clearly Niko had sugar-coated the details for my benefit. "Impaled?" I said, as though I hadn't any idea.

Frankie explained the killer's MO—the antlers, playing cards, the first victim they'd found in the oil drum that seemed unrelated to the others, except for the missing left hand and the King of Hearts that washed ashore hours later. "Since Mary Anne was in shock, Niko had her blink her answers. Once for yes, twice for no. Somehow, she mentioned the killer knew you or him. I'm not clear how it all went down. But look. Eyewitnesses are often unreliable, especially under those circumstances. That's probably why he didn't tell you."

Staring into her eyes, trying to decipher the things she did not say, I remained silent for several moments as she squirmed, her gaze flitting everywhere but at me. "Makes me wonder what else you aren't telling me. Because earlier, you specifically said something about being horrified by what Mary Anne said."

Frankie swatted the air. "I don't know what I'm sayin' half the time, lately."

"Uh-ha."

"Anyway—" she ambled farther into the kitchen— "can we

do what we gotta do? My crew will be here soon and if Niko catches me, I'll never get off suspension."

"You're suspended?"

"Shit." Frankie chewed her upper lip. "Technically, yes. After Niko found Chance's scalpel, he accused me of not being objective. Ridiculous, right?"

I didn't bother to respond.

"I've already memorialized the scene," she said as if the previous exchange never took place. "All I need for you to do is document the evidence collection."

"How do you plan to process it? I don't think you've thought this through. Niko will know the scene's been compromised, and he'll explode when he finds out we're the ones who did it. Basically, we'd be handing a mistrial to the defense, if the DA could even prosecute under these circumstances."

"Yeah, yeah, yeah. You're not tellin' me anything I don't already know. What the hell am I supposed to do? I can't just sit around and do nothing."

"I'm not saying that. Lord knows I couldn't either when Chloe…and now with Noah—" Tears built in my throat, and I swatted my comment away. "All I'm saying is, let's be smart about this."

"What do you suggest?"

"How the hell should I know? You're the cop. Do what you normally do without removing the evidence. Maybe photograph it instead, or look for clues, but do it without disturbing the crime scene."

"Great idea. To be safe, put these on, too." Frankie tossed me a pair of latex gloves. "We don't wanna leave prints." She checked her watch. "It's almost six. We don't have much time before the sun comes up."

Frankie withdrew a ballpoint pen from her inside jacket pocket and swirled an area in the blood pool that was so thick it was amazing the woman survived as long as she did. "Man, there's gotta be three pints here."

The pen made ripples in the crimson pool while she raised

several clumps of hair, two broken fingernails, and a square, white card.

"Let me see that." With a dish towel, I scrubbed off the blood. The business card read, *Chance Rocco, DVM.*

Chapter Sixteen

6:00 a.m.

The search of their home garnered very little evidence. The mutt must've worn gloves, because the only prints Niko's team found were from him and Sage. Maybe if Sage hadn't pocketed the baby monitor, it would've provided prints, but with her still not home, he could only guess.

A thickness balled in his throat. He should've never dismissed Sage's ramblings as paranoia. How could he be this lax with his family? After Mary Anne Goodman mentioned Sage, he should've run to her, held her, told her everything would be all right. But he didn't. He couldn't. The county depended on him. Why did the job always come first? Civilians had no idea of the sacrifices cops made on a daily basis and sometimes, with dire consequences.

Please don't let this be one of those times. I'm begging you, Lord, please keep Noah safe.

"How Am I Supposed to Live Without You" by Michael Bolton blared from the speaker of his cell phone—Sage's way of sending private messages via his ringtone. Emotions bubbled to the surface, impeded his strong façade, and he fought to keep his voice steady. "Sheriff Quintano."

"Sir, there's been another 187," said Doris from dispatch. "Sorry for calling your cell, but you didn't answer the radio."

"How many times do I have to tell you 187 is a gang term? New Hampshire ten-code for homicide is 10-50. Please make a note of it."

"Sorry, sir. We've had a report of a 10-50."

97

Niko resisted the urge to shake his head. "Address?"

"The east side of McDaniels Marsh."

McDaniels Marsh? He and Ben left there an hour ago. There must be more to the marsh, sections not visible from the main entrance. "I'll need the exact coordinates."

Doris rattled off the GPS location.

"Copy that. Call in Ben and Bradley, but not Campanelli. Am I clear?"

"10-62."

"A bomb? Where, the marsh?"

"A bomb! Oh, my goodness, I hope my Brian isn't anywhere near it. I couldn't bear the thought of—"

Baring his teeth, he fought the urge to berate her. Instead, he used a cool but firm tone. "Doris, please stop talking."

"I don't copy, sir."

Retirement couldn't come fast enough. "You said 10-62, which is New Hampshire's ten-code for a bomb threat. I'm assuming that's not what you meant."

"Oh, sorry, sir. Hang on while I check the chart."

"Just tell me what's on your mind."

"Here it is. I've got it now. 10-14 at McDonald's."

"Request granted."

"Thank you, sir. I'll radio Mathews and Bradley before I go."

"Copy that." As he thumbed the off button, he scrawled a mental note to place an ad for new help.

Twenty minutes later, he drove down a wooded trail to an obscure part the marsh, the icy water impassable due to a beaver dam. Nowhere near the main entrance, either. No wonder they'd missed the remains.

The early-morning sky muted with shades of navy, pink, and lilac, the new sun rising behind mountain tops. Bald eagles and crows hovered overhead in preparation to feast on the victim. Their cries distinct, excited, unnerving.

As much as he needed Frankie's help with this case— Noah's abduction messed with his head, but the state police insisted he steer clear of the investigation—he couldn't lift her suspension. It's his duty and privilege to get justice for the victims' families. Especially now, with a front row seat to the agony they experienced.

Dammit. Some days he really hated this job.

Chapter Seventeen

6:15 a.m.

By the time I pulled into the driveway Niko wasn't home. Maybe he found something to pinpoint Noah's location. I scurried down the walkway to the front door. When I stuck my key in the lock the baby monitor crackled.

"You home, Mommy?"

I pressed the intercom button. "I'm here. Tell me what to do."

Noah cried in the background, fracturing my existence, bringing me to my knees. "Oh, baby. It's okay. Mommy's here."

A sinister snicker echoed through the speaker.

"Tell me what you want. I'm done playing your twisted game. I want my son back. Now, dammit!"

"My, my. Still brave, I see. Good. You're gonna need it. At five p.m. sharp, drive to the corner of Pleasant and Lake Street and await further instructions."

"I'll be there."

"And Mommy?"

"Yes?"

"If I see one more cop at your house, the deal's off. You'll never see your child again."

How did he know? Was he watching us, watching me? An arctic chill struck my core, and I gasped. He had a partner, someone to stalk me while he stayed with Noah. "You won't. I mean, I understand." I paused to work up the courage to ask what I ached for most in this cruel world. "May I please speak to my son?"

The monitor crackled.

"Please... He's so frightened. I'll calm him for you."

Silence hung between us like a bloody scalpel, razor-sharp and ready to slice.

"Sir?" I raised the monitor high above my head...down low... to the left...to the right. "Sir?"

Tears washed my face, a niggling pang burrowing deep through my empty womb. "Noah," I cried, buckled over, my hands on my belly. If only he was still inside me, protected, safe, sheltered by his mother's love. I turned my gaze to the heavens. "Please let my child survive. I don't care what happens to me as long as he lives."

In the kitchen, I locked the door behind me. Not that it'd do much good now, but I couldn't think straight and watch my back at the same time. Ruger lumbered into the kitchen and opened his mouth for his morning pain cookie. Rimadyl worked wonders for arthritic fur-babies.

Setting the beef-flavored tab on his tongue, I uttered, "I love you so much. You know that, right?" I squatted to his level and locked him in a warm embrace.

Colt galloped into the kitchen, nuzzling his muzzle in between us. I lost my balance and fell back on the ceramic tiles. A dog on each side, they soaked my face with slobbery kisses, their breath hot against my cheeks, forehead, chin...nowhere was off-limits. I didn't resist. Their unconditional love renewed my soul.

To their detriment, since Noah's birth I hadn't given them the attention they deserved. We still cuddled on the sofa, but for years my whole world revolved around Niko, Colt, and Ruger. Unintentionally, I'd hurt their feelings, evident by the way they smothered me with love. They missed me. With Noah around, they probably believed he outranked them. He didn't. Not really. I had plenty of love to share.

Their sad eyes revealed so much pain. Did they feel guilty about not preventing Noah's abduction?

I maneuvered to an upright position, my back pressed against the cabinets, and cradled their blocky heads in my arms. "If you guys think you failed your brother in any way, let me put your fears to rest. No one blames you. That man drugged you, my puppy loves. None of this is your fault. Please forgive yourselves."

Ruger's head hung low and Colt refused eye contact.

"Hey." I stroked their backs. "You two mean everything to me. I love you so much, my heart aches to see you so sad. Come on." I scratched each one on the scruff of the neck and kissed their foreheads. "One tiny smile. Please?"

Colt caved first, with a long lick up the side of my face.

"Rugey, honey, you all right?"

Whimpering, he plopped across my lap, buried his face under his paws. In an instant, his sobs exhausted my strong charade, transformed me into a blubbering mess, his cries tangling my very essence into knots, abolishing any hope that they weren't affected by our family's destruction.

Consoling his brother, Colt rested his chin on Ruger's spine. The three of us bawled over our loss, huddled together on the creamy ceramic tiles, mourning Noah's absence.

Spears of sunlight reached through the kitchen window, lavished us as if God attempted to soothe our pain with warmth and adoration. If only it were that easy. An evil man robbed us of the lifeblood of this family. In a matter of hours, I had to confront him. Whatever fate awaited me, nothing could be worse than the guilt and shame I carried now, even if he stole my final breath.

* * *

An hour later, I was at my desk, researching buck antlers. Pages and pages of hidden meanings filled the screen. The first to catch my eye was their biblical reference.

He makes my feet like the feet of a deer; he enables me to stand on the heights. ~ Psalms 18:33

I read on.

Myths, legends, and cosmogonies told of spiritual animals, one being the deer, which symbolized the personification of virtues and a strong character. The antlers gave the animal superiority. Like a crown of thorns, the antlers grow beyond its body, reaching for the sky, making it sacred. In many cultures, the deer is the symbol of spiritual authority, because during its lifetime the antlers fall off and regrow. Thus, the animal is also symbolic of regeneration.

Some Christians viewed deer as a piety, devotion, and of God caring for his flock. The legend of Saint Eustace told the story of a Roman general who, before sainthood, was out hunting when he came across a magnificent deer. When Eustace gazed into its eyes the light of Christ shone through and he heard the voice of God. The following day he relinquished his love of hunting and became a Christian.

In Celtic tradition, two aspects of the deer came into play. The feminine, called *Eilid* in Gaelic, which symbolized femininity, gentleness, and grace. They believed deer called to man from the kingdom of fairies to free them from the trappings of this world, leading them into magical realms. The masculine side, known as *Damh*, related to the sacred and to forests, independence, purification, and pride. The protector of all creatures, great and small.

Native Americans believed the deer was a messenger, a power animal, and a totem that represented sensitivity, intuition, and gentleness. Some Cherokee tribes even conveyed a legend that deer procured its antlers after winning the race against a rabbit who cheated.

Buddhism told the story of harmony, happiness, peace, and longevity. When a buck and doe stood together they showed a direct allusion to the first teachings of Buddha, near Varanasi. By presence alone they represented the purity of a kingdom bereft of fear.

All the customs I found related the deer to kindness, softness, and gentleness, an animal connected to the gods, to the magical, and to the sacred. Their stare, agility, speed, and antlers inspired values and symbols throughout many cultures, but I found nothing to indicate an urge to kill, evil, or anything sinister connected to the deer or its antlers.

Unless the killer used them as a symbol for something else. The odd part was, with the exception of hermaphrodite deer, only males grew antlers. When placed around a female victim, they could indicate entrapment.

So, who in the killer's mind was he trapping again and again?

Chapter Eighteen

7:00 a.m.

Niko approached the barrel, washed ashore on the edge of McDaniels Marsh. He bent over to look inside. Empty. Did Doris give him the right location?

A quick scan of the area answered that question. About ten feet off shore a corpse floated face-down in the water. Chances were, the killer didn't fasten the drum's lid properly, so when putrefaction took place, the remains escaped its watery grave.

Crunching diverted his attention.

"What do you need me to do, boss?" Ben's uniform freshly pressed, he'd buffed his shoes to a glossy shine. Too bad they wouldn't stay that way.

"Get your waders on and nudge the vic to shore."

"What?" Shock registered on his face. "Shouldn't we wait for Gaines?"

"Do as I ask, please. I've already alerted Marine Patrol. Sergeant Banks gave the go-ahead to start without him."

Ben jogged to his department-issued SUV, and Niko called out, "Have Bradley cordon off the area."

Head cocked, Ben gave him a look like an untrained dog trying to understand the English language.

"Have…Bradley…cordon…off…the…area. He's right behind you."

Like Noah, Ben dragged out the process of slipping into waders in the hopes that Niko would change his mind. When Noah pulled this stunt, the move tickled his heart with fond memories of his own childhood. Ben's display had the opposite effect.

"Enough screwing around. Get in the water." One might've thought Niko ordered him into the death chamber by the way he dragged his size twelve boots toward the corpse.

Glancing over his shoulder at Niko, Ben's hands hovered inches above the body.

"Nudge her toward me, but be careful. Until I can get a better look, we don't know how fragile the remains are."

"Ya mean, she could fall apart? In my hands?"

"Let's not worry about that now. First thing's first. Bring her to me, please."

As Ben neared, a quizzical expression crossed his face. "I wonder why she's face-down."

Niko beamed like a proud parent. "Excellent question." He assisted Ben in lifting the left-handless victim onto the snowy shoreline. "Actually, most floaters are found face-down. When a cadaver sinks, the air in the lungs gets replaced with water. After submersion, during the putrefaction stage, the bacteria in the gut and chest cavity emit gas, which raises the corpse like helium in a birthday balloon."

"Gas?"

"Methane, hydrogen sulfide, carbon dioxide. That brings up another great point, though. Because she was found face-down, we know something else."

Ben crinkled his nose. "We do?"

"Think about what I just said, then tell me how we can use this information."

Head shaking ever so slightly, Ben stared at the corpse. "I've got no idea."

"Grab your notepad. Time for another quick lesson."

Prompting Niko to continue, he flipped to a fresh page.

"When the victim entered the marsh, the lungs filled with water like I just mentioned. The body then sank until the putrefaction stage, where bacteria in the gut and chest cavity accumulated—these gases normally aid our immune system while alive—which resulted in the body becoming buoyant. However, the extremities take longer to bloat, so the head, arms, and legs slumped forward as the body rose to the surface. This dragging of limbs causes the face-down posture. Make sense?"

"Because of the weight?"

"Yes. Very good. Okay, so, if the lungs have no air when a body enters the water, what does that tell us?"

"That she's dead?"

"You askin' me or tellin' me?"

"No air in the lungs would mean she's dead," he said, his tone etched with conviction.

"Correct. So now, since our victim was found face-down that tells us what?"

"That she was still alive when she went into the water."

"Actually, that was a trick question, but good guess. The answer is yes and no. We'll need to wait for the autopsy to pinpoint time of death. Because, believe it or not, unlike other organs, lung cells don't depend on blood flow for oxygen. When the heart stops beating, the lungs use the remaining oxygen in the air sacs and airways, which is what keeps the lungs from deteriorating. However, even if she was dead when she entered the water, the lungs can only survive for up to four hours after death. This helps us create a concrete timeline."

"Cool."

"Cool is right." He patted Ben's shoulder. "You'll make a fine sheriff someday. One last thing to remember. The buildup of methane, hydrogen sulfide, and carbon dioxide can take days or weeks to develop. Which tells us…?"

His face lit up; he knew this one. "By subtracting the time she went into the water by the TOD, we might be able to approximate a driving radius of where she was killed."

Niko's eyebrows lifted in amazement. "Very good. We'll need to factor in a few other things as well, but bravo. Bodies that have been dead a while have different floating patterns."

Niko squatted beside the corpse. Stuck between her teeth was some sort of paper. He pried open her mouth. "Grab that please."

Arm extended, the rest of Ben's body as far away as possible, he reached into her mouth with the apprehension of a novice diver examining shark's teeth.

To get a better look Niko bobbed and weaved his head. "Is it a note?"

"Yeah, it says, 'She can run, but she can't hide.'" He raised his face to look at Niko. "I don't get it. What's it mean?"

"Maybe he knew her." With the victim's lips still pried apart, he leaned in, his eyebrows drawing together. "There's something else in here. It's lodged deep in her throat. Grab me a pair of forceps from the kit, please."

Ben jogged toward the duffel bag, returned moments later, and slapped the forceps into Niko's palm.

Careful, steady, Niko gripped the edge of thin cardboard-like paper. This was almost too easy, like the killer purposefully wanted it found. When he unfurled the cryptic clue, his theory made sense. "King of Hearts. Why am I not surprised?"

Silent, Ben's gaze traveled the marsh.

"What's wrong? Talk to me."

"Where's Frankie?"

"Lemme see the note please."

He passed Niko the drenched scrap paper, with block lettering and bleeding black ink. Deciphering the mysterious message, Niko remarked, "Unless our victim isn't the right 'she'."

Gagging, Ben clamped his hands on his knees. "I'll never get used to this smell." His back swelled; Ben's gag reflex was in perfect working order. "Floaters are even more bogus than regular corpses. How is that even possible?"

"It's true." A wretched odor tunneled through his sinuses. Akin to rotted meat, decaying fruit, urine, feces, and blood, this god-awful stench penetrated everything in its path, including investigators' clothing, skin, and hair.

Early in their marriage, Sage requested he strip before entering their home. In Boston, it wasn't an easy task because the houses stood so close together. Once they moved to the country, however, the ritual became a breeze. He'd strip to his boxers in the mudroom, drop his soiled clothes in the hamper Sage left for this purpose—a hamper marked "Death laundry" in case there was any question—and then enter. She also left a change of clothes for him.

He chuckled to himself, and then an overwhelming sadness took him by surprise. Oh, how he missed her laugh. Why didn't he see it before? This change in her demeanor was his fault. During her forty-eight years on this earth, she'd been assaulted and emotionally scarred more than anyone should endure. If she hadn't married a cop, she could've lived a normal life filled with joy, children's laughter, a white-picket fence, and dogs frolicking in the backyard. Instead, Niko led death and destruction to their home.

Over time, while he shared the gruesome details of homicide case after homicide case, one sinful act more brutal than the last, her charming naiveté withered away like lily pads in a frozen pond. She had no choice but to face the harsh reality that wicked men roamed free. This world was not a safe place. A masked man drilled that message home one fateful night in Boston, five years ago, the night an elusive killer slipped through Niko's grasp.

Due to his profession and lack of common sense, he ruined the woman he loved most in this world. Why would she forgive him? And now, because of him, another sicko would soon tarnish the purity of their child.

With a vacant stare across the marsh, tears teemed in his eyes.

Ben's elbow brushed his, and he startled. Rubbing his watery lashes with the top of his gloved-wrist, he cleared his throat. "Where was I? Oh, right. Floaters are the worst due to the bloating mixed with putrefaction."

Ben buried his nose in the crook of his arm. "Got any more of that Vick's stuff?"

"In my truck."

While Ben jogged toward the SUV, Niko studied the note, the unknown gnawing at his side.

If he substituted "Sage" for "she" the killer's message became even more haunting: *Sage could run, but she can't hide.*

Chapter Nineteen

4:30 p.m.

As instructed, I drove to the corner of Pleasant and Lake Street a half-hour early so I wouldn't be late. What was I looking for? He never said. At first, I figured he meant a phone booth, but who uses phone booths anymore? My empty stomach tightened to a fist. Did I blow the one chance to save my son?

My iPhone® rang, and I fumbled to answer. "I'm here."

"You're where?" asked Niko.

"I can't talk right now."

"Where are you, Sage? If you heard from the kidnappers—"

"Kidnappers? There's more than one?"

"Gimme your location. If you're making a drop, I don't want you alone."

"I have to go. I'll explain later." I disconnected. With the spotty cell signals around here, I could always blame the abrupt end to our conversation on a dead spot. As much as I hated to do this by myself, I couldn't risk Noah's safety because of my husband's refusal to get involved. What were the state police doing to find him? As far as I could tell, nothing. Unacceptable.

I slid the shifter into park and killed the engine. Last Christmas, Niko had surprised me with the Land Rover. We thought it'd be a safer vehicle for Noah, never realizing he could be abducted from our home.

Multiple businesses surrounded downtown Bristol, the next town over from Alexandria. We shared the same zip code, neither with enough population to warrant division. State liquor store, hair salon, Bond's Auto Parts, hardware store…no place a lone thirteen-month-old could wander the streets unnoticed.

While I waited for instructions, I set the phone on the dash and reviewed my copy of Mary Anne Goodman's case file for clues that might lead me in the right direction. The autopsy report showed high levels of ketamine in her system. On the streets, drug users called it special K, which I'd learned when I researched street gangs. When we lived in Boston, I wrote a true crime novel, entitled *Deadly Dawgs*, about the inner workings of a blood gang called The Columbia Point Dawgs, the largest and most powerful street gang in the city.

Back in 1988, the Dawgs were "born in blood" when they murdered the leader of a rival gang who'd set up drug trafficking on their turf—aka the Columbia Point housing projects, one of the most crime-ridden, dilapidated areas of Boston at the time.

The Dawgs' violence, murder, and drug trafficking continued to this day.

A new housing project ran numerous gang members out of the Columbia Point projects and renamed the apartment complex Harbor Point on the Bay, which now charged residents three-thousand dollars a month. This change only worsened the Dawgs' activities as they wrestled drug dealers in other neighborhoods. Turf wars weren't only dangerous for gang members; we all worried when one broke out.

Could a member of the Dawgs be involved in Noah's kidnapping? Maybe a rogue member relocated to New Hampshire to "make his bones" by slaughtering non-paying clients.

Tears spilled down my face. My baby… the child we waited a lifetime for could be in the hands of a blood gang who enjoyed wreaking havoc and wouldn't hesitate to take his life, if they didn't get what they wanted from me.

A fierce shudder ran through me as if someone outlined a toddler-sized grave in orange spray paint. Was this about revenge? Did the Dawgs target my family because of my book?

Chapter Twenty

For hours, I waited for a sign, something to lead me to my son. Then, as I clicked on the headlights, a white panel-van pulled alongside the Land Rover. What happened to the dark sedan? Did he steal different vehicles to suit his needs?

The side-door slid open and the silhouette of a man cradled Noah in his arms. The van was so close to my vehicle I couldn't open the door.

Eagle eyes on my son, I tugged my door handle six or seven times.

The same raspy, sinister voice that haunted the baby monitor pierced the frigid night air. "Your life for his, Mommy." His tone dripped with ire. "That's the deal. Take it or leave it."

Noah screeched, his terror steeped in the horror of his experience. Breastmilk soaked through my blouse, the mother inside me unhinged, paranoid, petrified by what the stranger might do.

Without hesitation, I said, "I'll take it," and then swung one leg over the console to exit out the passenger side.

"Wrong way," he teased, and stopped me cold.

"How, then?"

"Through the window, Mommy. We don't need an audience. C'mon. Tick tock, time's slipping away."

Feet first, I slid out the window, on to the two-feet of pavement between the vehicles, and then opened my arms for Noah. "Give him to me."

"Get in the van."

111

"How do I know you'll let him go?"

"You don't."

The dome light flicked on.

In slow motion, he listed his head to the left, then to right, and I shrieked. He raised one white-gloved finger to his mask, a disturbing latex rendition of a killer clown. Tremors licked up my spine as I gaped in disbelief. The clown's mouth splayed open with razor-sharp teeth, blood dripped off fang-like canines. Hunter-green diamonds outlined piercing-gold eyes, reflective in the dim interior. The faux skin a grayish-white. The blood-red nose matched the lips, arched in a snarling grin.

When I reached for Noah, my arms trembled against my will. "Let me take him home and I'll go anywhere you want."

Theatrics afoot, he tapped his forefinger against his chin, the white-cotton glove masking his ethnicity, complexion, scars or tattoos—distinguishable features that might lead to his capture. "Fine. The brat does nothing but cry anyway."

I scooped Noah into my arms, and he nuzzled his face under my chin. *Thump, thump, thump* thundered through his onesie and well-worn blankie—also stolen from our bed. To comfort, to protect, and to show him I'd never let go, I enveloped him with my jacket. In his tight fists, he crumpled my blouse, and bawled.

"You renege and I will kill him. Got that, Mommy?"

Rote, one hand on Noah, I slid my Gemini charm across the chain. "Yes."

"Toss me your phone."

"Why? Abducting my child isn't enough for you, now you want to dig through my entire life?" The clown's cold stare erased the sardonic edge to my tone. "I'm sorry. I didn't mean that. I'm confused about why you need my cell."

In slow motion, he slanted his head to the right, then to the left. Each time he used this ploy, it rattled me. This creep took melodrama to a whole new level. "Because we don't need an audience. As it is, the cops in your house broke our deal."

"That wasn't my fault. I had no idea my husband called them till they showed up at my door." I fudged the facts.

If he knew he'd frightened me to the point of fainting, his omnipotence would intensify, and I was not about to give him that satisfaction.

"Fork over your cell, Mommy. I don't work on the honor system."

I slapped my phone into his outstretched hand, and he tucked my lifeline inside his leather jacket.

"Don't try anything stupid, Mommy. I'll be right behind you."

"Like I said, once he's home safe, I'm all yours."

Behind the mask, he sniggered as though he had specific plans for my ultimate demise.

The van door slid shut.

Within seconds, his vehicle reversed enough to open my back passenger door, then idled while I buckled Noah in his car seat. I swept his wispy locks off his face. "I love you so much, sugar plum." Breathing him in, my lips pressed against his forehead, I assured him I'd get him home safe.

Noah responded, his words incoherent through the tears.

A blazing car horn kicked my adrenaline into overdrive. The clown waved forward, gestured for me to hurry.

I locked the back door and slid behind the wheel. The entire drive home, I planned our escape. I couldn't leave Noah home alone, and I certainly was in no rush to become a casualty of a blood gang. As I hung a left onto Cass Mill Road, I reviewed every possible scenario. None ideal. This would not be easy, but I needed to summon the courage to protect my child. Too much had transpired for me to fail him twice.

Two miles down the road, I veered left and pinned the gas pedal to the floorboards. At the top of our road, I banged a sharp left into the driveway, the back tires fishtailing in the snow. Headlights jounced at the foot of our mountain. The van sped out in the slush, not heavy enough to gain traction.

I bundled Noah in my arms and sprinted down the walkway, into the mudroom, and kicked the door closed behind me. Scratches gouged the antique brass around the lock on the kitchen door, the key trembling in my hand.

Heavy boots stomped down the walkway. Before he reached us, I slipped into the kitchen and re-engaged the padlock. "I'll be right out," I called through the door.

He panted through the latex mask.

Hackles on end, Colt and Ruger skittered into the kitchen. Ruger whimpered for Noah, still locked in my arms, and I squatted to his level. Using the tip of his tongue, careful not to cause harm, he dried his brother's tears. A tiny giggle escaped Noah's wet lips.

"Good boy." With the back of my hand, I caressed Ruger's furry cheek—waited a beat—then pointed at the door. "Watch 'em," I said, low but firm.

Ruger snapped into protection mode.

I whispered to Colt, "Bring Mommy the phone." Colt zipped into the living room. With the cordless handset wedged between his teeth, he met me at the loft stairs. Before he blessed our lives, he'd trained to join the K9 Unit. Even though he never graduated, on more than one occasion his skills came in handy.

"Good boy." I mussed his fur. "Go help Rugey guard the door." Colt galloped into the kitchen and took his place next to his brother. Squared hips, heads held high, chests out, low growls rumbling in their throat. Two statuesque heroes, willing to sacrifice themselves to protect us. Not that I'd ever let that happen.

With Noah on my hip, I dialed Niko's cell phone, but got his voicemail. "Get home now. I've got Noah, but the man who took him is here. God, I hope you get this message in time." I paused, took a breath. "If you don't make it home, please don't let our son forget me. I love you, pup. Always remember that. Love you to the moon, 'round the world, and back again."

Chapter Twenty-One

9:00 p.m.

Earlier, a call came over the radio about another homicide, but Frankie only caught the tail end. Debating whether to call dispatch, she keyed the mic.

Dammit. Doris answered.

With her all-business tone, she said, "Dispatch, what's the 10-50?"

"Sheriff Quintano left me specific instructions not to contact you."

Lip curled in a sneer, Frankie ignored her. "Confirm location of 10-50."

"Deputy Campanelli, I will do no such thing."

"All right, all right, don't get your panties in a bunch."

Flabbergasted, Doris gasped. "Deputy Campanelli."

Snooty bitch. She flicked on the sirens. "In pursuit of a red Chevy Avalanche, New York plates, six-five-Henry-David-niner-three-Bravo."

"In pursuit? Oh, my. Running the plate now."

For the full effect Frankie held the mic toward the siren.

"Plate comes back to a Mr. Phuck Mehard"

Tears of laughter welled in her eyes. Screwing with dispatch never got old. Ever. She killed the siren. "Great idea, Doris. Maybe then you'll lighten up." Her cell phone vibrated in her pocket. Maybe Niko changed his mind. "Campanelli."

"It's Sage. How fast can you get to my house?"

"You all right?" Frankie flipped on the lights, banged a U-turn in the middle of the main drag. "What happened?"

115

"I have Noah, but the man—" Chaos exploded in the background. Dogs barking, growling, a male voice shouting obscenities. For two dogs who rarely got vocal, never mind violent, this *was not* a good sign. "Hurry. He's beating down the door."

"On my way. Don't be brave, Sage. Hide."

Voice barely audible, her frantic whisper muffled even more. "Please hurry. If he has a gun, I can't risk him shooting the kids."

"I'm goin' as fast as I can. Whatever you do, *do not* engage the suspect."

"If I'm not around by the time you get here, please help Niko care for Noah. Tell him, I'll never stop loving them. Promise me, Frankie. I can't reach him, and I don't know how much more time I have."

Vehicles refused to pull over to let her pass. Zigzagging in and out of lanes, the tires slipped on the icy road. Hand over hand, she regained control of the wheel. "Don't talk like that. I'm five minutes out." More like ten, but why add to her distress?

"Promise me."

Frankie pounded the steering wheel. "Listen to me, dammit. You're gonna be fine. I'm almost there."

"I know you're not big on the mushy stuff, but I love you too, you know." Her tone turned calm. Too calm, like she'd given up all hope of survival. "We would've never gotten through the tragedy two years ago without you. You've always been there for us. Take the time you need to process what's happening with Chance. Maybe you're not seeing the whole picture. I sure wasn't when I allowed my child to get kidnapped from our bed."

Gas pedal pinned, she blew through an intersection, through red lights and stop signs. Drivers flipped her off. Relentless honking. They're lucky she couldn't stop, or she'd shove the horns down their throats. "Please stop talkin' like this. You're freakin' me out."

"For that, I'm truly sorry. I don't know what more I can do here." Incessant scratching, barking, growling in the background demonstrated the dogs' willingness to stop the suspect at all cost, like they were ready to claw through the door, attack in a ravenous rage. "I need you to promise me, Frankie. *Please.* I can't leave without knowing my family will be well-cared for."

"Fuck!" Body temperature rising in intensity, she punched the dash. "I'm almost there." The car up ahead swerved all over the road, probably drunk. She couldn't stop. Saving Sage was all that mattered. "Okay, fine. I promise. Now you listen to me. You did nothing wrong. In the middle of the night, some psycho broke into your house. No one could've predicted that, so stop talkin' like it's your fault. It isn't." Hughes of blue tumbled into the blackness of the backroad. A few more minutes and she'd arrive. Till then, she needed enough information to plan her strategy. "Tell me exactly what's happening, the more detailed the better."

In the background, Colt and Ruger snarled and spit, itching for a fight. Noah wailed, his cries deafening as if screaming into the phone.

"Also," Sage continued on as though Frankie hadn't said a word, like bedlam hadn't erupted in her home, "cut Niko some slack. He depends on you more than you know."

"Snap out of it. You're talkin' crazy, woman." She gripped a clump of hair, almost yanked the strands from her scalp. "Listen to me." She stopped, rephrased, her voice calmer. "Go upstairs and lock yourself in the bathroom. Do you have access to Niko's backup piece?"

"I can't let him hurt Colt and Ruger. It's me he wants. If I go peacefully, maybe he'll leave my family alone."

"Move your ass! You've got a Rottweiler and mastiff to protect you. No one in their right mind would mess with those dogs." She quelled the heated attitude, worsened by the heightened urgency. "Please, Sage. Think of Noah."

"I *am* thinking of Noah."

"Dammit, Sage!"

"I'll leave him in his crib. Make sure you run to him first."

"Don't you dare hang up on me."

A dial tone hummed in her ear.

Frankie punched the roof, dash, anything within reach. "Fuck, fuck, fuck!" Rolling her head, she cracked the bones in her neck, took a deep breath, and keyed up the mic. "Dispatch, radio Sheriff Quintano and tell him to get home ASAP. Don't stop till you get a hold of him. Do you copy?"

"I'm not falling for another one of your sick jokes, thank you very much. You must take me for a fool."

"Doris, if you don't find Niko—"

"I do not take orders from suspended personnel."

She didn't have time for this crap. Anything could be happening to Sage—rape, torture, or worse. "It's about his wife, you frickin' moron."

Silence came over the radio.

Softly, Doris said, "Copy that."

The next few minutes dragged as Frankie sped up the mountain to the Quintanos' country contemporary. With the house in total darkness, she leaped from the driver's door, sprinted down the walkway. Dim solar lanterns barely illuminated a path to the door. Sideways, Frankie slipped inside the mudroom, pressed her back against the doorjamb of the kitchen entrance. "Sheriff's Department."

No response.

Slow. Cautious. She kicked the door open a few more inches, her flashlight clipped to her gun. Long tunnels of light ripped through the darkness as she cleared the kitchen and living room.

Louder than before, she hollered, "Sheriff's Department."

Still no response. Where were they?

Chapter Twenty-Two

10:00 p.m.

Staging lights around the crime scene at McDaniels Marsh helped Niko and his team find evidence they might miss in the dark. Crime scene investigators in hooded bunny suits—aka white Tyvek® coveralls—tagged and bagged evidence while crime scene photographers snapped pictures before, during, and after removal. What struck Niko more than anything was the silence. Death locations tended to elicit an unnerving quiet.

Massive amounts of wildlife flooded the area. Bald eagles soared through the sky, a squeaky *kuk-kuk-kuk* reverberating off treetops. Owls perched on branches around the perimeter of the marsh, Blue Herons fished in the shallow parts, beavers built dams, and muskrats constructed pop-ups, tiny heads bobbing under the murky water.

An Aramis cloud encircled Niko's head when Dr. Gaines took control of the body. Waving away the stench, he coughed. "Got a rough TOD for me, Doc?"

"Sorry, Sheriff. That will best be determined after I complete my autopsy. However, I will schedule it for first thing tomorrow morning."

"Thanks. Appreciate it." He called for Ben. "I'm running to grab a quick bite. Want anything?"

"Nah. The floater ruined my appetite."

"You gonna be okay here for a while?"

"Y'mean, I'm in charge?"

Niko chuckled. "Just do your job. I'll be back as soon as I can."

When Niko hit the parking lot, "Just Once" by James Ingram

blasted from his jacket pocket, Sage drilling her message home. "Sheriff Quintano."

"Sheriff, it's Doris. I've been trying to reach you for a solid hour. You need to get home ASAP. Deputy Campanelli radioed in an emergency."

"Did something happen? Is my wife all right?"

"All she said was that you needed to get home. She gave no specifics. Would you like me to find out?"

"No. I'm on my way." He clicked off the phone and slipped behind the wheel. Stomping the gas pedal, he barreled out of the lot, banged a right, then left, pushing the SUV to its max.

Niko made it home in record time. When he pulled into the driveway every light was on inside the house. Frankie's department-issued vehicle hung half in the driveway, the tail end in the road, the driver's door ajar. *Ding, ding, ding.* She'd left the key in the ignition—a sinister beat that elevated Niko's awareness.

Poking his head in the kitchen, he hollered for Sage, but got no response.

"Babe?" Gun drawn, he stalked into the living room.

Frankie appeared at the top landing to the loft, and her grave expression shook him to the core. "Up here, Niko."

"Is my family all right?"

"You need to come upstairs."

Every bone in his body warned him not to follow Frankie, but he had no choice. In the master suite, she swung her arm toward the bathroom. When Niko peeked inside, the heart severed from his chest, dangled somewhere near his feet.

Sage huddled in the bathtub, rocking Noah in her arms. Eyelids closed, lines of tears streaked both cheeks. Colt and Ruger faced the door—proud and strong—their hind feet on the bathmat. Formidable soldiers guarding the unlucky who dared to enter their domain.

Careful not to startle his wife, he squeezed between the kids and caressed Sage's cheek. Noah cracked open one eye, and Niko released a pained moan. Through their unnatural stillness both his wife and son revealed severe inner turmoil, the details of why weren't clear. He kissed Noah's forehead, slick from Sage's tears. One stroke of her hair, and her chest writhed harder, her anguish on display.

"Babe, talk to me. Are you okay?" Stupid question. Of course she wasn't all right. Why didn't he say something meaningful? The cop in him yearned for answers, but the husband longed for more, something tangible to explain what they'd experienced.

She nodded yes.

"Is he?"

She nodded a second time.

"Can you tell me what happened?" Wrong again. Maybe he should slide in behind her, tell her that together they could heal, together they'd fight, together they'd crush the man who did this. But he didn't. The very sight of Sage and Noah jumbled his thoughts.

He caused this. While the homicide investigation distracted him, his wife and child suffered a traumatic, even horrific, event, a situation that put both their lives in jeopardy.

"I'll be right back." He hooked an arm at Frankie. Outside the bathroom door, he dragged her farther into the master bedroom. "Why are they both in shock?"

"I'm not really sure. I found them like that."

"How'd you know to come here?"

"When Sage couldn't find you, she called me. She was talkin' crazy, Niko, like sayin' goodbye and stuff. I'd never heard her like that. Scared the shit outta me, too." As if remembering a detail, her face lit up. "Oh, she did say something about the dogs, which was weird. Doesn't she call them 'the kids'? Meh. Could've been a heat-of-the-moment type thing."

He peered around Frankie, into the bathroom. "What'd he do to my family?" Tears collected in his throat, quaking his voice. "I can't believe I wasn't here for them." He held a closed fist to his heart. "Help me understand. I put a car on her. I thought she'd be safe."

"Obviously, she shook the tail."

Pacing the room, he laced his fingers behind his head. "I don't

121

know how to fix this. Maybe I should move them to a safe house."

"You could try. Doubt Sage will go for it, though."

The moisture in Niko's mouth dried to dust as he battled his unrest. "Listen to me." A piercing ache throbbed inside him as he latched on to Frankie's biceps. "Go through Sage's phone. The mutt must've called her. I doubt he told her where to find Noah through the monitor."

"I'm on it."

In the doorway to the bathroom, gazing at Sage and Noah huddled together in the tub, he swallowed his emotions. "Maybe I should call a doctor. She looks almost catatonic."

"I think once the shock wears off, she'll be okay. Just give her a little time."

Niko knelt before his beloved family. "Babe, Frankie needs your phone. Is it in your bag?"

She shook her head in an emphatic no.

"Your car?"

Another no.

"Then where? We need the call history."

In a tone unfit for human ears, she uttered, "He took it."

He glanced back at Frankie, mouthed, "Ping it." Then refocused on Sage. "Lemme help you outta there." He slid his hands under her armpits. "I don't wanna hurt you, so you're gonna have to help me. Can you move your legs?"

Refusing to loosen her grip on their son, Sage slid her knees to her chest and Niko lifted her and Noah from the tub. With his family locked in his arms, Sage wept on his shoulder. Tears obscured his view when he laid them on the bed. Neither opened their eyes. Probably best. If she looked at him now, her stunning jade eyes might crush his barely-stable demeanor.

The tears came full force, soaking Sage's face, shattering Niko's soul like a boulder tossed through plate glass. For a moment, he curled beside her, an arm draped over Noah's back.

Oh, how he loved his family.

Propping his head on an open hand, elbow sunk in the pillow, he kept his voice low, calm. "How 'bout a nice cup of chamomile tea? That always makes you feel better."

Tears flowed under her thick lashes.

With his fingertip, he swept away her sadness. If only he knew how to help, but he didn't. This situation surpassed his capabilities. Sage was the nurturer in the family. No matter how minor or significant a problem, she found a solution.

He swung his legs off the bed. Slouched, his back to his family, Niko's chest caved. Head hung, tears fell in his lap. "This is on me. When you told me how scared you were I should've listened. Please tell me how to fix this."

Her non-response spoke volumes.

Chapter Twenty-Three

March 24, 2008, 5:13 a.m.

For hours, I stared at the ceiling fan, Noah asleep on my chest. Niko was out cold, too. At the foot of the bed, Colt snored so loudly the sheer scarlet curtains rippled in his wake. On the floor beside us, Ruger sat statuesque, his sight peeled on the staircase so no one could ambush us. Ever since Noah's abduction he hadn't slept much, an hour here and there if Colt stood guard. My poor baby couldn't forgive himself, and his pained eyes shredded my very existence.

With most of my family asleep, now was the perfect time to get answers.

Stealth-like, I slipped off the bed, petted Ruger's blocky head, and whispered, "You can stay, if it'll make you feel better to be near him."

I swiped my leggings off the dresser and tiptoed down the stairs. In the living room, lit only by the nightlight and the half-moon's golden luster, I searched for Niko's briefcase. I'd waited long enough for my husband to solve this case. If a connection existed between the murders and Noah's abduction, and I had no reason to think otherwise, I needed to uncover the killer's identity before he resurfaced. Next time, I might not have Colt and Ruger to protect me.

On the face of the briefcase lock I dialed in our anniversary—12-21-89—and slid two brass buttons aside. The lock popped open. I glanced over my shoulder, then fished out four file folders from under a stack of papers. If more murders occurred, Niko hadn't brought the files home.

At the kitchen table, I spread out the crime scene photos. All oxygen fled from my lungs. Three nude women with severed left hands, each victim impaled by buck antlers and iron spikes. Blood dripped down the birch trees from which they hung. A Suicide King left behind. The card's significance escaped me. In Niko's case notes he said the killer stole the hands. For what purpose wasn't clear. To display? To mount like hunting trophies? To massage his cheek as he reveled in the kill?

I swiped the cordless phone off the end table and dialed a trusted friend, my spiritual adviser, Mr. Chen.

By the end of the second ring, he answered.

"Mr. Chen, it's happening again."

"Talk to me, child." Originally from China, Mr. Chen was the most spiritual person I'd ever encountered. A master of the arts, his deep faith allowed his mind to travel beyond the realms of this world, into the unthinkable, the magical.

"I'd rather come see you."

"Married couples tell each other a thousand things without speaking." Mr. Chen offered his wisdom via Chinese proverbs. He'd held my counsel for so long, I knew almost all of them by heart.

"It's not about me and Niko. Well, not really."

"Come."

"I will. Thank you." Rather than risk waking my family, I dragged my calf-length sweater from the hanger in the coat closet. Dressed in my nightshirt and leggings, I buttoned it to my chin. By the back door, I swiped my keys off the rack and hustled outside.

Fifteen minutes later, I pulled into Mr. Chen's driveway and nudged the driver's door closed so I didn't wake the neighbors. I followed the slate walkway into the backyard, where he sat cross-legged on the high point of a bridge in his friendship garden, fingers clasped in an "O" on each knee. Around him, an icy brook rolled over four waterfalls, into a lagoon with an elevated ring of twelve animals—rat, ox, tiger, rabbit, dragon, snake, horse, goat, monkey, rooster, dog, pig—which represented the Chinese zodiac.

On each side of the bridge, candles in decorative paper

lantern bags floated on the water, flames flickering a mirrored glow. Around an outer circle of the lagoon stood symbols for the five elements—wood, fire, earth, metal, water—where we often meditated and communed with nature. Albeit, usually in warmer weather.

When I squatted to his level I didn't dare mention the nip to the air. "It's happening again, Mr. Chen."

He stared straight ahead and rattled off his standard line. "Tell me your fears, dreams, and worry. I cannot take these things. You must surrender them willingly."

"A man took Noah."

That got him to face me.

"He's home. Don't worry. Only now, the same man wants me dead." I paused to regain composure, but the events of that night replayed in my mind.

After I'd hung up from Frankie, the house erupted in total chaos. Colt and Ruger growled, barked, bared their teeth as the clown pounded on the door. The more I cowered, the more anxious they became, clawing at the wood, noses twitching, pained whines, low, guttural rumbles in their throats.

Snarling, spit flew off Colt's canines when he lunged at the clown who'd pried open the door with a crowbar. Ruger watched. Waited. Bided his time to plan his next move, evident by a transfixed glare. The masked intruder booted Colt in the ribs, and he yelped. Ruger pounced. To force him to drop the crowbar, he sank his teeth into the clown's forearm. Metal clanged on the tiles.

Mouth agape, Colt hurtled toward the man's throat, but he blocked himself with his forearm. Didn't matter to Colt. Nothing could stop him now. He latched onto the clown's thigh, whipped his head from side to side. Blood coated the fur around his muzzle as he shredded the flesh from the leg.

Ruger roared—a warning he'd also fight to the death. That I couldn't allow, so I stashed Noah in the coat closet and assured him I'd return. Then I scrambled to the kitchen and swiped the crowbar off the floor.

Weapon in hand, I cocked my arm. "Leave now, and I'll call

off the dogs. Don't, and I'll let them tear you apart. Either way, it makes no difference to me."

"You fuckin' bitch. I'll make you watch while I rape your son."

I sucked in a sharp breath. Backing away, the crowbar tremored against my leg.

"Call them off, or I'll snap their necks."

"Good luck with that." Spasms built in my toes and swept up my body as I faked a confident front. "Do we have a deal?"

He screamed in pain, and I grinned. Pinned against the wall, he agreed to my terms. As much as I hungered for revenge, I couldn't turn my puppy loves into killers. If it meant he walked free for now, then so be it.

Thumb and forefinger between my lips, I whistled for the kids. In a flash, they released him.

"We're not done here, Mommy. It might not be tonight, but you will suffer for this." With one last scowl in my direction, he turned and bolted out the door.

I dropped to my knees, praised their heroics, and checked for injuries. Both walked away unscathed. After a quick three-way embrace, I ordered the kids to stay while I retrieved Noah from the closet. Once the madness quelled, emptiness filled me deep inside, and I clambered up the stairs, into the bathroom, and climbed inside the tub, Noah locked in my arms. Spent. No fight left to offer. Nothing but a void where a happy wife and mother had once lived.

"Sage?"

"Yes, Mr. Chen?"

"Talk to me, child."

"Oh, right. If Colt and Ruger hadn't lunged at him when he barged through the door, I might not be alive."

I filled him in about the murders, Noah's kidnapping, the baby monitor, the van, and the moment I had my son back in my arms. In passing, I also mentioned my true crime novel, *Deadly Dawgs*.

"Then this morning, I found Niko's case files. The murders

are brutally vicious. Not only is the killer slaughtering innocent lives, but he's chopping off their hands. I don't know if he's saving them as trophies or what, but Niko's team hasn't found any of them."

"Left hand?"

"How'd you—?" Stupid question. How Mr. Chen knew most things remained a mystery. "I mean, yes. Always the left hand, never the right. What's it mean?"

"In dream, left hand symbolizes betrayal by brother. Dawgs is street gang, yes?"

"Yes. They're what's known as a blood gang. Their main turf's in Boston." My eyes widened. "You think they traveled north in retaliation for my book? You may be right. I've only encountered one guy, so I can't say for sure there's not more of them."

"Vengeful army will certainly win."

Stunned into silence, tears welled in my puffy eyes. "He mentioned John Doe, too."

"No time for tears. Remember teachings."

"I remember, Mr. Chen, but I'm so frightened, I can barely think, never mind look for a way out of this. Please tell me what to do."

Gazing into my watery eyes, he rested a soothing hand on my knee. "Not enter tiger den, how get tiger cub?"

"I know great rewards require great risk, but I have my family to worry about."

The hint of a smirk emerged. "A mountain cannot turn, but a road can."

"Are you saying there's another path I should follow?"

With a bow to his head, he confirmed, then offered one last nugget of wisdom. "Dripping water eventually wears away stone."

"I promise I won't quit. I'll never stop till I know Noah's safe."

Acquiescent, he bowed his head a second time.

"Thank you, Mr. Chen." Renewed, empowered, I rose to my feet. "I know what I have to do now."

Chapter Twenty-Four

6:45 a.m.

The morning sun raised its brilliant orange face above Mount Cardigan. Magenta, ruby, and deep purple streaked across the dawn sky like brush strokes on a navy canvas. Even with the homicides weighing heavily on his mind, Niko couldn't tear his gaze away as he slid his feet into wool-lined slippers. Standing in front of the loft's picture-glass window, he admired the spectacular view. In God's country, early spring offered majestic sunrises that lessened life's troubles. Except for when a serial killer targeted your family. Not much could diminish that fact.

When he shuffled down the stairs, the front door swung open. Sage strolled by with a tray of coffee and a box of scones. "Hey, pup. How'd you sleep?"

Niko stared in awe. "Uh...fine. Where'd you go?"

Busying herself in the kitchen, setting up Noah's high-chair, she refused eye contact—a telltale sign she was hiding something. "You just get up?"

"No. I've been up for a while. Where've you been?"

For a moment she stopped, probably shocked to learn he'd been awake. He hadn't, but she didn't need to know that. "I went to get scones, obviously. Here, I got you a mocha latte."

He un-wedged the Styrofoam cup marked "ML" from the cardboard tray. "Thank you." What the hell happened? Last night she was nearly catatonic.

"Excuse me." She brushed by him. "I've gotta get the fruit sliced for Noah's breakfast."

Aching for her touch, he moved in behind her and snaked

his arms around her waist. "We don't keep secrets from each other anymore, right?"

"Right." She unhooked his hands, wiggled out of his clutches, and spun to face him. "Why, is there something *you* need to confess?"

"Like…?"

"Like, oh, I don't know. Tell me about the murders. Did you ID the killer yet? Should I be worried about anything other than some freak possessing the baby monitor, kidnapping our child, and nearly killing me?"

He teed his hands. "Enough of this, Sage. This isn't us. If you wanna ask me something, spit it out."

"Fine." She slammed Noah's sippy cup on the table. "When were you going to tell me about Mary Anne Goodman?"

"Frankie told you."

"Damn straight, she did. You should've told me. You!" She pointed an erect finger in his face. "But no. God forbid you—" she flashed air quotes— "*worry me.* Isn't that the standard line these days?"

"That's not fair. You know how much I—"

She flashed a flat hand. "Save it. I think we're well past you protecting me, don't you?"

What could he say? Even he couldn't believe his lackadaisical response to the threat. Hanging his head in shame, he parted his lips to offer an explanation.

Sage wasn't finished. "I had to convince Frankie I already knew, because the last thing she'd ever do is betray your trust."

"Ha! That's rich. She didn't wanna betray me. What a joke."

"She didn't, Niko. She never does. Though, by the way you're acting, I have no idea why."

He raised an open hand to his chest. "The way *I'm* acting? What about her?"

"She's protecting the person she loves. Can't say the same for you."

Niko softened his tone. "Babe, I—"

"I know, I know, you're trying to protect me. Well, I'm sick of you protecting me. It's high time I protect myself. In fact, where's my gun? Is it still in the safe?"

His shoulders pulled back. "*Your* gun?"

"Yes, my gun. I think I've earned it, don't you?"

"Babe—"

Arms scissoring by her side, Sage soldiered into the living room, gripped the sides of the black bear oil painting above the mantel, and lowered it to the sofa. Fingers on the dial of the wall safe, she urged, "The combination please."

"Sage, honey—"

"The combination!"

Niko set his hands over hers. "Will you please listen to me for a minute?"

Her arms dropped to her side. "I don't know what the problem is. You said you wished I had a gun that night in Boston." As if erasing the memory, she shook her head. "What's the problem? I've been armed before."

"Yeah, and look how well that worked out. Besides, things are different now."

"They sure are. Another psycho wants me dead."

On the loft carpet, Noah scooted his rear-end to the top landing of the stairs. He wasn't allowed on the staircase without an adult, but this was not the time to reinforce rules. His face twisted with shock and grief. "Momma?" He wailed, dropping his tear-soaked face in his hands. Colt zipped up the stairs and licked away his tears as quickly as they fell. On the top landing, Ruger whimpered, his chin planted in Noah's lap.

Niko lunged up the stairs, swept Noah into his arms. "Good boy," he told Colt and then Ruger before turning his attention to his son's back heaving so heavily he might hyperventilate. "Nothing's gonna happen to Mommy. I'm sorry we scared you." He glared at Sage, mouthed, "Happy now?"

When she hurried to the bottom tread, she scowled back. Paused, and then opened her arms. Till he confirmed their son had calmed, he refused to let go. Noah raised his face from the crook of Niko's neck. Big, round teardrops fell like bubbles from

131

a wand, his rosy lips wet and quivery.

Sage wiggled her hands through Niko's vice grip, lifted Noah, and cradled him to her chest, her palm on the back of his head. That woman beamed when she held their son.

How Niko let this argument escalate to this level, he had no idea. He'd made a fine mess of things. If only for a moment or two, he might have a way to fix this. "Hey, who wants to play airplane?"

A tiny voice said, "Me."

Scooping Noah into his arms, he raised him high above his head, lowered the top half of his body to his face, and nuzzled noses. Playfully, he zoomed him around the living room. "Weeeee…Look at you, buddy."

Arms extended like wings, Noah's belly-laugh erased the tension in the room.

"Look how well he flies, Mommy." Niko stepped on the sofa to raise him higher, and Noah screamed with delight, a high-pitched screech that made Ruger bury his face in his paws. "Captain Quintano, this is air traffic control. What's your twenty?"

Noah laughed harder as Niko's gaze met Sage. Maybe he'd overreacted earlier. "Babe, the combination is Noah's birthday and the year we got married. The two best years of my life."

"Aww, pup." She interrupted "airplane" long enough to kiss him.

After he spent some much-needed family time, his priority was to find Chance. When he did, no one could stop the hell he'd rain down on him.

Chapter Twenty-Five

2 p.m.

With a copy of Mary Anne Goodman's phone records, Frankie paced back and forth across the kitchen. If Chance had in fact answered the phone that day, then the last number dialed should reach him.

With no plan on how to confront him and remain true to her badge, she dialed.

The phone rang and rang.

As she pulled the phone away from her ear to disconnect, he answered. "Chance, it's me. Don't hang up. I'm alone."

Silence came over the line.

"It's not what you think," he said. "I knew Mary Anne from the clinic. Here and there, she helped me out once in a while."

Whoa. Cheating never entered her mind, until now. Was Mary Anne his mistress? "Never mind that. We need to meet. If you're innocent, I can protect you, but you're gonna have to trust me."

"Where?"

"How 'bout the cabin?" With any luck her team hadn't arrived yet.

"Umm…the cabin?" he asked, guilty as hell.

"One hour. Don't keep me waiting."

"Fine, I'll meet you. This better not be a trap, though. I'm trusting you, Frankie."

"Just be there." She slammed the phone in its cradle. How dare he question her integrity. That cheating bastard had so much to explain. If she didn't wind up shooting him, it'd be a miracle.

133

* * *

3:00 p.m.

Frankie's department-issued SUV idled in the hunting cabin's dirt driveway. Debating whether to wait inside or out, she killed the engine. The front door was locked tighter than a virgin's legs at senior prom—a sure sign Chance hadn't arrived yet.

She entered.

Silence struck her hard. If he turned out to be the serial killer they'd been hunting, she'd lock his ass away. A question lingered, though. Sometimes Sage used "the man" and other times "the men." Plural. What if there's more than one killer? Would Chance ambush her with his goons? Lately, she didn't even recognize him. For months, he hadn't been the man who'd initially intrigued her, and now it made sense. Did he take Mary Anne here? Was this their love shack?

Emotions spiraling in her chest, fluctuating between sadness and rage, she took the stairs two at a time, careened around the railing, and into the master bedroom. In the closet, when she shoved the hanging clothes aside the hidden door creaked open. Not a lot, but enough to sheath her arms in goosebumps. Flashlight leveled beneath her Glock, she ducked through the doorway, into the storage area.

Down and to the right slumped the corpse with the same caramel-colored jacket draped over the shoulders, proving the evidence hadn't been touched. Before Chance arrived, she jogged down the stairs. Against the counter, she leaned as nonchalantly as possible. Not five minutes later, the back door opened by Chance's hand.

At first, she hesitated. Throw him against the wall, or sigh that he's safe? "Well? I'm listening."

"No hello first?"

"If you've got something to say, say it. I don't have time to play your frickin' games."

"All right, fine, if that's how you wanna be." He slumped into a kitchen chair, rested his forehead in his hands. "Years ago, I got into trouble with the IRS."

Across from him Frankie lowered to the chair.

"Then this opportunity presented itself and, well...you've gotta understand, I was petrified of losing my business. You of all people know how important my work is. I save lives. I couldn't lose the clinic because of a fleeting error in judgment."

Part of that was true. Five years ago, her Saint Bernard, Gunther, broke free from his outside run and chased a squirrel into the street. A blue F250 swerved, but not in time. The truck struck Gunther in the hindquarters and he rolled onto the windshield, contorted in ways she still couldn't wipe from her memory, then crashed onto the asphalt, fracturing his back femur. That day, Chance saved his life, and ever since, the man made her heart skip like a teenage boy on his way to getting laid.

The part of his story she failed to understand was his so-called error in judgment. He could dress up the word "fraud" all he wanted, but that didn't make it legal. "You screwed the IRS and got caught. Yeah, so?"

"Why do you always have to be a cop? Can't you, for once, talk to me like my fiancé?"

"I am a cop, Chance. Although now, I'm suspended 'cause of you."

Arms outstretched, he leaned across the table. "I swear to you, I didn't murder anybody."

Hmm...nothing about his posture or mannerisms screamed guilty. Except for acting like a dog in heat. Or maybe, he'd practiced this routine and had it down. Wouldn't be the first time a kickass liar got away with shit.

"Really? Then who's the dead guy upstairs? Next you'll tell me he just magically appeared like the leprechaun in Lucky Charms."

Chance dropped his face in cupped hands, his head swaying side to side.

Classic all-about-me body language. Hate that shit. What about the five dead women? In CODIS they'd matched two other homicides dated prior to Amy St. John, but the crime scenes were outside their jurisdiction, so technically the suspect murdered seven women so far. God forbid they became a consideration. If he didn't change his 'tude, and fast, she'd give him something to cry about. Literally. "Look. You're not the victim here. Man up."

"I am, though. I'm very much the victim in all this."

Heat assaulted her insides, burned like flames in a crematorium. "You didn't come here to confess. Un-fuckin-believable. You actually want me to feel sorry for you. Niko was right. I can't believe I risked my badge." She shoved the table and rose, and her chair flew into the wall. "Get. Up."

"Don't you want to hear my side?"

Grabbing his upper arm, she yanked him to his feet. "Lace your fingers on your head."

"Frankie, it's not what you think, I swear to you."

"Tell it to the judge, pal. I'm done listening to your bullshit." She wrenched his arm behind his back. Granted, maybe a little rougher than usual, not that he didn't deserve it. She slapped on the handcuffs. "Let's go." Walking behind him, she shoved him toward the front door. Again, maybe a touch harder than normal, but oh, well. Too frickin' bad. After the shit he pulled, he was lucky she didn't kick his ever-lovin' ass.

When they reached the front door, he stopped short. "They'll kill me, Frankie. Can you live with that on your conscience?"

"Who, Chance?"

He hung his head. "I can't tell you that."

"Uh-ha. Classic dirt-bag response." She shoved him out the door and down the steps. Too bad he didn't fall on his face. At the SUV, she set her hand on the back of his skull and had to resist the urge to slam his forehead into the door frame. "Watch your head." Gotta admit, part of her enjoyed making him suffer.

Slamming the back door brought more pleasure. Too bad his foot wasn't in the way. Frankie slipped behind the wheel, turned the key in the ignition. Right then, a guy with a black bandana tied around his face—a white skull silkscreened on the front—opened the back door and dragged Chance off the seat.

"What the—?"

Before she had time to react, a second guy leveled a shotgun at her head. Not a tiny dude, either. Dark-skinned arms flexed beneath a shockingly-white T-shirt, three sizes too big, the sleeves hitting the elbows. Both suspects wore baggy jeans that hung off their asses, boxers revealed, and brand new high-tops. The guy who guarded Frankie wore a do-rag while the dude who rescued Chance donned a crooked hat. Classic gang attire.

"Don't be a hero, lady. He ain't worth it." They jumped into a black Escalade and sped away. Massachusetts plates, probably stolen.

Frankie peeled out the lot.

Chapter Twenty-Six

5:00 p.m.

While Niko was at home with Noah, I ran to the grocery store, the first stop in a long list of errands. A quick trip to anywhere tripled in difficulty with a toddler, not that I'd ever complain. That said, if I had the opportunity to dash out while Niko babysat, I did. Lately, I hadn't gotten much writing done, either, and the deadline for *Scarred*'s sequel quickly approached.

Ninety minutes later, I was in the parking lot loading diapers, reusable sacks of groceries, and a *Wall-E* stuffed animal into the back of the Land Rover.

From behind me came a whisper. "Hello, Mommy." As I whirled around, a saturated cloth struck me in the face. The sickeningly sweet chemical weakened my knees, and my body melted into muscular arms.

When I woke, blackness encompassed the steel barrel; my cold, watery grave drifting to places unknown. Throbbing pains shot below my eyebrow, now flopped over the right eye. The thick scar from Boston tugged at my skin when I bent my head down to cup my off-centered nose. Tiny bits of bone swam under my right cheekbone, my lips swelling to twice their normal size. Wetness leaked down my fingers from an incised wrist wound, the sting comparable to miniature spears stabbing me. While unconscious, had someone attacked me? I called into the darkness. "Hello?"

Nature's sultry songs coiled outside the barrel. Screech owls rejoiced over their captured prey, coyotes howled in unison, and the subtle *swish* of water lapped against my unforgiving prison.

Tears hitching my voice, I called again. "Hello? Anyone

out there?" With my body mangled and bruised, I picked at the curved metal walls, dragged my broken fingernails across the lid, and clawed at the bottom of this maniacal trap. Normal breathing patterns no longer existed, my lungs weighted, my knees squeezed against my chest.

Once I escaped, algae rode the ripples, closing in on me like the Taliban invading our troops.

Before I even had a chance to gain my bearings, Lisa asked if I was free.

"I'm out," I said, "but, ah…" Five other barrels floated in the marsh, all at different submersion levels. I pressed her for more information, but her memory was sketchy. Then, as casually as possible, I asked her to bang on the barrel so I could find her, which only intensified her fright and confusion.

Whispering her name outside barrel number one, I caught the silhouette of a man streaking across the tree line, and I ducked neck-deep in the icy water.

Lisa didn't respond.

My head volleyed left and right as I scanned the darkened forest around the marsh. Thick brush obscured my view. Twigs cracked under the weight of heavy boots. Shielded behind barrel number two, I hushed, "Don't make a sound. We're not alone."

In an instant, all movement stopped. The wildlife came alive, owls hooting, wood frogs chirped back and forth as if discussing our dangerous situation. The full moon brightened only the marsh. The stranger had the advantage.

The freezing water needled my bones while I remained still, silently praying Lisa wouldn't announce my escape.

Chapter Twenty-Seven

8:00 p.m.

By the time nightfall hit, Niko had worn out the living room carpet as he checked and re-checked the main drag and driveway, panic sluicing through his veins. With his sleeping son on his hip, because he sure as hell wasn't entrusting him to some babysitter, he called his team before darting up the walkway. Once he buckled Noah in the back seat—Sage would kill him for not using a car seat, but they only had the one—he drove to the station.

The job had a way of making him painfully aware of his mortality, but he never considered Sage's life could come to an end, even after their past tragedies. At the very least, he counted on dying first, especially with the seven years between them. That way of thinking seemed naïve now. If only he could switch places, sacrifice himself so his wife could live. Sadly, the world didn't work that way.

In the department parking lot, he unbuckled Noah. No matter how much activity surrounded him, he rarely, if ever, woke. A bomb could explode and Noah's tiny nose would still whistle sweet melodies.

When Sage's pregnancy passed the first trimester, Niko allowed himself to fall in love with their baby. What he never envisioned were the day-to-day decisions. Which baby carrier had the safest statistics? Whether to put safety latches on the lower cabinets. Which diaper held the most pee? Endless questions with multiple answers.

If they didn't find Sage in time, he'd never recover—forever marred by the evil acts of a predatory killer.

The minute he reached the office, he put out a BOLO on the Land Rover and called in SWAT to raid Chance's cabin. When everyone arrived, he gathered his deputies around the whiteboard while the Special Weapons and Tactics field commander, Sergeant Reagon, addressed his team.

Late as usual, Frankie stormed into the bullpen. "Got your message, boss, but I need to talk to you first. You didn't give SWAT the go ahead yet, right?"

He waved a dismissive hand toward her. "I'm not pulling them off this case, if that's what you're after. I've pussyfooted around you and your boyfriend long enough."

"Five minutes. That's all I ask." Fire in her eyes, she slapped the nearest desk. "You owe me this, dammit."

Reluctantly, he followed her into his office.

She slammed the door behind them, the frosted glass vibrating in her wake. "Chance isn't the killer."

"I don't have time for this, Deputy." With an audible exhale, he strutted toward the door.

"I know he isn't the killer because I arrested him."

Almost robotically, he rotated toward her. "I'm listening."

Frankie explained what occurred at the cabin; how she found a corpse in the storage area; how she put Chance in handcuffs to bring him in, and how two men dragged him out of her vehicle at gunpoint.

Niko took a minute to process the information. "Did you get a good look at these men?"

"Black males. Both had black bandanas tied around their faces. Freaky too, with skull images on the front. Definite gang attire."

"Tell me everything you learned before, during, and after Chance's abduction."

"Mass plates. Escalade came back stolen. I'd swear they had an accent like yours, so they might be from the Boston area. After they shook the tail—I followed them for a good five miles before this bitch in a white Lincoln cut me off—I did some digging through Chance's clinic files. The name Dawgs came up more than once. Not sure if that's important. Just throwing it out there."

"And the dead guy in the cabin, what's that about?"

"No idea. Maybe a warning of some kind?"

Something Frankie said unearthed memories from the past, and Niko's eyes protruded from the sockets. "Back up. Did you say dawgs as in, D-A-W-G-S?"

"Yeah. How'd you—?"

"Oh, shit." Stumbling backward, he steadied himself by gripping the edge of his desk. "Years ago, Sage wrote a true crime novel about The Columbia Point Dawgs. I warned her how dangerous it was to shine a light on their activities, but you know Sage."

"So you think this is payback."

"Shit, shit, shit." Forearms curling around his head, he strode toward the bank of windows that overlooked mountain ranges, mist floating atop the tallest pinnacle. Sage loved this view. A lone tear trickled down his cheek.

Silent, his mind whirling with endless scenarios, he cleared the desperation from his tone. "What I can't figure is how Chance fits in to all this."

"No clue. But before we left the cabin he said something like, 'they'll kill me.' Aw, shit, Niko. You don't think—"

"Yup. They're serious bad guys, with extensive criminal histories. How'd Chance get mixed up with a Boston street gang? Either you're not tellin' me everything, or he's hiding a secret life. Crap." He hustled out the office door and over to the field commander, still coordinating efforts to storm Chance's cabin. Niko leaned over his shoulder, hushed, "We've gotta problem."

Sergeant Reagan told his men, "Give me one minute, guys." He jabbed his head toward a spot where he and Niko could speak in private.

"I received confirmation that the target is actually a kidnapping victim, but hang around, because we know who the suspects are. We just need to find them."

Sergeant Reagan agreed.

Ambling to the center of the bullpen, Niko smacked his hands together to quiet the chatter in the room. "Listen up. The suspects are The Columbia Point Dawgs, an especially nasty street gang from Boston who have warrants out for murder, trafficking girls and drugs, robbery. You name it, chances are there's a warrant. Let's focus our efforts on digging through the case files. Bradley and Childs, tear apart the victims' histories and get on their phone logs. I want to know what ties these cases together ASAP. Ben, did you run down the log cabin spikes?"

Ben flipped open his notebook to review his notes. "The closest match is to a Grip-Rite fifty-pound, steel-shank spike used for building log cabins and railroad ties."

"Nicely done. Did you get the list of suppliers I asked for?"

He stared at his boots. "Umm, not exactly."

"Whaddaya mean, not exactly?"

"They're pretty common. You can even buy them on Amazon."

"Shit. Okay. What about the antlers?"

"Fish and Game told me they're from whitetail deer, which are native to New Hampshire. Reported this year alone, they found over two-thousand deer that matched the points and measurements of our antlers."

Niko's eyebrows lifted in amazement. "That's a shit-load of hunters. Any way to narrow the list?"

"Not sure. Maybe. Because then, I tracked down a taxidermist in Alexandria who had a bunch of racks hanging around, but he said they were waiting to be mounted."

"Taxidermist, eh? That works."

Frankie butted in. "What about shed hunters?"

"What the hell is a shed hunter?"

"They hunt for sheds, obviously." She mumbled into her hand, "Guess you picked the wrong deputy for the job."

Niko caught the insinuation of Ben being groomed for sheriff, but didn't call her on it. "You lost me. What's a shed?"

"Deer and moose lose their antlers between January and March. They slip right off like late autumn leaves from a tree. Anyway, there's a class of hunters who search the woods for shed antlers. They're a bitch to find, too. The worst part, most people don't report them, even though technically they're supposed to if the skull is attached. I dated this guy once who—"

Niko teed his hands. "Make your point, Deputy."

"Right." She cleared her throat. "Shed hunters would have rooms filled with antlers because they can't part with them, even though they'd make a frickin' killing if they sold 'em."

"The more you tell me this shit, the less it sounds like the Dawgs."

"Maybe that's the point. Maybe that's exactly what they want us to think."

"So the Dawgs planted the antlers to throw us off. Cause us to look at local hunters so we don't make the connection to Sage's book."

Clearly proud of herself for making Ben look like he half-assed the assignment, she grinned like the Cheshire Cat. "Exactly."

"You might be right." He mulled over various possibilities. Without more to go on, chasing down antlers could be an endless task. "Could DNA lead us to a specific herd?"

"It might. At the very least it should pinpoint a region."

"That could take weeks."

"Easily. If not months."

"We don't have that kind of time." He glanced at Noah, asleep on the desk behind him. Admitting to himself that he didn't know his son's daily routine widened the pit in his stomach. "What'd you discover about John Dunn, the guy from Sage's book signing?"

"Yeah, about that..."

"Frankie," he warned.

"What?" Arms wide, she shrugged. "I looked into him. No need for the fatherly tone."

"And?"

"And he must've used an alias. The only John Dunns in Grafton County are pushing sixty and seventy. None looked strong enough to impale a woman with antlers, either. About how old was the guy, do you know?"

"According to Sage, around mid-to-late forties. Dammit." He

palmed his forehead. "I should've had her sit with a sketch artist."

"Cut yourself some slack. At the time, Sage thought everyone looked suspicious."

"Yeah, I suppose," he said, mentally kicking himself for not trusting his wife's instincts. "Ben, I want you to concentrate on Mary Anne Goodman. Tear her life apart. Since she mentioned Sage, she might be the key to finding her." He pointed at Frankie. "You're with me. Let's go."

He scooped Noah into his arms, and his mind twirled like a tilt-a-whirl at the carnival. Cherry-red digits descended to street level, silence enveloping the elevator. Numb inside, losing Sage was too horrific to consider. Was she with Chance? Would they watch each other die? One might think this would drive him and Frankie closer, but uncertainty hung between them like a blood-soaked machete, swinging in the dark.

In the parking lot, he passed Noah to Frankie, and her lip curled in disdain. "Seriously? That's why you brought me along, to babysit?"

"Gimme a break. The car seat's in the Land Rover. Can't you just ride in the backseat with your godson? What's the big deal?"

"What're you gonna do if we find Sage's truck?"

"I have no idea." His hands juddered. "I don't know anything anymore. My wife's missing. I can barely think straight, never mind figure out the safest option for our child. What if I screw up and put him in danger? I can't risk it. Not a second time."

"Okay, okay, calm down. We'll find her. But first, we need to drop Noah at the babysitter's."

"Are you deaf? I said, I won't do it."

"Then at least let Childs watch him." Deputy Lars Childs, another member of his team who loved to clown around. "No one's gonna mess with Noah at the Sheriff's Department. Besides, he'll have a blast with Childs. Mentally they're the same age."

Frankie's suggestion didn't wrench his stomach as much as the other option. Maybe she's right. Any number of things could happen on the road, especially at night. Thirty years in law enforcement proved that. "Okay, fine. But make sure you instruct him not to let my son outta his sight. I don't care if he's gotta take a piss. Under no circumstances is he allowed to pass my son to someone else. Actually, I should probably take him inside myself."

Frankie slid Noah to her hip, his head resting on her shoulder. "I think I can handle it."

A tightness balled in his chest as Frankie strode into the building. Had he made the right decision? With a heaviness on his shoulders, he wrung his hands. One wrong move and his family would never be the same. "Just Once" by James Ingram blasted from his cell phone. "I hear ya, babe." Tears threatened to escape. "I'll fix this. I promise." Thumbing the answer button, he cleared his throat. "Sheriff Quintano."

"Sheriff, we've got a twenty for the Land Rover," said Doris. "Walmart parking lot on Tenney Mountain Highway. Local patrol is on scene."

"Is my wife okay?"

The long pause of silence sent a shockwave through his system. "I'm sorry to report she was not inside the vehicle."

He winced. "Did they check the trunk?"

"The trunk? Why would anyone—? Oh my. Good Lord, I hope not."

"I'm leaving now. Tell them not to touch anything. Understood?"

"Yes, sir."

Barely managing his composure, Niko thumbed OFF.

Frankie opened the passenger door and settled in the seat.

Without a word, he hit the lights and siren and peeled out of the lot.

"Hey!" With a closed fist, she jabbed him in the bicep. "I barely had my damn foot in the car."

"They found the Land Rover." What if the killers stuffed her in the trunk? If they found her impaled by antlers, or submerged in swampland, he'd never erase the image from his mind. Never mind telling his son his mother was dead. How could he explain murder to a toddler?

Against his will, tears flooded his eyes, blurring his vision. He swept them away as quickly as they fell, but to no avail. They built and built, a sob tangled in his chest, heart shattering like an ice sculpture dropped on concrete. "When we get there, I need you to do me a favor."

"Name it."

"Check the trunk."

She nodded her agreement, then rotated toward her window. "Frankie?"

"Yeah?"

"I'm sorry about Chance."

Deep sadness cascaded over her face as a forced grin trembled her lips. "Thanks."

Silence enveloped the SUV when he veered into the Walmart parking lot. Near the crime scene tape Niko stopped, killed the engine. Never had he envisioned this. The day he surprised Sage with the Land Rover consumed him. From the moment they brought Noah home from the hospital his safety became a constant topic of discussion.

They'd lived so many childless years, being parents was a new endeavor, a rewarding but terrifying experience.

How anyone raised a child without transforming into a basket case remained a mystery. Not to mention the challenges of raising a child late in life. After endless conversations about her Ford Edge, Niko surprised her with a safer vehicle. All their lives he'd dreamed of tying a massive red ribbon around a shiny new car, and this was his chance. So, he woke early one Sunday morning and snuck down the stairs. At the door Ruger nudged Niko's knees with his forehead, insisting he tag along.

One tap to Niko's thigh, and Ruger galloped out the door and up the walkway. During the ride to the dealership, Niko petted his blocky head and asked which vehicle to buy. By decoding high-pitched barks, happy whines, and panting patterns, Ruger agreed the Land Rover was the safest option, evident also by his sloppy smile and wiggle to his hips. He never mentioned the part about it being an easier SUV for arthritic doggy legs to climb in and out of, and Niko wasn't about to dampen the excitement in the front seat.

Needless to say, their fur-baby was a huge hit with the dealership's sales force and customers, especially the females. Not often did they witness a dog Ruger's size act like a prancing toy poodle with a limp. However, it was his charming personality and good looks for why the manager—also female—deducted a few grand off the sticker price. From that day forward, Niko wouldn't even consider buying a new car without him. The dealership even had a driver follow them home so they'd have the new vehicle right away.

Tail swishing with excitement, Ruger followed Niko into the house. At the stove, Sage cooked their Sunday morning feast, Niko's favorite meal of the week. The aroma of bacon, heated maple syrup, and home fries with sweet onions wafted through the house.

Without a word, Niko snuck up behind his wife and turned off the burner and griddle for the pancakes, slid the spatula from her hand and rested it against the frying pan. Kissing his beautiful wife, he dipped her in his arms, and Sage tittered the way she did on their first date. By one hand he twirled her away, and back.

"Trust me, babe." Blinded by his hands, he led her out the door. Sage giggled like a schoolgirl as he escorted her up the walkway.

In the driveway he uncovered her eyes, and she shrieked with joy.

If only he could relive that day.

With his hankie, he dried his tears, blew his nose. Niko wasn't an emotional man, especially in public, but this situation was far beyond normal. The crime scene tape around the Land Rover snapped his heart in two. The vehicle his wife adored... the same SUV that flooded his mind with blissful memories... was now considered evidence in Sage's kidnapping. Or, perish the thought, her murder.

He swiveled toward Frankie. "I need you to run this investigation. Can you do that for me?"

"Does Raggedy Anne have cotton knees?"

"I'll take that as a yes. In return, I'll make sure we find Chance ASAP. Deal?"

She slapped her hand in his. "Deal."

"Thanks, Frank."

"Yeah, yeah. Just stay outta the way. I don't need you compromising my scene." She winked.

He managed a slight smile. "Yes, ma'am."

Before she closed the car door, she leaned in. "Call me ma'am one more time and I'll slap you into next week." No wink this time.

She slammed the door. Head held high, she strutted over to the police tape and flashed her badge. "Deputy Campanelli, I'm the lead on this case. Whadda we got?" After a short exchange with the first officer on scene, she glanced back at Niko, her eyes saddening.

Then she reached for the trunk.

Chapter Twenty-Eight

I had no concept of time. Outside barrel number two, I whispered, "Lisa, if you're in there, tap lightly."

While I waited for a response I surveyed the darkened woods. Now, even the wildlife didn't dare move, didn't dare speak. Something, or someone, forced every living creature into silent deportment, including me. Had I seen a black bear earlier, or the clown? Or something even more menacing, like a pack of hungry wolves?

I waded over to barrel number three, and a wretched stench announced Lisa was not inside. Whoever was in there had been dead a while. I'd only smelled the unmistakable scent of death twice in my life, but it was something I'd never forget, similar to a mixture of rotting meat, fruit, blood, urine, and feces.

About ten feet away, nestled in a dark spot of the marsh where the moon couldn't reach, a barrel thrashed from side to side. I dipped my shoulders beneath the freezing cold water and swam over. Breath rolled from my lips in frosted puffs. "Lisa?"

"Sage?" she said, her tone hopeful.

"I'm working on getting you out. Hang tight."

"Hurry," she cried, her voice tainted with fear.

"Shhh, you need to stay quiet. I don't think we're alone."

"Is it him? Oh, my God, Sage. Hurry. He'll kill us."

Using my fingertips, I felt around the edge of the lid for the latch on the metal bung. One last glance in all directions and I snapped it open. By the time I opened the lid, Lisa was hysterical, her face beaten and bloody, her body stuffed inside like trash.

Head first, she squirmed out the drum and threw her arms

around my neck. "Help. I can't swim."

A click echoed through the forest. I slapped a hand over her mouth and dipped under the water, Lisa latched to my side, her nails digging into my frozen skin. Exposed to only our noses, my limbs half-numb, white-hot pain riddled my body.

A blue flame shot from a butane lighter.

Fear rippled across my skin, icy tingles diffused across my back. The capillaries in my hands constricted—my Raynaud's syndrome peaked—as I slung Lisa's arm around my neck, hushed, "Paddle with your free hand."

Speechless, eyes splayed with fear, her chin dipped in confirmation.

Controlled. Methodical. Precise. I slid my arms forward... and back...forward...and back...forward...and back...gliding across the wintery marsh while Lisa struggled to hang on.

To the right of the butane lighter, we sculled halfway to the tree line and through an algae patch. Lisa panicked, her rigid arms squeezing my airway, nearly drowning the two of us.

As I peeled her off me, I choked on a mouthful of water. Lisa sank beneath the surface, and I dove under the algae to scour the murky swamp. Hair sifted through my fingers and I tightened my hand into a fist. Blonde locks twined around my painful wrist, I yanked upward enough to reach her armpits. When her face crested the water, I slung her on my back. Lisa didn't cough, expel water, or cry for help. In fact, she went oddly silent.

Chapter Twenty-Nine

10:00 p.m.

Tears bubbled over the rims of Niko's eyes. Please, let the trunk be empty. Without a body, hope existed. If he witnessed the end to the most incredible woman on the planet, surely he'd died alongside her. He missed her tender touch, her eyes that melted his heart with one glance, the way her hair smelled like fresh morning dew. A better person than he, Sage so freely shared her love with anyone lucky enough to befriend her.

Without question, without hesitation, he'd trade his life for hers. If only…the phrase repeated in his mind. If only he'd believed her when she first mentioned being followed. If only he'd paid more attention to his family, rather than worrying about Grafton County residents. How could he not chose his wife and son over the job?

The thin blue line consumed him. Dammit. When his family needed him most he wasn't there. Frankie gave him the thumbs-up, and relief poured through his long exhale.

Heart in his throat, he exited the SUV. The empty trunk gave him hope, but he'd been around long enough to accept this wasn't necessarily a good thing. Often times these manhunts lasted hours, days, even months.

Keeping his voice low—the fewer witnesses to his involvement, the better—he nudged Frankie in the right direction. "Call in the K9 Unit. Maybe the dogs can track Sage."

She whistled for Ben's attention. "Hey, golden boy. Call K9. We need the dogs here ASAP."

"But it's dark." He looked to Niko for confirmation, but he

didn't dare respond.

Frankie snapped her fingers in his face. "Hey, eyes on me. This is my scene. You have your orders. Now do it."

Colt! Without a word, he sprinted to the SUV, fumbled to get the key in the ignition, and then gunned it out the lot. Rather than wait for the K9 Unit, Colt could track Sage. Why didn't he think of this sooner? He'd almost graduated to K9 Cop before his expulsion due to his playfulness. If anyone could track Sage's movements, he could, especially with the bond they shared.

He sped up the mountain to his empty house, nestled in blackness. Instilled training warned him to proceed with caution—the lock on the kitchen door hadn't been fixed—but he didn't care. With his wife missing, the heart gutted from his chest, cleaved from the woman he adored, a broken soul wilting like dying rose petals.

The moment he strode into the kitchen Colt skittered across the tiles, paws out to stop himself from sliding headlong into Niko's knees. Ruger lumbered behind. Niko squatted to their level and tousled their fur. "Ruger, I need you to stay here and guard the house. Colt, wanna go for a ride?"

Colt's feet danced, his stubby tail swishing back and forth. Ruger groaned his disapproval.

"Please don't be upset. I'd take you both if I could." Ruger wasn't buying his excuse, evident by the sneer in his direction.

In the loft, Niko searched for worn clothing for Colt to sniff as a baseline, because he couldn't take the chance that he'd get confused with all the commotion at the crime scene.

Rifling through the hamper, he settled on Sage's favorite nightshirt, the material so thin it was practically transparent. Deep and long, he inhaled his wife's sweet nectar, the soft aroma of Shalimar. With the nightshirt balled to his face, he collapsed on the bed.

He could hardly remember a time without Sage in his life. Lips quivering, salted with tears, a longing burrowed into his soul. Energy drained from every part of him, his heart fractured beyond repair. He hiked his knees to his chest as he clung to the nightshirt like a drowning man with a floatation device.

The day they first met forever etched his memory. Sage had worn her sable hair longer then, waves cascading halfway down her sculptured back. When the waitress at the Hilltop Steakhouse passed her the menu, Sage's hands moved so elegantly, so delicately, so ladylike. At the time, Niko was a newly-minted officer who'd gone out for celebratory drinks with a fellow recruit, but Niko couldn't tear his gaze away from this stunning beauty, one booth over. It took three draft beers to work up the courage to say hello. When she smiled, warmth filled him inside, an unexpected experience he'd never known before.

On their third date, he asked for her hand in marriage, certain he'd die if he ever had to say goodbye. More than twenty years later, the memory remained sharp, vivid.

Colt hopped up on the bed, jarring him from the past. Head cocked, he didn't understand Daddy's pain.

Niko scratched the scruff of his neck, under the leather collar. "It's okay, buddy. I'm just—" His words faltered. "There's something I haven't told you." He sobbed, his speech almost incoherent. "Mommy's missing."

He dragged himself upright, and Colt flopped across his lap, whimpering like Sage was dead. "Hey." He mussed the fur on his back. "We'll find her, buddy."

When Colt raised his head, desperation shone in his eyes.

Heart crushed, Niko faked an upbeat tone. "C'mon, let's bring her home. Whaddaya say?"

A sloppy smile spread across Colt's face, his tail wiggling with excitement. Niko didn't have the heart to tell him what they might find. The last thing Sage needed was for him to fall apart.

* * *

10:30 p.m.

With Colt perched in the passenger seat, they drove through the entrance to the Walmart parking lot. The K9 Unit still hadn't arrived. Leash in hand, Niko scooted around the front bumper to Colt's side. Latching the clasp to his collar, he prompted him to start the search. "Find Mommy." Colt buried his nose in the nightshirt, and then took off, nearly separating Niko's shoulder as he tracked the scent around the Land Rover.

Frankie's heeled-boots *tap, tap, tapped* across the plowed pavement. "What's Colt doing here?"

"What's it look like?"

"I mean, why?"

Niko gave the leash a subtle tug for Colt to stop. "I can't wait around all night. You know as well as I do the first hours are critical."

"Yeah, but there's a reason Colt didn't graduate."

He tossed her a cutting glare, then gave the leash another tug. Colt snapped back into action. "Run your investigation anyway you want. We won't get in your way." He parted his lips to offer an explanation, but Colt dragged him toward another parking spot, several yards away.

"What is it, buddy?"

Wedged in a tire tread of slush, Colt alerted on a cell phone.

"Good boy." Niko snapped on latex gloves and pressed the call history. None of the phone numbers registered.

Frankie called out, "You find somethin'?"

Rather than shout across the lot, he wiggled the cell phone in the air. Once she approached, he ordered her to run the number. "It's got a Boston area code."

Snatching the phone from his grasp, she said, "I'm on it."

With any luck, Rainhorse will be able to trace the call. If it was a burner, they might be screwed, but even a long shot was better than no lead at all. Colt lost the trail. Whoever took Sage switched vehicles. Intersecting tire tracks crossed the impressions in the snow. Which meant, they'd never be able to determine which make and model left with Sage.

Chapter Thirty

Eternity passed before we hit an area where I could drag Lisa's limp body. One hand crossed over the other, I shoved the heel of my palm into her chest, the cold temps biting my skin. Lisa's body balanced on a snowy island no bigger than a twin bed—in the open for anyone to see, including the killer clown.

Nothing worked. Even her eyelids wouldn't twitch. Again, I compressed her chest, and she still didn't respond. I leaned her head back, pinched her nose, pressed my lips to hers, and blew sharp, forceful breaths.

Dammit. No signs of life.

"C'mon, Lisa. Stay with me." With a balled fist, I slammed her heart in an attempt to kick-start it into pumping. That didn't work, either. Over and over I gave mouth-to-mouth, then compressions, mouth-to-mouth, then compressions. I'd almost given up when her lungs expelled the water. I rolled her onto her side, and she coughed, choking on more water.

I winced, my gaze scanning the darkened tree line. Her outburst wasn't ideal, but at least she was breathing...for now, anyway.

Now came the hard part. Swim to the wooded shore with someone who could barely dog-paddle. If the clown caught us, he'd end our lives here and now.

"Rock a bye baby..." A sinister cackle rode the arctic breeze.

Lisa's panicked stare shot toward me. "What the fuck was that?"

The unknown strangled my words. All I managed was, "He's here."

We slipped beneath the frigid water, and Lisa's shoulders

sprang to her ears, her lips parted as if she was about to scream.

Before her voice pierced the blackness, I slapped a hand over her mouth. "Quiet. Does that sound like the man who took you?"

Eyes bulged in terror, she nodded yes.

I expected as much. "With the mountains, it's almost impossible to pinpoint where he is. We'll have to hug the shore without leaving the water."

"But it's freezing. I can barely feel my body as it is."

I grimaced. "Would you rather die?"

"Well, when you put it that way."

"One last thing. The closer we get to the edge the more weeds, muck, and algae there is, so don't be surprised if it brushes your legs. It might even— I mean, I wonder how high they reach." I swatted my comment away. "Not important. My point is, whatever happens, don't scream. If you do, we'll lose our only advantage."

"Might even what?"

My trembling hand could barely swat a second time. "Nothing. Forget I mentioned it."

"Might even what?"

My gaze roamed the darkened milieu, then settled back on Lisa. "From what I understand, bass and pickerel tend to nestle in weeds, so a few fish might touch you. Don't panic."

"What?" Her eyes opened even more. So much so it was amazing they didn't fall out the sockets. "Do they bite?"

Honestly, I had no idea how to answer. Niko wasn't a fisherman, and we hadn't encountered many people who fished in Boston. In New Hampshire, it was a favorite pastime, but we didn't mingle much with the locals. The only reason I'd learned about bass and pickerel was for a character in one of my books. Rather than upset Lisa, I downplayed the possibility. "I doubt they bite."

"You mean, you don't know?"

"Enough." I flung her arm around my neck. "I'd be more concerned about the serial killer than a few fish that may or may not come near us."

With Lisa weighing me down I swam toward the edge, my intuition screaming not to continue. We hugged the shore. Slimy weeds tangled around my legs, sifted between my toes. Fish and unidentified swamp creatures encircled my hips, shins, and feet. By the time we reached the muck on the ledge, Lisa was in the middle of a full-blown panic attack—hyperventilating, sweating in forty-degree temps, shaking, crying, impossible to soothe.

It's not like I couldn't relate. Over the years, I'd had my share of episodes, but this was not the time to fall apart. In a whisper, I kept my voice calm and serene. "You need to relax. Take a few deep breaths. C'mon, I'll do it with you. Inhale through your nose, exhale through your mouth. In…out…in…out…in…out…" Our breath crystallized mid-air. "Good. Now, grab hold of something. I need to crawl up the embankment, and I can't do it with you hanging on me."

Without a word, Lisa latched onto a clump of weeds on the marsh's edge, nodding deeply like a child acknowledging her parent. Through the mud and muck, I dragged myself on shore, and then assisted her out of the water.

The bitter night air compressed my lungs, making it harder and harder to speak. "Before we go any further, grab a handful of mud and rub it all over your body for camouflage. It's not ideal for open wounds, but at least our fair skin won't point to our location."

Lisa scooped the mud from the water's edge. "Oh, man. This stuff stinks. Can we please skip the face?"

The soil reeked of fish, moss, and an indescribable odor that soured my stomach. "I'm not exactly having a party over here, either. No. Face, too."

After painting our skin, we crept into the thicket of tall conifers. The moon couldn't penetrate the snow below. In our bare feet, we trampled over pine needles protruding through the snow. The muscles in my neck and shoulders tightened into balls and shivers chattered my teeth.

Twigs snapped behind us.

Lisa whirled around. "What was that?"

I grabbed her hand and dragged her behind me. "We need to keep moving. If we stop, we might freeze to death."

"I'm scared, Sage."

"I know. Me too."

"What if he finds us?"

Stopping, I rested my shaky hands on her shoulders. We both trembled uncontrollably, the cold tunneling bone-deep. "We need to make it to the road. Repeat after me. Ten more steps."

"Is that all it is?"

Grimacing, I ordered, "Say it."

"Ten more steps."

"Good. Keep repeating it over and over. Not out loud, though."

"Okay."

"Cool. Let's go." Legs weak, I stomped over vines. The thorns punctured the soles of my feet and dragged their teeth across my bare calves. Flashing a flat hand at Lisa, I warned her. "Careful when you come through here. Whatever you do, don't scream."

"Is it gonna hurt?"

"Probably, but you have to suck it up."

As if she was walking on hot coals, Lisa hopped through the vines a lot better than expected. We zigzagged around trees, over fallen logs, through snow-coated pine needles and dead, crunchy leaves that made way too much noise in the stillness of the night.

"Hello, Mommy."

A maniacal snigger stopped me cold.

Chapter Thirty-One

11:45 p.m.

Frankie was wrapping up the search at Walmart when Niko returned from dropping off Colt. Cell phone in hand, he leaped from the driver's seat and tossed her a look that meant the news wasn't good. "Did they find Sage?"

"Not yet, but…uh…I need to speak with you privately."

"For what?"

"It won't take long." He strode to his vehicle and climbed inside.

Frankie leaned against his opened window. "What's up?"

A somber expression crossed his face. "Get in."

"What's so important?"

"Please get in."

She shuffled around the front bumper and hopped in the passenger seat. "You sound so serious. What's goin' on?"

"Hikers training for the Bristol triathlon found a body in the woods. Holt Trail on Cardigan Mountain."

"Another murder?"

His eyes tilted downward. "Afraid so."

"Okay, well, I'm just about done here if you want me to ride with you."

"There's more." His monotone chilled the blood in her veins. "The victim's been ID'd."

"Okay, great. What's the problem?"

"Frankie, I should've trusted you when you said—"

A volcanic blast exploded in her chest, and she wagged her finger in his face. "No. Don't you dare finish that sentence."

160

The look on his face resembled a frightened puppy—head hung low, eyes big and round, a quivering smile. "I'm sorry to inform you—"

"No." Arms crossed, she kicked the dash. "You're wrong."

"Frank." He rested his hand on her knee. "I'm not wrong. We found his wallet."

Incredulous, she covered her ears. "Stop. You're wrong. Anyone could've planted it." She tugged on the door handle. "I've got work to do."

Niko grabbed her shoulder, but she stared straight ahead. "I'm so sorry."

For a moment, she laid her hand over his.

Refusing to face him, she yanked her hand away. "For all you know, it's another decoy by the Dawgs. Street gangs do that shit all the time."

"It's him. I saw the crime scene photos."

She spun in her seat. "Who was first on scene?"

"What's it matter?"

"Seriously? You know as well as I do half the local patrol officers have their heads up their asses and the other half can barely tell a donut from a croissant, never mind something as important as checking for a pulse. Maybe they dosed him with special K and he's sleeping it off."

"If you need some down time, say the word."

"Why would I need down time? You're wrong about this. In fact, I'll prove it to you." She gestured for him to drive.

He didn't budge. "Maybe I should drop you at home. You shouldn't see this."

"Drive, dammit!" When she kicked the dash a second time her heel left a dime-sized ding in the glove compartment door. Heart sinking in her chest, she stared out the passenger window. *Chance couldn't be dead. Could he?*

* * *

Midnight

Lights swirling, sirens blazing, they sped through the parking lot of the AMC Cardigan Lodge. An American flag rippled in the breeze that rolled off the mountain as Frankie hip-checked the door closed. She hadn't been hiking a day in her life, unless you count the time she thumbed home from Shields, the cop bar in town, after kicking her date in the balls. Long story.

Gaines and Billy Michaels—the mayor's prodigal son who assisted the Medical Examiner only part-time after an "incident" between him and an attractive female corpse; pervert—lugged a stretcher to the OCME van. A black body bag laid on top. Something deep within warned her not to look inside, but she needed to see for herself.

Waving her arms, she signaled the Medical Examiner to wait. "I need to see the vic real quick."

Gaines' frantic gaze shot toward Niko, who returned a slight nod.

With the zipper tab between her thumb and forefinger, she dragged the slider down the chain a few teeth at a time. Blond curls peeked through. She stopped, slowed the mounting pressure in her ears, and then continued. Chance's battered face walloped her like a strike to the gut. His bluish lips and eyes gaped open as though he saw the final strike ahead of time: that he'd soon die by the hand of an enemy.

Tears built and built. She couldn't speak, couldn't witness the finality. Shoulders slumped in defeat, she spun on her heels, jogged back to the SUV.

Moments later, Niko slipped behind the steering wheel. "Gaines assured me he didn't suffer."

"Bullshit. Don't you dare handle me like some vic. Even if he didn't suffer, he sure as hell knew he was gonna die. Did you see the look on his face?"

"You're right." Eyes closed, he shook his head. "I'm sorry. I shouldn't've tried to—"

"Stop. Just stop already." Hatred dripped off her snarling lip. "I can't talk about this now." For the illusion of solitude, she focused on Cardigan Mountain, smoldering in the moonlight. This celestial place had the ability to wash away one's darkest hours, or so said the locals. Didn't do shit for her tonight.

If only she could escape up the trail, push away from the sadness, away from the guilt and shame, maybe then she could heal the emptiness inside. Chance's last memory of her was when she cuffed and stuffed him, threw him in the backseat like some dirt-bag. How could she ever forget? When he needed her most, she sided with her brothers in blue. If only she'd believed his story, no matter how farfetched it seemed at the time.

Once Niko dropped her at home, Frankie stood in the road as his taillights trailed into the darkness. She slogged up the drive to the garage. Gnashing her teeth, she slipped behind the wheel of Chance's Mercedes, the car he hand-washed every Sunday with a cloth diaper, and probably what he drove for his secret rendezvous' with Mary Anne Goodman. A dull ache knotted in her chest, a heaviness widening the pit of her stomach.

What she neglected to tell Niko was that she'd also found a receipt to a storage unit when she searched the clinic records. She patted the lump in her front pocket. With any luck, the key she'd swiped from Chance's desk would fit the lock.

Ten minutes later, she putted down each row at Newfound Self-Storage in Bristol. By excluding the larger units, she narrowed the list to ten possible doors, behind which might hold the key to his killer's identity. Or at least, help her plan her next move.

Flashlight leveled, she shuffled to the first door and slid the key into the padlock.

It barely fit to its second notch.

At the next door down, she tried again.

Still didn't fit.

The third door, she skipped. The cheap lock was nowhere near the right size.

Door number four, five, and six looked promising, though. She jimmied the key into each one. The last lock popped open. *Figures.*

Folded at the waist, she curled her fingers around the handle and raised the door. Her jaw slacked in disbelief. "Wow. You stupid bastard. No wonder they came after you."

Chapter Thirty-Two

March 25, 2008, 12:30 a.m.

After dropping Frankie off, Niko swung by the office to pick up Noah and hopefully, discover if his team was able to track down The Columbia Point Dawgs. But first, he stopped into Tom Rainhorse's office, their IT guy on the fifth floor. "Any luck tracing the call my wife made from the nursery?"

"Came back to a burner cell. The serial number indicates it was bought at Tedeschi's in Lowell, Mass. I tried to ping it, but got no love. I was able to track down your wife's iPhone with Whitepages, though."

"You're speaking French. End result it for me."

"Technically, iPhones need to be connected to a network in order to ping them, but like most things in life, there's an app for that. Whitepages allows you to do a reverse search for any phone number and zero in on the location."

"And?"

"And I found it."

"Well, where is it? Why didn't you call me right away?"

"Because I doubt it's gonna help much."

So damn done with playing these games, Niko slapped the desk. "Tell me where she is, dammit."

"Umm, well…"

The delay pushed him to the edge, and he envisioned himself grabbing Rainhorse by the shirt collar and slamming him into the wall. "Spit it out, already."

"It's in the middle of McDaniels Marsh."

The world crashed around him. Sweet Jesus. He couldn't

speak, couldn't form the words to thank him before leaving the office. Pure emotion saturated his face as he jogged to the elevator. Cherry-red digits descended.

When the door slid open, Frankie was pacing back and forth, waiting to waylay him the second he arrived. "I know who killed Chance."

"Not now, Deputy." He brushed by her.

"But Niko, I—"

Over his head, he tossed, "Rainhorse just located Sage's cell. I can't talk now."

Her heels *tap, tap, tapped* to catch up. "I'm coming with you."

"Frankie, I gave you some down time. I suggest you use it."

She snagged his arm and twirled him around. "If you don't tell me where he found Sage's cell, I'll ask him myself."

Against his will, his chin trembled. "In McDaniels Marsh."

"Aw, shit. You want me to call the dive team?"

"Not yet. I wanna check it out first. Maybe the mutt tossed her phone to dispose of it, and she's still all right." His eyes popped wide. "Does Childs still have Noah?"

How could he be so careless? Finding Sage consumed him, and he almost forgot about his son. Without her near, he couldn't think straight. If anything happened to her…if the mutt punished her for writing about the Dawgs…how could he raise their boy alone? The job wasn't fair to spouses, even harder for a single parent. Ben was nowhere near ready to take over his position. All angles of how this might play out spiraled his mind like a hurricane. None ideal.

Outside the Sheriff's Department door, he stopped dead. "If this goes badly, I need you to take my place. Do you think you're up for it?"

"Whaddaya mean?"

"As sheriff. I can't do this job and raise my son. Something's gotta give."

She raised splayed fingers to her chest. "You're asking *me* if I want the sheriff job?"

"You're the best fit. You'll need to make several changes. Like dressing the part, for one."

Her gaze ran down the front of her low-cut blouse. "What's wrong with the way I dress?"

He resisted rolling his eyes, but barely.

"What about Ben? I thought he was next in line."

"Do you want the job or not?"

"Yep."

"Good." He swung open the door to the bullpen, and searched for Noah.

Childs reclined in his padded chair, crossed ankles propped on his desk, fingers laced behind his head. Niko swept his feet to the floor, and Childs straightened in a flash. "Boss." He cleared his throat. "I was just—"

"Where's my son?"

He pointed to the floor, where he'd laid several layers of blankets, Noah tucked inside. Careful not to wake him, he sat beside him.

"He's such a good kid."

A smile spread across Niko's face. "Thanks. Sorry about before. I guess I panicked when I didn't see him right away."

"No worries. I get it."

In the palm of his hand he allowed Noah's wispy locks to sift through his fingers. If this didn't have a happy ending, he could never tell him what happened to his mother. Above all else, he needed to protect him from the horrors of this world, at least until he was old enough to understand. When was the right time to talk to children about murder? Eighteen, twenty, thirty? Was there ever a right time to shatter their view of the world?

Look what happened to Sage when she got a firsthand look at the evil within psychopaths. She never fully recovered. And now, another monster had her in his lair. Even if she did survive, would she ever be the same?

Chapter Thirty-Three

Lisa latched onto my arm, her nails biting into my bare skin. Not that I could blame her. The wooded terrain was even spookier than the water, because not only could we run into the killer clown but we might come face-to-face with a black bear, moose, blood-thirsty coyotes, or a lone wolf scouting for food.

"Mommy," he sang out, sparking chills from head to foot. "Where are you going, Mommy? The party's this way."

I tugged my arm away from Lisa and weaved her fingers with mine. "C'mon. If w-we can m-make it to the stretch of m-moonlight," I stuttered, the freezing temps chattering my teeth, "w-we m-might be able to track his footprints in the s-snow."

"But it's s-so d-dark here. I c-can't s-see my own—" Lisa's hand slipped from my grasp and her body tumbled into a ravine or off the side of an embankment. Where, wasn't clear. I got down in a squat and felt around the ground. "Lisa?" I whispered.

No answer.

I crawled toward the area where I last heard movement. Surprisingly enough, she never screamed. "Lisa, c-can you hear m-me?"

The scuffling of dried icy leaves drew my attention.

I crawled closer. "Lisa?"

More leaves crunched under someone's feet.

"Answer m-me."

A low, almost unrecognizable, whisper said, "Over here."

I crawled toward the voice. "Keep t-talking s-so I can follow your v-voice."

No response.

"Lisa, you s-still there?"

"Closer."

I crawled a few more feet.

"Closer."

Something wasn't right. Why wouldn't she talk to me? Earlier I could barely shut her up, but now, getting her to speak was like trying to tame a black bear. Actually, the bear might be easier.

A low, guttural growl stopped me cold. Hand over hand, I backed away. With my injuries, feral animals could probably track me. Were they attracted to blood like chum in shark-infested waters?

I didn't dare move, didn't dare breathe too loud for fear of a blitz attack. Before the murder spree rocked our quaint New Hampshire towns—Alexandria, Campton, Hebron, and Springfield, none with populations over sixteen hundred, including out-of-state residents who owned weekend getaways— I'd watched a documentary about black bears. One can never have too much knowledge, and being a parent, I figured it wise to learn about what lurked in the forest, around our home.

Most often, black bears would steer clear of humans as long as no one fed them and brought their bird feeders in the house at night. When bears did attack, the circumstance usually revolved around a mother protecting her cubs. Or if they perceived the person as a threat.

As if on cue, a huff sounded. A massive paw stomped the earth, vibrating the snow beneath my knees. Another huff, the chomping of teeth—all signs that a bear viewed *me* as a threat.

Shockwaves shot through my system, now painfully aware of the danger ahead. According to the documentary, I needed to stand in order to appear large and powerful without being confrontational so he or she didn't go on the defensive. The weak link, especially in nature, got snuffed out the quickest.

In hindsight, this sounded a lot easier at the time.

Knees knocking from the cold, I rose to my feet. "N-nice b-bear. Please d-don't eat m-me." In all the man-versus-nature attacks I'd researched after the show, an interesting but bogus tidbit emerged. Bears in general often cracked open the skull to slurp up brain matter. Apparently, to them our brains were a delicacy. The sound alone caused every tiny body hair to snap to attention.

Step by step, I backed away while staring into the blackness in the hopes of making eye contact. Contrary to belief, playing dead never worked with black bears. Grizzlies, maybe, but their northern cousins didn't fall for the act.

*Huff...loud breath...*claws swiped the earth.

Uh-oh. This time he, or she, sounded closer.

"S-scram," I said, my tone firm and confident as if my legs weren't buckling beneath me. "M-move along, b-bear. I'm n-no threat to you." I smacked my hands together, the clap ricocheting through the darkened woods. "Shoo. B-beat it." My heart slammed against my chest wall. If this stand-off didn't end soon, I might have a coronary right here and now. From the day of Noah's birth, I swore to protect him, even if meant fighting to stay alive. What I never considered was a few-hundred-pound bear as my opponent.

A gunshot rang out.

I hit the forest floor. In a flash, the bear disappeared, evident only by the swishing of tree limbs, marking the escape. For several never-ending moments, I stayed flattened against the snow, ice nipping at my exposed skin.

Who fired the shot?

"Oh, Mommy," a voice sang out. "I saved you, Mommy."

To my right, I tucked into an opening, encased by dirt and snow. With my luck, it probably belonged to a fox. Or, God forbid, the bear. Had I blocked the entrance to her den, cubs nestled inside, and that's why she'd perceived me as a threat?

Where's Lisa? Did she get knocked unconscious in the fall?

Something moved behind me, and I catapulted out of the hole. Please don't let fur brush up against me. Or worse, teeth.

Lisa screamed, her voice boomeranging through the forest. Beavers chewed logs in the marshland. A lone wolf howled a long, steady bay. Wood frogs chattered louder than before, as if discussing the danger that awaited me. Eagles and owls flapped their impressive wings, hunting their prey, *whoosh...whoosh...*

whoosh…emanating high above my head.

The commotion stunned me into silence. With no way to identify Lisa's location all I could do was wait, an ear cocked in her direction.

"Help!" Lisa's high-pitched shrill pierced my bones. "P-please, Sage. You c-can't leave m-me out here to d-die."

I rose to my feet. "I'm c-coming."

"Over here."

That didn't help any. The marshland played with sounds. They bounced off the water, ricocheted off trees, zigzagged to and fro. To pinpoint something in particular I needed to be close enough for contact.

"W-where?" I did my best to keep my voice down, but I doubt it did any good. If the creepy clown chose to attack, he had the advantage, especially if he had night vision goggles. I, on the other hand, could barely make out shadowy figures farther than a few feet away.

Maybe the bear was onto something. "Lisa, s-stomp your f-foot as hard as you c-can."

The snow-covered earth didn't move. So much for that idea.

"Lisa?"

No response.

"Lisa?"

A faint gurgling consumed my full attention, and I bustled toward the noise. Problem was, I had to veer off the well-traveled animal trail. For generations, wild life used the same routes over and over. In this case, they matted down their path. Now, however, I marched in knee-high snow, slowing me to a crawl. Ice crystals stung my shins, my feet well past the point of hypothermia.

When I approached the silhouette of Lisa sitting on the ground, leaning against a tree, I slipped in a patch of warm liquid, flattening me in an instant. Squirming, trying to regain traction, I rose to one foot…fell…crawled to my knees…fell. When I finally managed to scramble to my feet, I took one less-than-ideal step, which sent me flying headlong into a massive conifer. My body tangled in the branches, pine needles in my hair, sap stuck to areas

I'd rather not mention.

Lisa's head slumped forward, left hand cleaved at the wrist.

I pressed two fingers to her jugular. If she had a pulse, it beat too faintly to identify with nearly-numb hands. Behind me, a snap of a tree branch caused me to whirl in its direction.

"My, my, Mommy. You found your partner in crime." He sniggered behind the same latex mask. Only now, blood stained his white gloves. Lisa's blood. "Shame you're dying from hypothermia. You can barely save yourself right now, never mind her."

Sirens wailed in the distance.

"M-my husband's c-coming." *Please let that be true.* "If I w-were you, I'd r-run."

"This isn't over. Watch your back, Mommy. I'll see you soon...and that little brat of yours, too."

"N-not if I see you f-first." *Where the hell did that come from?*

"If you survive, we'll see how brave you are when we're alone."

When he fled my immediate vicinity, I drew in a sharp breath that barely penetrated my lungs, and my confident front shriveled like cut flowers on a child's grave. For all I knew, he could be hiding up ahead, waiting to ensnare me in a trap.

The image of Lisa's grieving family flitted through my mind. I couldn't leave her body here, out in the elements for wildlife to pilferage. So, I clasped my fingers around her forearms and slung her on my back, her dead weight bowing my spine. I stuck out my right foot, dragged forward my left, trudging through the snow. Stuck out my right, followed with my left. Her body weighed a ton. First the right, then the left. Right...then left...right...then left...right...then left. By the time I reached the animal trail, I'd gained momentum, but then her body shifted to one side, threw me off-kilter and I fell to my knees.

Lisa rolled off me. When she hit the thin layer of ice beneath the pine tree, the gentle tings—like rain on a metal roof—amplified in the dead silence. Face up, her eyes had a haunting, blank stare toward the heavens.

Gazing in horror, I chewed my numb lip.

"I'm s-so sorry I f-failed you." I readjusted my grip and got back into position, her long, blood-soaked hair dripping down my bare breasts. My body weakened, so damn tired of the fight, of the madness overshadowing our lives, but if I gave into the darkness, into the sadness and pain, I'd never see my family again. That, I couldn't allow.

Chapter Thirty-Four

1:45 a.m.

Siren blazing, lights swirling on the roof, cascading colors into the early morning gloom, Niko floored the SUV toward McDaniels Marsh. A million things raced through his mind in the course of a few seconds. What if he arrived too late? How could he prepare to find his murdered wife? Was she alone? Or still in the arms of a serial killer?

One hand on the dash, Frankie turned to face him. "You were right about the Dawgs. Chance had a storage unit full of ketamine."

"The horse tranquilizer?"

"Yeah, y'know, special K in street lingo."

"Right. Sorry. I don't know where my head's at."

She mumbled, "I do," but he let it slide. "Anyway, no one would suspect a vet of ordering large quantities of that shit. He had the perfect cover. But what I can't figure is why he stopped supplying them. If they'd threatened to kill him, why didn't he tell me? We could've put him into protective custody."

"Maybe he was ashamed. Men do all kinds of stupid things when they can't admit they're wrong."

She rolled her lips. "Preachin' to the choir."

Niko hung a right on to George Hill Road and pinned the gas pedal to the floorboards. Up ahead the headlights caught movement by the guardrail. "Hey." He backhanded Frankie's arm, then pointed at the silhouette. "Look."

A nude woman, her skin painted with blood and bright-red from the cold, swung her legs over the guardrail, then reached back and dragged a body underneath.

His heart skidded to a stop. "Oh…my…God. Is that Sage?"

"I…" She squinted. "I can't tell."

He swerved to the side of the road and leaped from the door. "Sage!" Arms pumping to increase momentum, he charged toward her, sobbing, overwhelmed by her condition. As he neared, he slowed, a hand shielding his opened mouth. Gaping at his precious wife, he couldn't find the words. What do you say in this situation? Nothing seemed appropriate.

Sage dropped the woman's wrists. Rote, arms dangling by her side, her vacant stare lasered through him, like she had nothing left inside, like her soul had traveled to places unknown to escape the horror.

Heedful of her injuries, careful not to startle her, his hands hovered inches from her body. "Can you speak?"

She didn't respond.

"Is this your blood?"

She stood with an unnatural stillness, her back arched, shoulders rolled forward. At any moment she might collapse, so he tucked her into his chest, shielded her from whatever, or whomever, was out there. Why didn't he protect her sooner? As a husband and father, he failed. No amount of wishing could change that; no amount of prayer could lessen the damage caused by his abstracted view.

Chin rested on her head, his tears soaking her scalp, he held her tight. "I can't believe I found you." Shifting his gaze to Frankie, who'd driven alongside them, he mouthed, "Get a blanket."

Frankie hopped out of the truck and hurried to the back door, where she dragged a Mylar bag from the first-aid kit. To spread out the bi-colored material—one side almost tinfoil-like; the other an emergency orange—she gave the insulated blanket a good, hard shake. Silver side facing in to reflect body heat, she wrapped the material around Sage, and tucked the sides around her chest, still cocooned in Niko's arms.

Technically, he shouldn't be compromising trace evidence that clung to Sage's blood-red skin and hair, but at that moment,

SOP was the farthest thing from his mind. Back in his arms, Sage was safe. Nothing else mattered.

Unlike Niko, Frankie remained cool by following standard operating procedure. With gloved hands, she plucked sticks, twigs, and foreign matter from Sage's wet hair, scraped debris off her legs, and preserved any evidence she could find without disturbing her and Niko. This too was out of character. Perhaps her silent keening ran deeper than she let on.

Blinking away his tears, Niko nuzzled his cheek against Sage's head, murmured, "Babe, can you tell me who did this?"

Eyes closed, Frankie shook her head in a long, drawn-out no.

"I mean...I love you. When you didn't come home from errands, I was so scared. You, Noah, and the kids are my whole world. Without you, I'm nothing." Pressing his lips to the top her bloody scalp, his chest heaved. "You were right. It's time I retire. You guys deserve so much more. Can you ever forgive me?"

As if struck by a Taser, her whole body stiffened. Her teary eyes tilted upward as if begging him for answers. "N-Noah?"

"He's safe. Childs has him at the station."

Like her bones had turned to ash, her eyes rolled back in her head, lashes fluttered twice, and she crumbled to the asphalt. A resounding *crack* from her skull striking the pavement made Niko wince. Urine melted the icy road beneath her.

It all happened so fast. He had no time to react. Kneeling beside her, he pressed two fingers to her carotid artery. "She's still got a pulse, but it's weak."

"Should we start CPR?"

"No. She's hypothermic. That could kill her." He swiped the Mylar bag and covered her. "Call a bus. Then grab the army blankets in my duffel bag. We need to warm her."

While Frankie rattled off her badge number to dispatch, Niko climbed on top of Sage to use his body heat. His gaze strayed to the victim wedged under the guardrail. "Call Gaines too. But first, I need those blankets."

She covered the mouthpiece of her cell phone. "I'm on it."

In a flash, the image of Chance's corpse flitted through Niko's mind. Dammit. He'd been so preoccupied with Noah, and then with Sage, he never considered how Frankie might be coping. With her gruff exterior, she hid her emotions like a trick-or-treater stashing the last snickers bar. Once EMTs transported Sage to the hospital, maybe he could steal a few moments alone with her. If past experience shined a light on the truth, he'd tell her how well-guarded secrets could destroy someone quicker than end-stage renal failure. He'd learned that nugget of wisdom the hard way.

Under the moon, partially obscured by clouds, Niko balanced on his hands and toes to keep his full weight off Sage. She could have broken ribs, a punctured lung, or a snapped neck. With all the blood, distinguishing what injuries she sustained became a near impossible task. The longest fifteen minutes of his life ticked by, his heart-rate soaring far above normal limits.

The ambulance skidded to a stop. Two EMTs leaped from their doors and dragged a stretcher from the back. Niko rose to his feet and stepped away to let them work. Unwilling to let her out of his sight, his head bobbed around the paramedics.

"She's hypothermic," said the male EMT. "Core body temp., eighty-eight degrees."

Hands held in prayer, he cringed when he asked, "Can you save her?"

"We'll do our best. She needs a hospital."

Heat incinerated his insides and he grabbed his head in both hands. "Then go."

"What about her?" The female paramedic jabbed a chin toward the corpse.

"She's the ME's problem. Concentrate on my wife."

They loaded the stretcher into the back of the ambulance. Before jumping in with Sage, he turned back to Frankie. "You can handle things from here, right?" Meaning, memorialize the crime scene, search for evidence, drag information out of Dr. Gaines, and keep everyone in line. The latter wasn't in question.

"Not a problem. Go." She waved him away. "I'll keep you posted."

As the ambulance fled through the early-morning streets, the moon peeked around the clouds as if announcing better times lay ahead. If only that were true.

Exhaustion tugged under his eyes as he gave his wife's hand a gentle squeeze. The entire ride he refused to let go, even when the EMTs dragged the stretcher out the back and rolled it through the automatic hospital doors, or when the doctor rushed over to check Sage's vitals, then spouted orders about heated blankets and warm fluids, or when two nurses rolled her gurney into the ER and dragged her body onto a fitted mattress filled with warm water.

For the rest of his time on this earth, he'd never let go. The future was too uncertain. Over the last handful of years, more than thirteen-thousand people had lost their lives to hypothermia. Granted, that included the elderly. Even so, moderate hypothermia—core temperatures ranging from eighty-two to eighty-nine degrees Fahrenheit—was a serious condition, never mind the injuries she'd sustained.

The nurse called out to the doctor, "Eight-seven point eight. She's down two-tenths."

"After-drop. I was afraid of that." He pried open Sage's eyes to check her pupils. "IV of warm saline stat. Heated to one-hundred-and-ten-degrees in the microwave." He peeled off his latex gloves. "I'll scrub for surgery."

"Surgery?" A sudden jolt stopped his heart mid-beat. "I don't understand."

The jagged line of Sage's heartbeat flashed across the EKG screen, then dipped. A technician shoved him away from the table, then dragged a curtain around the bed.

Frozen in place, Niko couldn't move as nurses ran in and out of the sectioned area. An entire team now worked on his wife.

He bolted out the exit and dialed Childs' cell number. It rang three times before he answered. "It's Niko. Can you bring Noah to Dartmouth Hitchcock Medical Center? I can't leave."

"Sure, boss. He's such a great kid. I'm gonna miss hanging out with him."

As much as he appreciated the sentiment, he didn't have time for a drawn-out *tête-à-tête*. "Childs, I need him here right away. Please."

"Okay. Leaving now."

"Thanks." When Niko pulled the phone away from his ear Childs called his name. "What?"

"Heard about your wife. She okay?"

Now was not the time to share the details of Sage's condition. Not yet. Not until the outcome became clear. "Time will tell. Thanks for askin'. See ya when you get here."

Hospital setting or no, Noah needed to see his mom, feel her heartbeat against his, in case the Good Lord decided to take her home. If nothing else, Noah could spend time with the woman who gave him life, as much as her death pained him to consider.

Should Sage's soul return to heaven, beauty and love awaited her—a celestial parallel plain where pain disappeared, no fear existed, good triumphed over evil, and killers plummeted to the maw of hell. Sadly, that gave him little comfort. With each passing hour, their future together looked more and more grim.

Chapter Thirty-Five

2:40 a.m.

While Frankie set up the lights around the perimeter of McDaniels Marsh, Bradley cordoned off the area. Waving away the stench of Gaines' cologne, she leaned over the body of Lisa Cassidy, ID'd by her prints, cataloged from a DUI charge five years ago. Well, the right hand, anyway. The killer lobbed off the left and took it with him, the sick, twisted fuck.

Neck severed with one clean swipe, her face, head, arms, and stomach revealed numerous incised wounds, which had bled profusely, trailing crimson lines over her waxy, putty-like skin. Her splayed-open foggy eyes and blue lips alluded to a scream at the moment of impact.

Someone quieted her forever.

Contrary to Niko's theory of the case, Frankie didn't buy the connection between Chance's death and the murdered women. For one, Chance still had both hands. For two, the killer didn't leave a Suicide King at Mount Cardigan.

Unlike the others, the killer didn't take his time with this vic. What, if anything, did this signify? "I'm assuming TOD is nearly impossible now," she said to Gaines. "Obviously, she was hypothermic when she died."

Gaines' face brightened. "Very good. You are correct. The waxy skin is a telltale sign. Manner of death is homicide. The ironic part is, if the killer waited, Ms. Cassidy might have succumbed to cold. The organs shut down, including the heart and brain. However, much like a bypass machine, in frigid temperatures the body can last for hours in a suspended state. It is really quite fascinating."

179

"Yeah. Great. So…TOD?"

"I will be better equipped to tell you more once I complete the autopsy. I should warn you, however, the time of death window will be difficult to narrow."

"That's fine. I'm sure Sage can fill in the blanks."

"Have you heard from Sheriff Quintano?"

"Not yet. Why?"

"Well, if his wife is in a similar condition, she could be in for a tough battle, a life or death struggle."

In a flash, Frankie straightened. "Are you sayin' she could die?"

Gaines parted his lips to speak, but Frankie stopped him. "For Sage's sake, don't guess. You didn't exam her, so you can't really say for sure."

A somber expression crossed his face. "You are correct. I have no way of knowing what condition she is in. However, more people die in the hospital from complications of hypothermia than out in the elements." He glanced over his shoulder at Billy the perv.

The image of the mayor's son getting down and dirty with a corpse made Frankie's skin crawl, and she shuddered.

"Help me get her loaded into the van, please."

When Gaines rose to his feet, Frankie hooked his arm. "Am I missing somethin'?"

"In reference to…?"

"The weather, genius." She tsked her tongue. "Whaddaya think I'm talkin' about? Sage's condition, obviously."

"I thought the matter was closed."

"Whatever. Go play with your corpse." She stormed over to check on Ben, tagging and bagging evidence in the woods. "Got anything for me?"

"Huh? Oh, yeah. Found the card." At eye level, he jiggled a clear evidence bag. The King of Hearts fell to one side.

"Where?"

Beside a thick birch tree Ben pointed to an area in the snow, the blood slurping the moisture like a massive swarm of tics. The papery bark's crimsoned edges revealed castoff spray.

"Wow." Frankie examined every inch. "This must be where he sliced her throat. Did you photograph the bloodstains yet?"

He gave her a look like a homeless puppy.

Without Niko here, she might as well have a little fun. "See the droplets of blood on the bark, Benny boy? What velocity is it?"

Ben studied the dots. "Medium."

"You're guessing."

"No I'm not. Knife wounds cause medium-velocity spatter."

"No shit, Sherlock. But suppose you didn't know she was stabbed. How can you tell this is medium-velocity spatter?"

His neck turtled in his shoulders.

"Step aside, kid." She shoved him out of the way. "Watch and learn. Impact spatter will form larger drops and be more concentrated in the area adjacent to the action while forward spatter from a gunshot will form smaller droplets spread across a wider area."

"Huh?" He crinkled his nose. "Which is medium, then, forward or impact spatter? Niko didn't tell me there were different kinds of spatter, only velocity."

"Velocity is determined by the type of impact spatter, golden boy. Look here." She pointed at fine lines of blood across the birch tree. "See how all the tails go in the same direction, forming a line? The tails determine directionally. Meaning, they point to where the victim was standing. The vic is the source of the blood, so the tails would face her."

"Yep. I remember."

"Okay, cool. We need to photograph the blood before I show you how to use markers. I videoed before anyone entered the scene, so we're good there, too."

"I took the pics already."

"From every angle?"

He smirked like Chester Cheetah, the spokes-cat for Cheetos. "Yep."

"Lemme see the camera real quick. Niko will kill me if I screw up." Frankie scrolled through several photographs. What do you know? The kid did it right. She passed the camera back to Ben. "Snap more pics while I measure." She positioned a ruler— shaped in a forty-five degree angle with measurements on both inner edges—next to a blood droplet. "This is almost an eighth of an inch. Remember, we don't measure the tails. So that tells us this is medium-velocity spatter. When the killer sliced her neck, the blade went across her throat and swept outward with his arm. That's how this spatter got on the tree."

Ben's blue eyes widened in awe. "Cool."

Deputy, her ass. She was so ready for the sheriff job.

One by one Frankie measured each drop as Ben worked the camera. "Now let's cast these shoeprints. We probably should've done them first, but that can be our little secret, right?"

Head hung, staring at the ground, Ben didn't respond.

She biffed his arm. "Right?"

"Oh. Yeah. Right."

"What's up?"

"Niko should be grooming you for sheriff, not me."

"Hate to break it to ya, kid, but he already asked me." Wow, that felt good. She derived even more pleasure from Ben's shocked expression. "Casting in snow is simple as long as you've got this stuff." From her kit, she withdrew Sirchie's Snow Impression wax. "This protects the snow from the heat of Shake 'n Cast. Once the spray contacts the snow it locks in the ridge detail while the casting material hardens."

"I know. I've used it."

"Well *pardonne moi.*" She bobbed her head like a chicken. "Someone's got their panties in a bunch. Whatever. Do it yourself, then." Shoulders back, head held high, she strode away. Too frickin' bad if his feelings were hurt. Now he knew how she felt these last few years.

In the main lot, she surveyed the marsh. If the killer brought Sage and Lisa Cassidy here, maybe this was another dumping ground. Hands cupped around her mouth, she called out, "Has anyone checked the water?"

"No." Bradley's panicked reaction caused her hand to tighten into a fist. "Why?"

"Call it a hunch." As much as she hated to bother Niko, she had no choice but to call. When he answered, she first asked about Sage.

"The doctors are pumping her with warm fluids. She's not great."

"Aw, shit. I'm sorry, Niko."

"What's happening there?"

"Umm...well?" With no easy way to put this, she spit the words out fast. "I need to call in the dive team."

"What? Why?"

"If the killer brought two women here, who's to say he didn't bring more? Maybe this is another dumping ground, like the woods." A long pause of silence came between them, and Frankie mentally kicked herself for reminding him of Sage's ordeal.

"Do it," he said, his voice crackling with pain.

"I'm on it." She paused. "Niko?"

"Yeah."

"Give Sage a kiss for me, okay?"

"Will do. Thanks, Frank."

"Yeah, yeah. Don't go all mushy on me." After she disconnected, she dialed the State Police. Leads dried up faster than steam on a bathroom mirror. With any luck, the mutt left something behind that might reveal his identity.

Ninety minutes later, Frankie supervised the dive team as they raised barrel after barrel from their swampy grave. Two empty, the other four held naked women with no left hand and a Suicide King driven down their throat, the final message from a demented mass murderer.

Why leave Sage alive? Why not kill Lisa Cassidy right away? There must be some connection between the two.

Chapter Thirty-Six

8:30 a.m.

In a far-off land a steady hum reawakened my senses, but I could not distinguish the sound. Like a subway train it mushroomed toward me, a rush of loudness. Strings of words. A woman's voice. I lifted my eyebrows in an attempt to open my eyes, but my body refused to comply.

"Mrs. Quintano, wake up." Someone nudged my shoulder. "You're in the hospital. It's okay. You're safe now."

Total exhaustion weakened my resolve, and I could barely move.

"Babe?" Niko's voice. "Can you open your eyes?"

I nodded my head, but remained unclear if it moved.

"C'mon, babe. Let's see those stunning peepers of yours."

I raised my brows a second time, but the eyelids would not follow.

"She's still out of it," he said.

"Her blood pressure is quite low, Sheriff. Even so, she should be responsive by now."

A tiny voice said, "Momma."

I forced open my eyelids. One eye slitted with blurry silhouettes, the other hazy but sharp enough to see. Glaring light blinded me; it shot through my forehead like a flaming arrow, searing my brain from the inside out. My thoughts jumbled. I'd been gone a long time, but where, wasn't clear. What happened? Did I get in a car accident?

"You might experience some amnesia," said the nurse. "Don't panic. After what you've been through, it's perfectly normal."

"Amnesia?" echoed Niko. "Y'mean, she can't tell me what happened?"

"She may not know."

"Permanently? Or will her memory return over time?"

"Hard to say. Everyone's different."

All my muscles rusted shut as if they hadn't been used for years while Niko and the nurse spoke about my condition like I wasn't in the room. The pressure on my chest felt as if an invisible elephant sprawled on top of me, his full weight bearing down, crushing my bones.

"Momma?"

Even though every inch of my soul longed to hold my child, the struggle to move was too intense. Niko lifted him to my level, and Noah's bottom lip jutted and quivered.

With a hoarse voice, I hushed, "I'm okay, baby."

Instinctively Niko knew I needed our son more than anything, so he laid Noah on my chest and ensured he didn't tumble off the side. Noah snuggled under my chin. His silky hair tickled my skin, baby shampoo rising through my sinuses, warming my insides more than hospital fluids could ever do. The IV tugged at my skin when I slid my hand to his back, his shoulders bouncing while he cried on my chest. Even with prodding from Niko, he refused to look at me.

Did my appearance frighten him?

Surprise in her tone, the nurse said, "Will you look at that."

"The power of a mother's love." Niko grinned. "Amazing, isn't it?"

"Her blood pressure is rising too. I've never seen anything like it."

"He completes her." A tear trickled down his cheek. "And she completes me." He edged onto the mattress and swept my bangs from my eyes, lowered his face, gently kissed my cheek, and then the top of Noah's head. "Love you to the moon, 'round the world, and back again."

"Excuse me, Sheriff Quintano." The nurse leaned over us. "I hate to interrupt, but would you mind putting on a smock?"

A smock? I shifted my eyes to find out why the nurse requested he cover himself. Gaping, my jaw slacked. Dried blood stained his uniform from the neckline to the knees. Like a whipping tornado, images flooded my brain. Lisa. The oil drums in the marsh. Our trek through the woods. My encounter with a black bear, and Lisa's gurgle when she struggled for one final breath.

Sharp pain shot to my right cheekbone, upper lip, and nose— all battered under gauze bandages. Some details remained fuzzy. Did Niko save me? Did he kill the clown? Or did he flee, able to return to finish what he started?

Chapter Thirty-Seven

11:45 a.m.

At her desk, Frankie dug through Lisa Cassidy's background for a link to Sage. What restaurants she frequented, where she did her banking, who she called on a regular basis, and her favorite clothing stores.

She had to admit, Lisa had good taste. The selfie on her computer's home screen showed her in faded, capri-length jeans with strategically placed tears. Frankie had the same pair; she looked way hotter in them, too. Where Lisa failed was in the shoe department. In most pics she wore sketchers.

Who ruins a kickass outfit with sneakers?

She spun her chair to face Ben. "Hey, what'd you find out about Mary Anne Goodman?"

"What're you looking for?"

"I don't know yet. Gimme a rundown."

Ben's gaze lowered to his computer screen. "She went out to eat a lot. Village Pizza, Pat's Seafood, Purple Pit, Kathleen's Cottage, Cheerful Garden."

"Not Fugaky's? That's the best Chinese food around. Why wouldn't she—?" Her empty stomach grumbled. "Anyway. What else?"

"She worked as an ER nurse at Franklin General, but you probably already knew that. No criminal record."

"Did we get Lisa Cassidy's tox screen back yet?"

Hand raised, Ben shook the report. "Got it right here."

Frankie snatched it from his grasp. "With Niko gone, this should've come to me." She skimmed the report. No ketamine in her system, which proved her theory that Chance's death had nothing to do with the murdered women. But why, then, did Mary Anne Goodman have high levels of the drug in her bloodstream? Did Chance and his mistress party after hours?

For argument's sake, even if she believed Niko's theory that this was payback for a book Sage wrote years ago, then why leave the Suicide King and take the left hand? And how did the antlers figure in?

She whirled around. "Bradley, pull the security footage from Cumberland Farms, the one next to the Minot-Sleeper Library."

"Huh?"

"Am I speakin' French?" She rolled her lips. "Y'know what? Never mind. I'll do it myself." She dragged her Sheriff's Department jacket off the back of her chair and hustled out the door.

Fifteen minutes later, she drove into the convenience store's parking lot. Badge in hand, she swung open the heavy glass door. A line formed from the register and extended down the middle aisle. Frankie elbowed her way to the teenage clerk who looked like he'd rather be anywhere but here. "Important Sheriff's Department business. I need to speak with you." She turned back to the line of customers, pissing and moaning about having to wait. "Oh, relax. He'll only be a sec." Jabbing her head toward the office door, she prompted him to move. "Let's go. Now."

Once the clerk followed her into the office, she asked to see the security footage.

"Over here." He shuffled to the back wall where a monitor displayed split-screen images of six different camera angles.

"Perfect. All right. You can go. I've got it from here."

"Umm, don't you need a warrant or something?"

"Nah," she lied. "It's all good. Your customers are waiting."

With Mr. Wannabe Lawyer out of the way she searched for the tape dated the day of Sage's book signing. If this lead panned out, the sheriff job was in the bag.

For over an hour she scrolled through image after image.

Until a brawny man in a knit hat with a book tucked under his arm, sauntered into view. "Hello, Mr. Dunn." Frankie's gaze followed as he got into a dark sedan, parked at the gas pump. When he pulled out the lot exit, she zoomed in on the car. The grainy image only revealed a partial plate.

On her cell, she called dispatch and rattled off her badge number. "Need you to run a partial plate for me. Chevy Impala, black or navy, NH plates starting with six-three-niner-delta."

"One moment please." For once, Doris didn't give her shit. "Registered owner is Mr. Milton Laurent. Vehicle was reported stolen."

"You're shittin' me? Wendy Laurent's soon-to-be ex?"

"Deputy Campanelli, there's no need for that type of language."

"My bad. Was the vehicle ever located?"

"Actually, yes."

"Local or state police?"

"Local. Vehicle was recovered on Cardigan Mountain Road. CarTed Trucking towed it."

"Did the owner pick it up yet?"

"He did not."

"Interesting. Do me a favor and call the tow company. No one touches that car till I get there. Got it?"

"I understand, yes. I'll call over now."

Without a goodbye, Frankie disconnected. No wonder they never recovered Wendy's vehicle. It was registered in her spouse's name. Why wouldn't the ex-husband mention it when she'd notified him of Wendy's murder? Which sucked, by the way. Up until that point, she'd never done a death notification without Niko, and she was in no hurry to do another.

The car fell into the Investigation 101 category. How'd Niko miss this? Especially with one of his favorite lines being, "Before you look for an outlaw, look for an in-law." Stupid question. With the bullshit with Chance, Noah's kidnapping, and Sage appearing on the roadway covered in blood, it was a frickin' miracle they'd unearthed any leads at all.

Waving over her head on her way out the door, she ambled to her SUV.

Before she chatted with the alleged grieving husband, she needed to check out the car. If Dunn left latent prints, they might lead to his real identity. Maybe the husband hired him to off his wife. It wouldn't be the first time someone tried to cover up a murder by killing more than one person. Stupid move, really. Eventually they always caught their man. Sometimes it took months, sometimes years, but nowadays it's almost impossible to get away with murder.

* * *

1:45 p.m.

The impound lot had more cars than a sleaze-ball had pick-up lines. Frankie asked the dude behind the counter at CarTed Trucking where they'd stashed the Chevy Impala towed from Cardigan Mountain Road.

He took off his greasy cap, scratched his oily brunette hair, and drooled spit from his chewing tobacco, into a plastic cola bottle. Frankie's stomach tumbled forward, then back. If this joker had half a brain, she'd consider it a win. Judging by his ZZ Top beard packed with unidentifiable debris, there was little chance of that.

Without a word, he slogged toward the doorway, his filthy jeans pulled low from his gigantic beer-belly, exposing the crack of his startling-white ass. Poor bastard probably had no idea how cringe-worthy he was.

Already she'd had enough of this asshole. "Listen, pal. I don't have all day."

As he filled the doorway, he raised his dirt-caked fingernail, grease pitted in the lines of the knuckle, and pointed to the right-side of the lot. Basically, the moron waved in the direction of thirty possible matches to the Impala.

In the hopes of escaping this shithole ASAP she imitated Niko. "Use your words."

In the snow piled next to the door, he spit more amber spew.

Real classy, jerkoff.

"Back corner," he grumbled as though she had the audacity to ask him to work.

Perish the thought. No wonder he had the lazy-guy gut. The grease monkey probably woofed two large pizzas for lunch and had a fifth of Jack stashed for five o'clock, if he made it that long. Which might explain the stench of garlic mixed with BO.

Note to self: if she was ever called back to this hellhole, bring Bradley or Ben.

"For your sake, buddy, it better be there." If his incompetence forced her to trek back to the office, she'd kick his ever-lovin' ass. Course that would require her to touch his skeevy— Scratch that. There weren't enough tetanus shots in the world.

Please tell me he didn't breed.

When she rounded the corner of the building, the sun glinted off a cool Ski-Doo's new Corvette-orange paintjob, the keys still in the ignition. What the hell? She swung her leg over the seat and turned on the gas. With a glance back at Cro-Magnon man, she jabbed her chin. "You don't mind, right?" Then revved the engine so he couldn't respond.

The brisk afternoon air nipped at her face as she swerved in and out the rows of impounded vehicles, some ready for auction, others begging for a crusher to save them the misery of trying to turn-over. In the far corner sat a Chevy Impala with the same plates as in the surveillance video. On the seat sat a deck of playing cards with a flawless bloody fingerprint on the box.

A thrill zipped up her spine. Sheriff Frankie Campanelli had a nice ring to it.

Chapter Thirty-Eight

March 29, 2008, 4:30 p.m.

After my body temperature regulated, the hospital discharged me. The cosmetic surgeon decided to forgo operating on my orbital floor fracture—aka broken eye socket—and fractured cheekbone until the swelling decreased, approximately ten to twelve days after the attack. They scheduled my pre-op consultation appointment for next week.

Blood-red stained the whites of my two black eyes from the broken nose and swollen cheek. Multiple stitches and bruises littered my face, so wherever possible I avoided mirrors. Noah still wasn't used to seeing me all banged up, but at least I didn't frighten him anymore. Nonetheless, my scars became a constant reminder of how I'd failed Lisa. Nightly, I prayed for forgiveness. She played a starring role in my nightmares, too, as I relived that terrifying trek through the woods, my soul longing for absolution.

When I arrived home, little things alerted me to Noah's inner struggle to heal from his own horrifying experience—his downturned mouth and slumped posture, his lack of interest in anything but television. Obviously, he couldn't process his abduction or the chaos that ensued, because he did not yet possess the life skills to fully grasp the situation. During his thirteen months on earth, he'd survived more tragedy than most adults. Niko said he needed time, and maybe he was right. Still, I pushed for a child psychologist. Niko agreed; he didn't dare ignore my intuition twice. Look how well it worked out the first time.

So, earlier today, we took Noah to see Dr. Krieger—the best child psychologist in the area—who assured us he would not remember the time he spent with a serial killing clown. Seriously? Needless to say, his so-called professional opinion was less than ideal. Regardless of age, that creepy mask was not easily forgotten.

We'd been home for about an hour when Noah fell asleep in his fort. On the sofa, Lisa's cries cluttered my mind. She seemed like such a nice girl. She didn't deserve what that animal did to her. Why didn't he kill me too? More importantly, what did he want? Something—call it intuition, instinct, or just plain common sense—told me he was nowhere near done toying with me.

Colt jumped up on the sofa, circled twice, and plopped on my feet. Ruger rested his chin on the pillow under my head, his wet, black nose pressed to mine. "Hey, you." I stroked his blocky head. "Did Daddy give you your pain cookie this morning?"

In his Lay-Z-Boy, Niko lowered *Scarred*. Mind you, he'd read it twice already. "Yes, I did." His voice pitched, high and squeaky. "Didn't I, buddy?"

Ruger didn't move; he kept staring into my eyes as if clawing through my false façade. He always could tell when something bothered me. "I'm okay. I promise." When I forced a smile, I winced from the pain.

Niko must have noticed, because he rose from the chair and was at my side in a millisecond, wiggling his butt on to the edge of the sofa next to Ruger's face. Gazing lovingly at me, he stroked my hair. "You okay?"

Nodding, I offered him a quivery smile.

"You ready to tell me what happened?"

Tears welling in my eyes, I shook my head no.

"Babe, talk to me. Please."

"I can't. Not yet."

Audibly, he sighed. "When, then?"

I flipped over and faced the sofa cushions. "I don't know."

"Don't you trust me?"

I nodded yes.

"Then talk to me. I can't help you if I don't know what happened."

I didn't respond. I couldn't.

"Did he r-r—" He couldn't say the word. "Y'know, touch you inappropriately?"

"I don't think so."

He rose to his feet. "How can you not know something like that? Either he did or he didn't."

Flipping to my side, I then propped my head on a bent elbow. "It's not that simple."

"Then tell me." He lowered to the sofa, and I dove against his chest.

"What happened to Lisa is all my fault. She depended on me to save her. And now, she's dead."

With an open hand, he massaged my back in a circular motion. "Babe, you can't blame yourself. My God, you were both suffering from hypothermia. You're lucky to be alive."

I wiggled up to meet his gaze. "You don't get it. When I freed her from the barrel, I promised I'd save her. I promised her, Niko." I pressed a closed fist to his heart. "I promised her, and she believed me."

"Wait. Back up. What about a barrel?"

"The oil drums in the marsh."

Eyes squinting, he pulled back. "Oil drums?"

"Oh, my God, that's right. There were six total, including mine."

Ever so slightly he shook his head. "You were trapped inside an oil drum? Why am I only hearing about this now?" He tilted to one side and dug into the front pocket of his khakis.

"Are you calling Frankie?"

"Yeah. She had the dive team out there. If the marsh was filled with oil drums, they would've found 'em. Yet, this is the first I'm hearing about it."

"Don't blame her. She's running the investigation by herself. Even you get stressed dealing with multiple victims. Has she ever notified parents of their child's death? I can't even imagine what it's like to witness their heart-wrenching reaction." My eyes popped wide, and I pushed out of his strong embrace. "Mr. Chen. That's right. Hang on. Let me check something real quick." I hobbled over to my desk and flipped open the Chromebook, searching for the significance of the left hand.

Cell phone in hand, Niko hovered over my shoulder as links to dream analysis websites filled the screen.

"Mr. Chen mentioned something about brothers."

"You lost me. What do severed hands have to do with brothers?"

"Remember when I wrote *Deadly Dawgs*? I think Noah's kidnapping and my abduction is in retaliation."

"Uh…" He hesitated. "I didn't wanna tell you till you fully recovered, but Chance is dead."

I jolted back in my chair. "What? How?"

"Apparently, he's been supplying the Dawgs with ketamine. Then he must've had a crisis of conscience because he shut 'em off."

"And they killed him for it?" Eyes wide, I slapped a hand over my mouth. "Poor Frankie. Where is she?"

"Probably at the station."

"You didn't give her time off to grieve?"

"Well, I did, but…but then… Hey, she knew she could… you were gone. I didn't know where you were. Noah was crying, missing his mommy. Don't look at me like that. I'm human. I screwed up, okay?" He opened his arms wide. "Whaddaya want me to do? Either she runs the investigation or I do."

"Uh-ha," I said, glib.

"I thought you wanted me to retire."

If he left the sheriff's office for the wrong reasons, he'd end up resenting me. That, I couldn't handle. "I never said that."

"Maybe not outright, but every time I'm late for supper, or if I get a call when we're heading to bed, you always have some comment. After what happened, I just assumed you didn't wanna be alone."

"I can take care of myself, thank you very much."

"Now you're twisting my words." He softened his tone. "Babe, all I meant was, we almost lost you."

Averting my gaze, I hung my head. I didn't deserve his

kindness, his unwavering adoration. Through my incompetence, a woman was dead and our little boy was permanently scarred, and all because I pried into a blood gang's activities. Add that to what happened to Chloe, my twin sister, and I could barely face myself.

A question gnawed at me. How could I protect my family if I didn't recognize the killer without the mask? He could be my neighbor, the kid who bagged my groceries, or the UPS driver who delivered my books. With his identity concealed, I'd never see the danger till it was too late. Next time, I might not make it out alive.

Chapter Thirty-Nine

5:30 p.m.

The crazy March weather fluctuated between beautiful and sixty degrees to freeze-your-ass-off, which hovered around thirty-two degrees Fahrenheit. Today, snow flurries fell from muted-charcoal storm clouds as Frankie soldiered toward Laurent's front door. From digging through Wendy's life, she discovered Milton had moved out of the family home and scored himself a bachelor pad—aka an expensive condo at Newfound Lake—amid strings of side-by-side identical townhouses. How the residents told them apart was anyone's guess.

Frankie's heeled boots left imprints in the snow on the walkway. For the money the condo association charged for fees, it should be spotless. Around here, if residents could view the lake, they paid an insane amount of money for that pleasure.

When she knocked at the door of unit nine, a young boy answered. Cupped hands on her knees, she squatted to his level. "Hi there. Is your dad home?"

The door swung fully open. Milton Laurent stood behind his son, and he did *not* look happy to see her again so soon.

Mm-mm, Wendy had good taste. When she did the death notification, she'd missed his chiseled jawline and strong shoulders.

Frankie shook his manicured hand. Now it made sense. Any guy who went to the salon more than she did was an automatic no effin' way. Except Chance. Somehow he pulled off his flawlessly-groomed appearance without looking effeminate. "Mr. Laurent, we met earlier. Deputy Campanelli from the Grafton County Sheriff's Department."

"What can I do for you, Deputy?"

"I need five minutes of your time. May I come in?"

"Sure." He turned his attention to his son. "Milo, go play in your room so the adults can talk."

With a stomp to his feet, he whined, "But Dad…"

"You heard me." He tapped Milo's ass the way one might urge a horse to trot. "Off you go." He swung his arm toward the living room. "This way please, Deputy."

On the front mat, Frankie wiped the snow off her boots. When she followed the alleged grieving husband into the kitchen, Mr. Laurent pulled out her chair, and Frankie almost decked him. What'd he think this was, a date? Or his lame attempt to avoid murder charges?

"I prefer to stand, thank you." She flipped open her notepad.

He sloughed off a half-assed shrug. "Suit yourself."

"I should've asked this before, but I wanted to give you time to process your loss." That was bullshit. The best time to interrogate a suspicious family member was to catch them off-guard, like during the death notification for example. If only she'd seen through his crap sooner.

Careful not to reveal too much—a good investigator danced on the edge of truth-and-bald-faced-lie—she hinted about his wife's vehicle. "On the last day you saw Wendy, was she driving? Or did she leave the house on foot?"

"This is important, why?"

"Please answer the question." *Jerk off.*

His gaze flicked around the kitchen but didn't land anywhere in particular. "Hmm," he said, indifferent. "I'm not sure. Does it matter?"

"I wouldn't ask the question if it wasn't relevant." *You smug bastard.*

"Let's see." He stalled, tapping a finger to his full lips.

Classic avoidance. Frankie made a note of his hesitancy as she lowered to the chair across from him.

Mr. Laurent's neck stretched toward her like a giraffe nibbling a leaf on a high branch. "I haven't answered yet, so what are you writing?"

"Just taking a few notes." For fun, she made him squirm by doodling. Old cop trick. Keep the suspect on edge. "Also, I'm wondering why you wouldn't cooperate in your wife's case." Now her gaze met his.

As if swallowing a wise comeback, Milton Laurent's lips pressed together. "If memory serves, she stayed home that day. Oh, right, she must have, because I reported her vehicle stolen the day before."

"The day before?" Crap. Doris neglected to mention the date. "If you two were divorcing, why would you report the vehicle stolen?"

"I'm the registered owner. Do you think the guy who stole the car is the same man who killed her?"

"I never said a man's responsible. What made you leap to that conclusion?" Granted, this wasn't her best interrogation ever. Whatever. From here on out, she was winging it.

"Statistics show there are more male serial killers than—"

"Yeah, yeah. Let's get back on point. Why didn't you pick up the Impala from the tow lot? Records show they notified you."

He jerked a thumb toward his chest. "You think *I* had something to do with Wendy's murder?"

"I'm merely asking a question, Mr. Laurent."

"Oh, sure, blame the future ex-husband so you don't have to do any real police work."

The balls on this guy. Though it wasn't easy, she bit back the anger. "Why didn't you pick up the vehicle, Mr. Laurent?"

He clasped his hands behind his neck. "Fine. I'll get the damn car."

"Not now, you won't. It's being towed to the state police barracks as evidence in a serial homicide investigation. We'll be going through it with a fine-tooth comb, so you better start praying now."

He shoved the table away and rose. "Get out of my house."

Frankie took one last shot. "Would you be willing to submit to a polygraph exam?"

"Absolutely not." He pointed toward the door. "Get out. Any

more questions can be directed to my attorney."

"If you've got nothing to hide…" Snide and cold, she smirked. "What's the big deal?"

"What would be the point? The results aren't admissible in court."

"You're right, but it's a great tool to exclude family and friends from the suspect list. We use them a lot for that purpose, actually." Another lie.

Over the last five years they'd used polygraphs a handful of times. The threat of one worked amazingly well in judging the innocence or guilt of a potential suspect. If they got the family or friend to agree, all the better. Most potential suspects didn't want anything to do with the exam, so it wasn't surprising the Husband of the Year refused.

"I'll show myself out. Thank you for your time." *Asshole.*

On her way out the door, she tossed over her head, "Don't plan any trips out of town." As she strutted down the walkway, the upstairs window slid open.

The little boy called out to her. "Sheriff, wait."

Why correct the kid? "Yes, Milo?"

So he didn't have to yell he waved her closer. "Did Daddy kill Mommy?"

Frankie's hands went limp as she let out a long, low sigh. "Of course not. Look. I don't want you to worry. I'll find the man who hurt your mom. Okay?"

Acknowledging her promise, Milo's baby-blue eyes closed, and then reopened.

Cute kid. Shame he had an ass for a father. "Now get back inside before your dad catches you." She winked. "This conversation will be our little secret."

The window slid down the tracks, and Milo waved through the glass. Holding a tight smile, Frankie waved back. No wonder Niko hated this job some days.

If Milton Laurent turned out to be the killer, she could never again face his son.

Chapter Forty

While Niko washed the supper dishes—he'd made a delicious roast with potatoes, carrots, spinach, and *au jus* sauce; first time he'd cooked in twenty years—I dug into the case files. If the Dawgs weren't responsible, I needed alternate suspects. With my child's life at stake, I couldn't take the chance of being wrong. The oddest part of the MO, aside from the missing left hand, was the King of Hearts playing card. This cryptic clue had a special meaning for the clown. Otherwise, why leave one at every crime scene?

Searching the internet resulted in numerous articles. The four kings represented real-life rulers. The King of Diamonds embodied the wealthy Julius Caesar. The King of Clubs illustrated the vicious Alexander the Great. The King of Spades paid homage to the strong but kind David of Israel, and the King of Hearts—also known as the Suicide King—personified the emotionally disturbed Charles VII of France.

Could the killer relate to Charles VII of France? To brutally slaughter so many women it didn't seem that farfetched.

I dug further.

Charles VII of France was the eleventh child of Charles VI, who suffered from recurrent madness. In fact, his father implied Charles VII was illegitimate because his mother, Isabelle of Bavaria, was known to sleep around. Nonetheless, Charles VII became heir to the throne till the English victory over the French at Agincourt. But by Treaty of Troyes, his father disinherited him in favor of the English king, Henry V.

It wasn't until Joan of Arc, a peasant girl living in medieval France who believed God had chosen her to lead France to victory, convinced Prince Charles of Valois—as Charles VII was known at the time—to allow her to lead the French army to the besieged city of Orleans, where they achieved victory over the English and their French allies, the Burgundians. When Charles VII was crowned king, Joan got captured by Anglo-Burgundian forces and tried for witchcraft and heresy and ultimately, burned at the stake in 1431, at the tender age of nineteen.

After her death, the other Kings of Europe tried to retry Joan of Arc's case, but King Charles VII wanted no part of it. If they proved he obtained his throne and crown because of help from a convicted witch and heretic, he would no longer be worthy to rule France; his coronation would be null and void. Not only did Charles VII not help Joan of Arc while alive, but he refused to reopen her case after her death so he could retain his power.

Nice guy. But how did the killer relate to him? Did his father abandon him, too? Did his mother have men in and out of his home?

The more I dug, the more information I found.

Others believed the King of Hearts represented Charlemagne, who history remembered as a ruler who overtook the Roman Empire. Pope Leo III declared him emperor of the Romans after his armies helped defeat a rebellion. Not exactly the sort of guy who'd commit suicide, so why depict him as the Suicide King?

Hmm…I clicked the next article. Playing cards had a fascinating history, especially the King of Hearts. It derived from a late medieval design showing a king wielding a battle axe. The belt, patterned-cloak, and the stance on one leg—except in the double-ended version—remained the same. By 1800, a sword replaced the battle axe, and around 1870, English cards became fixed with the suit on the left-hand side to assist in fanning the cards in the player's hand.

Odd that the King of Hearts was the only card to depict four hands in the double-ended version; the sword always held in the king's left hand.

That couldn't be a coincidence.

Many mysteries surrounded the King of Hearts, including why he held a blade to his head. Was he ready to commit suicide, or raising a sword in battle? As iconic as the one-eyed Jack, the reason for his apparent sacrifice remained one of the biggest mysteries in a modern deck of cards.

Without more to go on I could be here all night.

Niko crept up behind me and slid his hands on my shoulders, and I startled. "Whatcha doin'?" His gaze darted back and forth across the screen. "Find anything that might help?"

"Actually, yes." While he pulled a chair next to my desk, I told him what I'd learned.

"The left hand can't be a coincidence."

"That's what I said."

"Tell me, what does your crime writer brain make of it? In other words, how does it relate to our guy?"

I couldn't believe he asked for my opinion. After the attack and Noah's kidnapping, I assumed he'd want me as far away from this case as possible. "Maybe we should play our game to find out."

A chuckle. "How'd I know you were gonna say that?"

Batting my lashes, I had him right where I wanted him. "What'd Frankie discover?" Before supper Niko had called her, fired off questions the way bullets shot from an AK47.

Making me work for the information, he grinned. "Several things, actually."

"Such as…?"

"I promised Noah I'd read him a bedtime story." He kissed my cheek. "To be continued?"

What could I say, no? "Of course. Don't forget to help Rugey up the stairs. If he can't lay in front of the crib, he'll whine all night."

He patted his hip for Ruger. "C'mon, buddy. Let's tuck in the little guy."

Ruger lumbered to the stairs and set one paw on the bottom tread. Niko grabbed the handle of his harness, lifted him a scooch to take the pressure off his joints. "The things we do for love," he sang, gazing down at our fur-baby.

Once I returned home from the hospital, our marriage grew stronger than ever, even though part of me wished he'd return to work. With him home during the day, I got nothing done, and Jess, my agent, wouldn't stop pestering me for a new book. I never told her about Noah's abduction or my fight for survival. Instead, I bought myself time by sending her an outline for a novel I never intended to write. Weeks ago, I found it languishing on my hard drive. Like many writers, I had pages and pages of story ideas, some planned, others not. For once, my reluctance to trash any of my writing came in handy. If only I had a plan to deal with the creepy clown. Certainly, he had a plan for me.

Chapter Forty-One

8:30 p.m.

With Niko due back at work tomorrow, Frankie took the time to check in with a few CIs—confidential informants from her days in patrol—who moved to the area around the time she transferred in from Colebrook, her hometown two hours north of Alexandria.

In front of The Water Cooler Lounge, a popular local hole-in-the-wall, she parked Chance's Mercedes near the front entrance and paid the bouncer twenty bucks to watch it. Dressed in skin-tight black jeans with gold zippers down the outside seams, her heeled leather boots clicked across the pine floor as she made her way to the bar. Sliding onto the stool, she leaned forward to reveal the cleavage bursting the buttons of her raven, shoulder-less blouse.

Don't judge. She needed answers about Chance's murder. If she had to use her feminine wiles to get them, then so be it.

"Jack and coke," she told the bartender who couldn't peel his gaze off her. Really, who could blame him? She had to admit, her outfit kicked ass.

He didn't move, like he'd been struck by lightning, his feet melted to the floor.

Here we go. Another loser who thinks he has a shot in hell. Like she'd ever. Vomit lurched up her throat from the very idea of him going anywhere near her.

She snapped her fingers in his face. "Hello? Sometime today, please. I'm thirsty like you read about."

The bartender rousted. "Right. Sorry. Jack and coke coming

right up. Rocks or no?"

"Rocks, obviously. Who drinks that shit warm?"

When he returned with her cocktail, a biker slid onto the stool next her. "Jack and coke."

An identical order meant it was safe to talk.

Over the years, they'd practiced this routine numerous times. No one ever caught on. Even Niko had never met Ozzy, her snitch, who got the nickname after an unfortunate incident with a bat. Not a full-fledged biker himself—he prospected for about two years now; earning the patch would take months, if not years, longer—his association to the Sinister Cycles Motorcycle Club made him a valuable asset.

"Foxy as ever, I see."

With her voice low, she leaned aside. "Looking for a Dawg member. D-a-w-g, ever heard of 'em?"

Without a turn of the head, he confirmed. "Yup. Nasty crew outta Boston. Had a couple of 'em in here the other night, bragging about killing some vet. The dude with the spider tattoo crawling up his neck almost got a beat-down too. At the time, several good ol' boys who fought in Nam were here."

She biffed his rock-solid bicep. "Not that kinda vet, you moron. They murdered my fiancé."

"The doc?"

She stared into her glass, didn't answer.

"Shit, Frankie. I'm sorry."

"Thanks." She could still hardly believe he was gone. "Anyway, I'm lookin' for 'em. Any idea where they went after they left?"

"Nah. All they said was, they had one stop to make before heading home."

"Did they say where?"

"Nah. Just something about special K. They were fuckin' wasted."

"Lemme ask you somethin'. If you were gonna hit a place, how long would you scope it out beforehand?"

"Depends on where it is."

"Let's say it's a storage facility."

"Shit, they got security cameras." He swigged his Jack and coke. Ice clinked against the glass. "If I was stupid enough to take the job, I'd need at least two nights to find the blind spots." He smiled a toothy grin. "Hypothetically."

"Feel like taking a ride? I could use the backup."

His wispy eyebrows V'd. "Don't you got cop buddies for that shit?"

"This isn't exactly what you'd call 'on the books.'"

"Ah, foxy lady wants revenge. I'm down with that."

She slapped two twenty dollar bills in front of him. "Call it a down payment."

He slid the cash into his leather-vest pocket. "Meet you in the parking lot in five. Gotta take a leak first."

Thirty minutes later, with binoculars in hand, Frankie camped out at Newfound Self-Storage with a biker named Ozzy. Admittedly, she'd had better nights.

Chapter Forty-Two

9:00 p.m.

Before climbing the stairs to the nursery, I waited ten or fifteen minutes. As much as I adored tucking Noah in at night, he and Niko needed father/son time. Especially because my injuries still bothered him. Even though he was unable to put his emotions into words, I had no doubt my swollen face and numerous stitches zigzagging across my left wrist, neck, upper lip, right cheek and forehead reminded him of the time he spent with a murderous clown.

When I tiptoed into the nursery, Niko was asleep in the rocking chair with *Hop On Pop* by Dr. Seuss opened face-down on his chest. Spread-eagle in his crib, Noah breathed deep and long. His upper-cheek twitched, his head rolling side to side. A mother could only control what occurred during waking hours. If nightmares climbed into his subconscious mind, I couldn't stop the terror without waking him.

Ruger must have sensed my disquiet because he gazed up at me with pained eyes. After I kissed Noah's cheek and pulled his pastel quilt over his narrow shoulders, I knelt to sit beside Ruger. Gray hairs around his muzzle revealed his age as he rested his chin in my lap. "He's safe now, honey." My tone betrayed my certainty.

When it came to his family, Ruger felt things so deeply. For a moment, I considered bringing him to a doggy psychologist, then decided against it. They couldn't do any more to help than we could. This time, Niko might be right. In theory, time could heal his emotional scars, but I doubt he'd ever forget the night a sinister clown stole Noah from our bed.

208

If only he'd forgive himself. The guilt he carried showed in every move he made; the way he hung his head when he lumbered into a room; how he never took his gaze off Noah, and no matter how hard we tried, he refused to crack a smile. Colt bounced back—playful and jubilant embedded in his DNA—but I doubt he'd ever forget, either. Shame over their failure to protect their brother overshadowed their lives, even though Niko and I made it a point to reassure them. Noah's kidnapping was no more their fault than my subsequent abduction and torture. I was the adult in the home. If anyone was to blame, it's me.

For the hundredth time, I explained this to Ruger, but it didn't seem to help. From that fateful day forward, he hadn't slept a full night. I scratched his furry head. He didn't budge. So he'd feel safe and loved, I lowered his muzzle to the carpet and spooned my battered body around him.

Niko woke from the rocker. "He all right?"

"Not really, no."

He crawled on the floor with us. "Maybe we should have a vet look at him. They might be able to prescribe something."

"Like doggy Prozac? No. Not yet. I'd rather not put him on medication. He already takes Rimadyl. At his age, the less meds, the better."

Facing us, Niko sat cross-legged and laid his hand over Ruger's heart. "We love you so much, buddy." Tears welled in his eyes as he lowered his face to kiss our first born on the snout. He nuzzled his face in the crook of Ruger's neck. "Please forgive yourself."

A tiny cry escaped Ruger's lips, eviscerating all hope of staying strong. While Noah slept, silently tortured by his experience, we cuddled with Ruger, Niko from the front, me from the back. Colt zipped up the loft stairs and into the nursery. When he found us, he stuck out his paws to stop short. Using his nose, he lifted my arm and wedged his muscular body between me and Ruger. With his full weight, he stepped on my hip, knees, ankles, and pinned my hair to the floor. In his eyes, there wasn't any place he couldn't fit. In reality, he'd passed lap dog size years ago, but he never let that stop him.

Niko sat upright and tousled Colt's fur. "You're a good boy too. Huh?" He scratched his fuzzy tummy, and Colt's back leg pedaled like riding a stationary bike. "That's the spot. Huh, buddy?"

Groaning, Ruger was not amused. Colt's nails scratched his lower back with each revolution. Before this got out of hand and woke Noah, I dislodged from the tangle of furry arms and legs. Niko rose, too, which Colt didn't like. He sprang to all fours and pawed Niko's leg for more attention.

"Daddy and Mommy have a game to play, buddy. Come downstairs with us."

Hope soared like a new kite out for the first time. "You mean that, Niko?"

"Can I ever say no to you?"

"Aww, pup." I threw my arms around his neck. Colt wedged in between us, and I giggled. "Give me one sec. I'll be right down."

"All right. C'mon, buddy, let's give 'em a few minutes alone."

After their footfalls trailed down the stairs, I checked on Noah, still fast asleep. My heart ached for him and for Ruger, who rose to all fours, circled once, and plopped back down. "Night-night, my loves." On my way out the nursery I flicked off the light.

When I limped down the stairs, Niko had case files spread across the coffee table. I sat on the edge of the sofa and pretended to be surprised by the crime scene photos. The photographs I'd reviewed days ago remained my secret to bear.

Close to his chest, Niko held two case files. "These might not be easy to look at. You sure you're up for this?"

"What are they?"

"Remember when Ben came to the hospital?"

"Yes."

"He brought me copies of the murder books for the last three victims."

I dropped my chin to my chest. "Lisa."

"Yeah. She's one."

"Who's the other two?"

He didn't answer.

"Oh my God. Chance."

"Not exactly. Because his homicide didn't have the same MO, I think we're dealing with two separate killers."

"Okay. So the Dawgs aren't responsible for what happened to me and Noah, then."

"Doubtful."

"Then who?"

"That's the question, isn't it?"

I planted a fist on my hip. "This is ridiculous. Will you show me the files or not?"

"Babe, I—"

"Don't babe me." I held out a flat hand. "The files, please."

With some reluctance he passed me the murder books. When I flipped open the top file I fell back onto the sofa. In the photograph, Niko's hands hovered in front my chest while I stood naked, blood and mud swirling across my skin, my hair matted to the sides of my face, deep, black circles under each eye with an eyebrow flopped over the right, purplish-yellow bruising on my cheek, broken nose, and split lip. Lisa's bloody corpse lay face up at my feet, her left hand cleaved at the wrist.

I couldn't speak. I couldn't move. I couldn't tear my gaze away. The photograph held me hostage, my fingers gripped to the edges, knuckles white from lack of blood flow.

Niko said, "Babe?"

The events of that night rushed back, flooding my mind with the terror of outrunning a serial killer who thirsted for our blood. The room whirled, and I rocked back and forth, my consciousness right back in that darkened marsh. No escape. No way to summon help. Feral animals roaming the woodland and a psychopath lying in wait.

Niko's touch propelled me back to the present. "That night I came face-to-face with a black bear."

He edged onto the coffee table in front of me. "You did?"

"It was my fault, not hers."

"What was your fault?"

Teardrops moistened the photograph. "She was protecting her cubs the way a mother should." I filled him in on the events of that night. "I don't remember anyone taking this picture. I don't even remember you being there."

He filled his hands with mine. "I'm not surprised. You weren't in the best shape when we found you."

"Did I speak?"

Warmly, he smiled. "You asked about Noah. Once I told you he was safe, you stopped fighting. Your only concern was your cub...protecting him the way a mother should."

Against my will, my chin dimpled.

"Maybe it's time you forgave yourself too."

Overwhelmed by emotion, I could only nod.

He slapped his knees and rose, and then offered me his hand. "C'mon, let's catch this bastard once and for all."

With a zing of empowerment, I slapped my hand into his. "No matter what it takes."

Chapter Forty-Three

9:30 p.m.

While Niko showed me the case file of a bloated corpse, he explained, "This is Kathryn Fontaine, the floater we found at McDaniels Marsh a few days before...well, you know." He cleared his throat. "The MO matches the first few homicides, as well as the last. I still think temperature plays a role."

So he wouldn't find out I'd broken into his office, I played stupid. Even if I confessed, I'd put Frankie's job at risk. "You lost me. Are you talking about the women in the woods?"

"No. Sorry." He passed me the crime scene photo from one of the initial murders, a murder he neglected to mention till now. The only reason I'd heard about the crimes was because of WMUR News 9, New Hampshire's local news station, reported on the case. "As you can see, the MO is identical on each victim."

For comparison, he passed me the other photographs. This could be me. Nerves spiraled to a frenzy, but I managed a murder cop's cool, detached front. If I freaked out, my husband would stop sharing. That, I couldn't allow.

"For our purpose, let's concentrate on Amy St. John. Beaten like the others, she was stuffed inside an oil drum, the left-hand severed at the wrist. Actually, the barrel ran ashore. We found her half-sprawled in the sand, half in the drum. Aack."

After finding me in a similar condition, this could not be easy for him, evident by his hangdog expression.

"Originally, the mutt used desolate bogs, marshes, and swamps to dispose of the bodies. If it weren't for survivalists who hiked those out-of-the-way trails, we might never've found them."

"Did he leave the King of Hearts at those crime scenes too?"

"Two were outside my jurisdiction. With Amy St. John, yeah, but I haven't figured out why yet."

I grinned. "I might have a theory about that."

"Care to share?"

"I'm still working it out."

"So, I should continue?"

I gestured for him to go ahead.

He passed me the photographs from the women in the woods. "Here we see the MO has changed, but it still resembles the previous scenes with the King of Hearts and missing hand."

"So he's evolved. He's perfected the art of murder."

"Originally that's what I thought, too. But now, I'm not so sure. Maybe his fantasy was always to entrap women in oil drums, but the weather made it more difficult."

"Perhaps. Or he had a partner, one killed in swamplands, one in the woods. Each with a similar but different fantasy."

"That's always a possibility, but my gut tells me this is the work of one guy. Let's play the game and find out. Victim or killer?"

As much as it pained me, I said, "I'll be the victim, but only because you know the case better."

"You sure? You might find playing killer more empowering."

"I know, but the victims were all female."

"All right, but tell me if this gets too real and we'll stop."

"Deal." I mentally prepared for this deadly sport of ours. "First things first, where am I?" I cringed. "Never mind. I know where I am. Out doing errands."

"Babe, if this is too much—"

"No, no. I'm fine," I lied, as my abduction replayed in my mind. I swiped my bag off the back of my chair and slung it over my shoulder. "I'm alone in the parking lot when you strike." Spinning away from him, I braced myself for the attack.

Within seconds, he slapped a hankie over my nose and mouth. "Chloroform was found in their bloodstream, so first I knock you out."

I slumped into his arms like I did that day at Walmart, and he carried me to the sofa. "Do I bind your wrists?"

Out of the corner of my mouth, I said, "What did the autopsy show?"

"No ligature marks found on the right, but there was bruising. Since he severed the left hand at the wrist, it's difficult to say if he handcuffed them to something in case they came to."

Acting unconscious, my eyes shut tight, I extended my left arm to show him the stitches around my wrist. Normally, I slitted an eye to watch, but I couldn't bear to see the pain on his face when he made the connection.

He pecked my wrist with tiny kisses.

A few minutes passed, so I checked to ensure he was all right. With a slight shake to the head, he inferred erasing the image from his mind, the reality that I'd been restrained by a madman.

"I handcuff you to the armrest in your own backseat. Well, not the Land Rover, but most of the victims had their cars stolen."

"You okay, pup?"

"Yeah. I…ah…it's just that…" He ran a finger under his shirt collar. "I need to keep my eye on you through the rear-view mirror. Hmm…where am I taking you?" He paused to think it through. "Someplace deserted where I can bring my darkest fantasies to life." His face lit up. "I'm taking you home. I must own a few acres if I'm not concerned with neighbors."

"Very good," I whispered.

"Thanks, babe." He patted the top of my hand. "Now be quiet. You're supposed to be unconscious. Wait. Do you mind if we jump to the vics in the forest?"

"Not at all. Why?"

"Because that MO is more convoluted. Besides, I don't think it's the best idea for you to relive the oil drum scenario."

Best idea for me or him? "Your call. You're the killer."

"Great." He rubbed his palms together as though he couldn't wait to play his part. "I've got you at home, where I strip off your clothes." He tore open my blouse and wiggled my legs out of my jeans. My wounds stopped him cold and he brushed his fingertips across my scraped knees, sliced shins, and the blisters on my feet.

"Pup?"

Tears pooled in his eyes. "I'm so sorry I didn't protect you."

I ran my fingers through his close-cropped hair. "Ruger and I aren't the only ones who need to forgive themselves."

While he took a minute to compose himself, he pressed my palm against his cheek. Until this moment, I didn't realize how much my abduction had affected him. Sure, he told me how much he loved me every hour, and he'd pampered me once I left the hospital, but he hid his devastation well. Even after all we'd lived through as a couple, he'd never been this upset. Why hadn't I noticed it before?

"Where were we?" he asked, jarring me from my thoughts.

Rather than respond, I let my gaze run down the front of my nearly nude body.

"Right. Stupid question."

Playing my role of unconscious victim, I fell back into position, my body limp for realism.

"I want you humiliated. That's why I strip you. None of the victims were sexually assaulted, but your nakedness angers me. I strike you over and over. Gaines reported the blows were from a fist. Crime of passion. Meaning, blinding rage fueled my outburst. Once you're beaten bloody, it's time to make you pay." Again, he paused, thinking. "How, in my view, did you cross me?"

As I often did, I helped veer him toward a conclusion. "Maybe it's not me you're mad at."

"Of course. You symbolize someone else in my life. Perhaps an abuser who made me feel lesser of a man. Excellent theory, babe."

This was why the game worked. By discussing possible scenarios while acting out the night of the homicide, it helped Niko conclude how, and often why, the killer created his unique *modus operandi*.

Again, Niko slid his arms under me, carrying me around the living room to illustrate the killer driving to the darkened forest. No one drove those snowmobile trails after dusk. Hence, why it made the ideal spot to dump a corpse. With no witnesses for miles, the killer had more than enough time to create macabre crime scenes.

With a bent arm, Niko pinned me against the wall. "I had this place picked out in advance. In fact, I visited several times to prepare. Afterward, I returned to relive the kill. Here's where it gets tricky, though." He readjusted his grip on me, placing one hand around my neck with the pressure of a young boy holding his first butterfly. "If you're standing, I could easily hammer in the spike. But the victims were suspended off the ground." He released me. "Hang on."

As he examined the crime scene photos with a magnifying glass, I remained flattened against the wall. "Does this look like the edge of an object to you?" He showed me two angles imprinted in the snow. "I remember them from the scene, but I didn't make the connection then."

"Connection to what?"

An evil little glimmer shone in his eyes. "He stood her on a milk crate, nailed her chest to the tree, and then took it away."

"Excellent. Let's do it."

Niko hammered the imaginary spike through my chest. "Now the antlers. Wait. How did I carry a grown woman, supplies, and a rack of antlers this far into the woods?" He smirked a Cheshire cat's grin. "Via skimobile. There's tracks all over the area. No way would the police be able to match a single tread to my sled." He pretended to lug over the antlers. He wedged the rack open and set them over my torso. Releasing an animalistic cry, he shoved the fake animal skull until the points punctured my skin."

I tittered. "Shh…you'll wake the baby."

"Oh, right. Sorry. Got carried away there for a minute. I'm about done anyway. Close your eyes."

And so I did.

"One final touch. I stick the King of Hearts on the end of one point, then escape into the darkness." Arms opened in wide shrug, he fell back into his Lay-Z-Boy. "I don't get it. Why the antlers?"

I slipped my arms into the sleeves of my blouse and held it

closed. "Want my two-cents?"

"Please."

"Rather than concentrating on the MO—we could analyze the psychological ramifications forever—we first need to figure out how he chose his victims. I know you don't want to hear this, but I think I'm the key."

"How so?"

I sat across from him, and Colt dove on the sofa behind me. "When Lisa first heard my name, she asked if I was 'the author'."

"Yeah, so, maybe she reads your books."

"Even you've gotta admit, I'm not exactly a household name."

"Yet."

"Aww, pup, you've always been my loudest cheerleader." I hopped in his lap and kissed his lips. "Lisa knew instantly, though. No hesitation at all."

"Okay." His palm caressed my bare legs. "And that means…?"

"What are the chances of an author and one of her fans being trapped by the same serial killer?"

In a flash, his back straightened. "Million to one."

"Exactly." I moved to the sofa and flung my arm around Colt, whose gaze shifted between the two of us.

Leaning forward, Niko steepled his hands. "Where could the killer run into a group of your fans?" The color drained from his face. "The book signing."

With an intentional flutter of the eyelids, I confirmed. "At the Minot-Sleeper Library."

"But Frankie ran John Dunn's name. It's an alias."

I limped to the Chromebook and punched in "Minot-Sleeper Library book events." When the website filled the screen, I blinked. Blinked again. "You'll never believe which book their bi-monthly book club is reading?"

"*Scarred?*"

"Yup. No wonder the signing was such a huge success."

"When do they meet next?"

I swallowed hard. "Tomorrow night."

Chapter Forty-Four

March 30, 2008, 12:01 a.m.

For hours Frankie waited in the car with Ozzy, and his BO splintered her skull. Waving away the stench, she said, "There's this new thing called the shower. Ever hear of it?"

To smell his own breath, he blew into a cupped hand. "I wash. You caught me on a bad day, is all."

"Phew." She rubbed her nose. "I'll say. Lucky me."

"I can go and you can handle these dudes by yourself. No skin off my back."

He probably had a hairy back, too. Her stomach flipped and flopped. "Don't be so sensitive. I'm just sayin'. You might get lucky more if you used soap once in a while. A little deodorant couldn't hurt, either."

Blood flushed into his face and neck. "Bitch, you're crossing so many damn lines right now."

Her hand slid to the weapon on her hip. "I know you didn't just call me a bitch. You do realize I can throw your ass in jail, right?"

"Once a cop, always a cop."

She turned the key to lower her window. "Dammit. Where are these assholes?"

From the shadows that edged the parking lot a dark figure emerged, with the same black bandana with white skull tied around his face. Behind him, another guy stepped into focus. He wore a do-rag like the guy who leveled the shotgun at her head.

Backhanding Ozzy in the arm, she then pointed out her side window. "That's them. Let's go." When she yanked the door handle, Ozzy stopped her.

"Not yet. Let's make sure there's only two." He reached into his ankle holster and withdrew a Glock 27.

Frankie jabbed her chin at the gun. "That legal?"

"You really wanna know?"

"No. Lie to me. I love that shit." She flashed her palm. "Actually, don't tell me. I'd rather not know."

The two men crept around the edge of the storage units, then veered down the row where Chance kept his stash of ketamine. Without waiting for the okay, Frankie killed the dome light so it wouldn't turn on when she opened her door.

Leaning through the driver's side, she urged, "You comin' or what?"

With a hand on the top window frame Ozzy hoisted his massive body out of the Mercedes. Frankie skulked to the first row of units and pressed her back against the metal wall, her hands wrapped around her service weapon, trigger finger along the gun's slide.

Glimpsing a sneak peek at the empty aisle of storage containers, she jabbed her head, signaling for Ozzy to move with her to the next row. Ozzy stayed on her heels as she darted from one row of units to the next, stopping at each one to ensure the gangbangers didn't notice till it was too late to react.

The prying of a crowbar alerted her to their location. Not that she had much doubt about why they were here. Poor bastards didn't know she'd found the container and took control of its contents, logging each piece of evidence to use against them at their upcoming murder trial.

At the end of the aisle, she and Ozzy flattened against the end unit. She leaned aside, hushed, "On three," and then fell back into position and counted off the seconds with her fingers. She mouthed, "One…two…three."

She rotated around the corner of the unit, arms triangled in front of her, left hand supporting her right. "Sheriff's Department. Don't move or I'll blow your frickin' head off."

The clang of the crowbar against cement echoed in the silence. The dude in the do-rag reached for the gun in his waistband and

Ozzy fired a warning shot that skimmed his ear.

"Muthafucka gonna die now." The gangbanger raised his pistol to chest level, his hand cocked to one side like a gangsta.

Again, Ozzy fired. This time, the bullet struck the dude dead-center in the forehead and he slumped to the ground.

How the hell could she explain this to Niko?

His partner raised his hands in surrender. "Don't shoot."

"Grab some metal, tough guy." Meaning, for him to place his opened hands on the storage unit. Ozzy pinned his wrists while Frankie patted down each leg. "Anything gonna stick me?" she asked before reaching into the pockets of his jeans, pulled halfway down his ass.

"Only if you want it to, chica."

With the butt of her gun she biffed him upside the head. "I'd rather die a slow, painful death. I *am not* your chica, pal. The name's Deputy Campanelli and you're under arrest for first-degree murder, conspiracy, kidnapping, torture, and any other charges I can think of on the way to the station." She leaned in so close, her nose almost touched the bandana. "That doctor you gunned down in cold blood was my fiancé, you prick." She spit on the toe of his stark-white Michael Jordan high-tops. "You make me sick."

While she lowered one of his wrists to slap on the handcuffs, Ozzy nudged the dirt-bag's fallen brother with his boot. "Uh, Frankie?"

She brought down his left hand to meet his right. "Little busy here, Oz. What it is?"

"He's dead."

As soon as the words left Ozzy's lips the gangbanger whirled around, sucker-punched Frankie in the face. Dazed, she stumbled backward, hands cupped over her nose, blood leaking through her fingers. His Michael Jordan's squealed across the thin layer of snow as he raced toward a thicket of trees.

Frankie took aim. "Stop!"

The final gunshot rang her eardrums.

Chapter Forty-Five

6:35 a.m.

The morning sunlight cascaded through the picture-glass window above the bed, warming my face in its soft, golden mist. When I swung my feet to the floor an awe-inspiring view awaited me. Deep lavender bands stretched across a navy-blue horizon, magenta hues beneath its muted edge, with a copper sun that ignited the pinnacle of Cardigan Mountain, melting away the blackness of night.

No doubt about it, Alexandria was a majestic place. Which made the murder spree all the more menacing. A sadistic killer stalked our country streets. He hid in the shadows. Watching. Waiting. Planning. Without more information, we had no way to ID him.

Jarred by the empty bed, I called for Colt, and he shot up the stairs. Exhaling a deep breath, my heartbeat slowed to a *pitter-patter, pitter-patter.* "Where is everyone?" I mussed his furry head. "Honey, is that bacon in your jowelies?"

A sloppy smile spread across his face.

"Daddy made breakfast, I take it?"

His rear end wiggled almost as fast as his stubby tail, and I giggled. "Adorable. Go on. I'm right behind you."

No one had to tell him twice. In a flash, he was gone, his nails clicking across the hardwood as he rounded the bottom of the stairs, hightailing it back to the kitchen before Dad stopped offering to share his meal.

I ambled into the kitchen and twisted off the Rimadyl cap. Ruger lumbered over and opened his mouth. Our usual morning routine, I set a pain cookie on his tongue, and he chomped it into bits, his jowls sagging and spitty. "How are you feeling today, puppy love? Get any sleep last night, or were you too busy guarding your baby brother?"

From the table Niko said, "Actually, he was asleep when I went in to get Noah."

"You were?" My pitch rose with joy, my palms cradling his blocky head. "What a good boy." With my newly-reset nose, I gave him Eskimo kisses. "You've got bacon breath, too. Lemme guess. Daddy dropped pieces on the floor by accident."

"That's our story, and we're stickin' to it." Niko lowered the morning newspaper. "Aren't we, boys?"

Noah tittered. Colt and Ruger couldn't hide their guilty faces to save their lives.

"A little bacon once in a while is good for the soul." I broke a piece in half and held out my hands. Colt nearly gobbled down my fingers, but Rugey gummed the savory treat from my grasp.

I kissed Noah on the crown of his perfect head. "How's my big boy today?"

Niko washed our son's fingers and face with a wet nap, and then slid the highchair tray away. When he got up to clear the dishes, I stole his seat so I could gaze at my sweet boy. "You seem better today, too."

His arms reached for me. I unbuckled the safety belt and lifted him from the highchair. Squeezing him close to my heart, I rocked from side to side. "Thank you, sweetheart. You give the best huggies."

Now Ruger's change in demeanor made sense. As Noah healed, so did he. They had such a special connection. Shame it took a tragedy for me to recognize it.

Niko set a plate down in front of me, loaded with scrambled eggs, home fries, bacon, and wheat toast. "Childs is coming over to babysit."

Over my shoulder a tiny voice said, "Yay!"

With my palm I rubbed Noah's back. "Do you really think that's a good idea?"

"I need you today, babe. Judy always glares at me like she wants to rip my throat out. Besides, you know more about what we're looking for than I do." He tapped the face of his watch. "Childs will be here within the hour, so you might want to eat and get dressed."

A sudden blast of cold struck my core. "You know that picture of me in the case file?"

"Yeah. What about it?"

"Did your whole team see it?"

"Just me and Frankie." He raised his favorite mug—emblazoned with #1 Dad on a gold shield; I had it redone when Noah was born—to his lips and sipped his caramel-apple coffee. "Do you really think I'd allow that?"

"Well, by your own admission, Ben delivered the case file, so how can you be so sure he didn't flip through the crime scene photos?"

"Oh, yea of little faith." Setting the mug on the table, he added, "I know he didn't because Frankie sealed the picture inside a manila envelope. Before our game, I broke the seal myself."

Staring at my plate, I forked the scrambled eggs. "You're not just sayin' that to make me feel better, are you?"

"Of course not." Gesturing to eat like his Italian mother used to do—God rest her soul—he rose from the table. "*Mungia, mungia*. I've got dishes to wash."

* * *

9:00 a.m.

I delayed as long as I could, but I needed to make sure Noah felt comfortable with us leaving. As much as I hated to go, my only saving grace was that Childs carried a firearm. They adored each other, too, because Childs was not opposed to clowning around to make him laugh. But did he have the skills to protect our child?

The familiarity of Noah's giggle filled me with warmth as I closed and locked the door behind us. Niko weaved his fingers with mine and led me up the walkway. "Don't worry," he said. "Childs might goof around, but he's a fine deputy. His father was a cop. His grandfather was a cop. Both his brothers are cops. In an emergency, his training will instinctively take over."

"Colt and Ruger seem to love him too. That alone says a lot about the type of man he is."

"Exactly. If he was at all off in some way, they'd pick up on it."

With my free hand, I patted his arm. "You're right. I'm being silly. Of course I trust him." We crested the top of the walkway and Niko opened my door. As I swung my legs into the passenger seat, I asked, "Do you think the day will come when we don't obsess over every little thing?"

"I dunno." With the back of his hand, he caressed my cheek. "We waited a lifetime for him."

Milk seeped through the pads in my bra. "Dammit." I checked to make sure I didn't have wet spots on the front of my blouse. "I haven't been able to nurse him since the hospital."

"Is that a bad thing? I mean, he eats solid food now. Maybe it's time to stop." Before I had a chance to respond, he closed my door and jogged around the front bumper to the driver's side.

When he slipped behind the wheel, I explained, "Before that awful night, he was starting to lose interest in nursing, but after I rescued him, I think the closeness soothed him. So, I planned to let him decide, which is what my doctor recommended, but with all the meds they pumped into me at the hospital, I didn't dare nurse."

"It's not like we have a shortage of milk. 'The girls' stocked the fridge." His gaze lowered to my breasts. Ever since the baby came they were off-limits, and he never ignored an opportunity to show me how much he missed "the girls".

With two fingers under his chin, I raised his face. "Did you show Childs the proper way to heat a bottle?"

"Will you relax? Everything's under control."

"You're right." I fastened my seatbelt. "Of course you're right."

At the end of Cass Mill Road Niko hung a left onto Rte. 104. "Last night you said you had a theory about the case. Wanna run it by me now?"

"Okay." Unbuckling the restraint—never wore seatbelts, anyway, except on the highway—I twisted to face him, my foot tucked under one leg. "While you were reading to Noah, I dug deeper into why the killer could relate to the Suicide King." I told him the story of Charles VII and his family roots. "Most serial killers are bed-wetters well past the normal age due to messed up childhoods."

"Agreed."

"So what if he used Charles VII as a way to show the police how he suffered at the hands of a cruel mother?"

"Go on."

"If I were to guess, I'd say she was a prostitute. At the very least, she was promiscuous, similar to Charles VII's mother. She could've sexually abused him, too, which is often the case with serial killers."

"Okay," he said, unconvinced.

"Hear me out. Early sexual abuse can lead to recurrent masturbation on the child's part, regardless of age or sex. During my research, I've read cases where three-year-olds couldn't stop masturbating in an attempt to control their environment, the poor kids."

"You're right. It happens, unfortunately."

"Okay, so, what if he was born a lefty and his mother punished him by tying it behind his back? Or she caught him masturbating and burned his hand on the stove. Which might explain why the clown wears gloves."

Niko pulled his gaze off the road to look at me. "So he's reenacting the abuse he suffered?"

"Exactly."

"Interesting theory. That might explain why he takes the hands with him, too. But what's he doin' with 'em?"

I faced front. "The only way to answer that question is to find him." The notion of coming face-to-face with my attacker twisted my stomach into knots. Sadly, that's exactly what we needed to do.

As the world sailed by my window, I summoned the courage to help my husband stop a madman who seemed hell-bent on making me suffer. Why, though? What did I do to illicit this much hatred in another human being?

Chapter Forty-Six

9:20 a.m.

At the Minot-Sleeper Library, Niko held open the glass door as his wife strolled through the entrance. Shoulders squared with her hips, she held her head higher than she had in days. Perfect posture, a warm smile plastered on her lips. Sage didn't normally wear a lot of makeup, but she insisted on covering the bruises. Niko rather enjoyed her maroon lipstick, the way it accented her gorgeous pearl-white teeth, but he kept that to himself.

At the front desk, Sage caught him staring, and winked. Even after all these years, she had the ability to send tingles to all the right spots.

Judy Cohen—head librarian and founder of Passive Aggressive Queens—set the book she was reading on the desk and bustled to the counter. "My, my. If it isn't Sage Quintano, blessing our quaint little library so soon after the book signing."

"Hello, Judy. Nice to see you."

When Judy turned her head toward Niko, his face snapped toward Sage. Better to stay mute and let his wife handle her. Safer that way.

Marble-like navy eyes peered over half-moon reading glasses—her way of rattling the person who dared to interrupt her reading time. "What can I do for you?"

"I noticed on your website that your bi-monthly book club is reading *Scarred*."

"Yes, that's correct. The director of the library, Patti Warbeck, suggested it. From what I've heard they all love the book, if that's what you're asking."

Through the makeup Sage's cheeks blushed rose. No matter how many fans complimented her work, she remained as humble as the day she scored her first publishing deal. "That's so nice of you to say. Thank you." As if conjuring the courage to ask about the man wreaking havoc in their lives, her shoulders pulled back, her chin high and proud. "Do you have a list of book club members, by any chance?"

"Patti probably does. It's a closed group, so members need to be approved before joining. However, it's against library policy to give authors that information. If members want to sign up for your newsletter, we'll provide them with your website."

"That's not why I'm asking. We need to...what I mean is... we're looking for..." Sage fumbled to find the right words.

Niko chimed in. "Where can we find Patti?"

"Last I saw, she was in the mystery/crime section."

"Thank you for your time." By the arm, he gently pulled Sage away from the counter. As they strode toward the stacks, he hushed, "You okay? You seem a little flustered."

Head down, Sage stared at the floor. "This is much harder than I thought. What if he's in the library?"

Safeguarding his wife, Niko rested his arm around her shoulders. "I'll kill anyone who dares to mess with you." He meant it too. Already he'd failed her far too many times. No way would he allow it to happen again. "Do you know who Patti is?"

"Yes. She's very pleasant."

"Great. I was wondering why you didn't ask for a description. Shoulda known better."

They rounded the corner into the mystery/crime section. A sharp-dressing woman in her mid-thirties, clad in a pinstriped pantsuit, returned books to their proper shelves.

The moment Sage recognized her, she sped up the pace. "Patti, hi."

"Oh, hey." She dumped a pile of novels on the cart in order to shake hands. "You must have ESP. We were just talking about you at our last book club meeting."

"That's why we're here, actually." Her voice was as somber as a funeral director. "Judy said all members need to be approved by you in order to join the group. Is that correct?"

"Regular members, yes. But if you'd like to join us, just swing by. The group will get a kick out of it."

"That's so sweet of you. Thank you." Her cheeks pinked even more. "Where are my manners? This is my husband, Niko."

Patti shook his hand. "I feel like I already know you. I'm a huge fan of your wife's work."

"That makes two of us."

Focused on the task at hand, Sage continued as if she hadn't heard their exchange. "The reason I'm asking is because…uh…is there any way we could take a peek at the list of members?"

"Absolutely. May I ask why?"

"Actually, it's for a new book I'm writing, where a serial killer—"

Gasping, Patti covered her ears. "No spoilers please. I'll get you that list." She dashed to the end of the stack, stopped, and turned back. "Will you be here? Or should I meet you out front?"

Sage looked to Niko for the answer. He said, "To keep it on the DL and not reveal any spoilers, it's probably best if we stay here. Don't you think, babe?"

"Absolutely."

"How exciting." Hands clasped together, Patti bounced on her toes. "Back in a jiffy, then."

Once they were alone, Niko said, "You know you've gotta write that book now, or she's gonna be so disappointed."

"All I have to do is include one scene with a book club, and she'll never know the difference." Again she winked.

Patti's business heels tapped across the natural wood floors, alerting them to her return.

"That was fast," he whispered to Sage. "What'd she do, run?"

She shushed him.

Arm extended, a manila file folder in her hand, Patti hurried toward Sage. "Here you go. I'll get out of your hair so you can concentrate. That's a copy, so I don't need it back." She disappeared as fast as she arrived.

"Let's hope we're right." Lowering her gaze, Sage flipped open the cover.

Niko hovered over her shoulder to scan the list of names. "All fifteen are women. So much for that idea."

Sage dragged her finger down the list, stopping at the tenth name. "Correction. Fourteen women and one man."

Squinting at the name, he said, "Dimitris Kokkinos. Can't be many with that name in the area. I'll have Frankie run it. You up for a ride? Or do you want me to drop you at home?"

As if her bones had turned to granite, her whole body stiffened. "You mean, confront him face-to-face?"

"You're right." He tucked her into his chest. How could he be so stupid? "After what you've been through, you shouldn't be anywhere near him. I shouldn't've asked." With his wife still wrapped in his arms, he dug in his pants pocket for his phone and dialed Frankie's cell number.

It rang and rang before a recording announced, "Mailbox is full."

"That's odd."

Sage broke their embrace. "What?"

"No answer."

"This area's loaded with dead zones, you know that."

Eyebrows furrowed, he stared at his phone. "Yeah, but her mailbox is full. Frankie always checks her messages." He shouldn't worry Sage. What if it was all very innocent? Her battery could be dead. The charger could be on the fritz. Or even, she lost her cell. "Ah, no matter. When we get to the truck I'll run the name myself. C'mon, let's get you home."

What he didn't mention was the way acids corroded his gut. Between Chance's murder and the stress of running the department in his absence, he'd seen cops eat their gun for less. Actually, he hadn't heard from Frankie in over twenty-four hours. That wasn't like her, either.

A cold shudder ran through him. Did she go after the Dawgs on her own?

Chapter Forty-Seven

10:00 a.m.

My husband didn't possess the skills to hide his feelings. Concern for Frankie etched his entire face, deep lines around the eyes and across the forehead, a grave expression. Did he worry that Frankie ran into the killer?

While Niko ran Kokkinos name I fiddled with my half-bitten fingernails.

He tilted the computer screen toward me. "Is this John Dunn from the signing?

"I can't tell. Maybe I should take the ride with you." Even though facing the killer clown would be brutally difficult, I prayed this meeting would help me regain some semblance of normalcy.

Shaking his head non-stop, I could tell he wasn't thrilled with the idea. "No way. I don't want you anywhere near this guy."

"You've got no choice. I'm the only one who can ID him."

Did I make the right decision? What if he killed us both? Who'd care for Noah and the kids?

"Besides, I need to do this for me."

"I don't like this, Sage. This guy almost killed you." Niko drove out the parking lot exit and hung a left onto Pleasant Street. At the lights, he took a left onto Rte.104 and followed it to Bog Road, where he banged a right. The cracked asphalt caused us to jounce in our seats. Halfway down the road, the plowed pavement turned into a dirt/snow mix.

"I said, I'm going with you. Why are you taking me home?"

"I'm not. According to DMV, his last known address is up ahead on the right."

"You've gotta be kidding me. Our house is two minutes from here."

A half-mile down the road Niko pulled curbside in front of an old farmhouse, the chipped white clapboard aged gray. Killing the engine, he twisted to face me. "Please stay in the car. You can ID him from here."

"Fine, but at least let me roll down the window."

He turned the key in the ignition, and I zipped my window open.

"When he comes to the door, I'll step aside. Gimme a nod if it's him."

"Okay."

As Niko strode around the front bumper I turned my gaze to the house. Snow melted off the shingled roof. *Ting, ting, ting.* The water striking a rusted antique milk can shot chills up the back of my neck. When Niko set his foot on the porch stair, the old wood cracked. Even from ten feet away the sound echoed in the silence. He swung open the screen door, glanced down, then over his shoulder at me—a harrowed stare I didn't understand.

I could not sit still another second. Something was wrong.

Niko whirled around. "Get back in the truck."

Ignoring him, I soldiered closer. "What's wrong?" My gaze lowered to the storm door. Specifically, to the dried blood on the doorknob. Now his reaction made sense. "Exigent circumstances, right?"

A hint of a frown tugged on his lips. "Sometimes I wish you weren't a crime writer. You shouldn't know these things." With a tap of his boot the door creaked open. "Sheriff's Department." Gun drawn, he tucked me behind him as we entered the home. "Mr. Kokkinos?"

A mouse scurried across the dingy hallway, and nearly stopped my heart. We edged into the living room. Stacks of old newspapers stood waist-high. I kicked an empty whiskey bottle, and it rolled into the leg of an ancient wooden table, butted against the window with soiled sheer curtains like one might expect to find in a Count Dracula film. The place reeked of rotten food, stale booze, and an indescribable odor that made my stomach wrench in protest.

We stalked through the maze of junk and emerged at a closed dark-stained door that required a skeleton key. Niko glanced back at me, and I jabbed my chin to signal I could continue, even though no part of this journey sat well with me.

When he twisted open the doorknob, my lungs depleted of air like they did inside the oil drum. Photographs papered one wall from the unfinished hardwood floor to the stained plaster ceiling. Pictures of Niko, Frankie, Lisa, Patti, Judy, Mary Anne Goodman, and several other women who looked familiar, but from where? In the center hung a photo of me and Noah at the Minot-Sleeper Library on the day of my book signing, symbolizing the heart of his obsession. Under our picture, the word "Mommy" written in blood with a finger swipe.

"Oh my God, Niko. These women were all at my table. I spoke to them when I autographed their paperbacks of *Scarred*. He's killing my fans."

Snapping photos with his cell phone, Niko surveyed the room, and I followed with my gaze. Against the back wall, a metal shelving unit held glass jars filled with formaldehyde. Inside each one, a human hand floated in the liquid. Pink, mauve, red, and wine-colored fingernails. Eight in total. A separate jar sat on an antique pedestal table by the twin bed. The hand had thin, bony fingers like one might see on an elderly woman. Could this be his mother's hand?

Niko said, "We need to go. Now."

My feet rooted to the floor, my body frozen in place.

"C'mon. We need to get outta here."

Fear strangled my words as though the creepy clown had his white gloves around my throat. Niko weaved his fingers with mine and dragged me out of the room of lunacy, through the maze of madness, out the front door, and down the porch stairs, and he didn't stop till we hit the SUV. When he whipped open the passenger door to hurry me inside, I steadied my gate by leaning against the front quarter panel.

Speechless, I gulped the fresh piney air. Sedated by the evil acts of a solitary man, all emotion gutted from my chest. Dead inside. My soul cleaved...like the embodied hands.

By the upper arms Niko shook me to jar me from my trance-like state. "Are you okay?"

"I...I..."

"Talk to me, babe. You're scarin' me."

My mouth worked, but my voice couldn't escape. When the clown kidnapped our son, did he trap him inside this house of horror?

With both hands, Niko tapped my cheeks the way you might prevent someone from slipping into coma. "Say something, anything. Tell me how stupid it was to bring you here."

I couldn't respond. The serial killer's lair held me hostage, an invisible rope tightening around my larynx. Unable to move, I was in his thrall.

Chapter Forty-Eight

10:00 a.m.

On the drive to the station, Frankie replayed the events of the early morning hours. Niko could never discover what went down. Ever.

Two dead gangbangers lay within twenty feet of each other, blood seeping out the bullet holes. If Frankie called it in, the crime scene might look like she'd taken revenge against the men who murdered Chance. At the very least, she could kiss her badge goodbye. Not to mention she'd let Niko down. He'd depended on her to run things by-the-book while he dealt with his traumatized family. Last night was anything but, especially what occurred after she confronted the suspects.

Whatever possessed her to bring a biker on a stakeout? If Ozzy hadn't shot the first suspect, she might have an easier time explaining how she killed the gang member who fled. Granted, the sucking wounds looked equally unlawful because the hollow-point bullet traveled through his back and out his chest. But after what he did to Chance, she couldn't let him escape. With no prints and no ID, if he fled back to Boston, he was in the clear. No way could she live with that.

Ozzy had said, "What do we do now, foxy lady?"

"Shut the fuck up and let me think." The musical trill of her cell phone coiled through the darkness.

"That your boss again?"

She checked the caller ID. "Yeah. Something must be wrong for him to call this many times."

"Then answer."

"What are you, my shrink? Listen pal, you're the reason we're in this mess." With both hands, she shoved him a good two feet. "Why'd you have to shoot?"

"Hey, the dude had a gun. I ain't gettin' killed 'cause you don't wanna color outside the lines."

"Whatever. It's too late now."

Head volleying between the two corpses, only one option sprang to mind. She passed Ozzy a pair of black-latex gloves. "Make yourself useful and grab this scumbag's legs."

"And take him where, exactly?"

"I don't frickin' know, but we can't leave 'em here. For now, we'll stuff them inside the storage unit. Make it look like a drug deal gone bad."

"Are the drugs still in there?"

Her upper lip twitched. "Shit."

"I'll tell ya what. I know a guy who can deal with this. Want me to make a call?"

"How much?"

"Eh. Couple a get outta jail free cards oughta do it."

Not one bone in her body thought this was a good idea, but she didn't have much choice. "Fine, but under one condition. The free pass is only for minor shit. Your boy commits murder, rape, torture, assault and battery, or any other violent crime and he's on his own."

"Deal."

"Damn you, Chance," she grumbled as she sealed the pact with a handshake. "This better not come back to bite me. I mean it. One whiff that I've been screwed and I'll come after you, my friend. Count on it."

"It's all good, foxy lady. Now get outta here and lemme do my thing."

Before she left the storage facility, she'd collected her brass and unhooked the handcuff from the wrist of the gangbanger she shot in the back.

Breaking the law went against everything she believed in. Sure, she'd bent it a few times, but never disregarded it to this extent. Even when Niko accused Chance of multiple homicides she didn't dare cross the thin blue line. Maybe a little, but nothing that would keep her up nights. Having some cleaner dude cover-up a sting gone bad would stay with her for years to come. No doubt about it.

In front of the Grafton County Sheriff's Department, she slammed the car door, and then jogged into the building. No sooner did she step off the elevator and her cell phone rang again. "Campanelli."

"Where are you?" asked Niko. "I've been calling you all night."

"Yeah. Sorry 'bout that. I didn't realize I had the ringer off."

"Did you decide to take some down time? It's fine. I just wanted to make sure you were okay."

Phone still pressed to her ear, she strolled into the bullpen. Niko had everyone around the whiteboard. When he saw her, he clicked off his cell. "I take it that's a no?"

"I'm fine. Whadda we got?"

"We've ID'd our guy as Dimitris Kokkinos. Remember when I asked you guys to dig through the victims' backgrounds? Not one of you found the link to a book club at the Minot-Sleeper Library."

Ben spoke up first. "That's my fault, boss. Frankie told me to check their calendars and I forgot."

Huh. The kid was covering for her. Someone get that guy a brownie point. "How'd you find the connection?"

"I didn't. Sage did."

"How is she?"

"Not great. She's in my office."

"She is?" Frankie scuttled into Niko's office. Reclined, Sage hugged a toss pillow, her ankles crossed on the sofa arm. She wiggled her butt on to the sofa, and Sage sat upright. "What happened?"

Lines of tears ran her mascara, but she didn't speak.

"Sage?"

"We went to his house." Her lips quivered. "It was awful. All those hands."

"Aw, shit. The sick bastard had them on display?"

Her gaze fell to the floor.

"I take it Kokkinos wasn't there."

Sage wagged her head in a drawn-out no.

"Do you need anything? I'm gonna have Niko debrief me." When she rose, Sage latched onto her arm. "What it is? What can I do?"

"We know where he's gonna be tonight. Don't let Niko make me stay home. I need to see that monster caught."

Deep and long, she sighed. "I can't make that promise, but I'll do my best."

"I'm so sorry about Chance."

"Thanks, but what happened is on him. It had nothing to do with the murders."

"You sure? Maybe the Dawgs came to the area because of my book, and that's how he met them."

"No. They didn't. They came for drugs, drugs Chance was all too happy to provide. It had nothing at all to do with you." She tried to lighten the mood with, "Your makeup looks like shit, you know that, right?"

Sage let loose a giggle.

"I'll be back in a few. In the meantime, pull yourself together, woman. We've got a killer to catch." She winked.

"Thanks, Frank."

"Yeah, yeah. Don't go all mushy on me." As she closed the door behind her, Niko turned and stared as if tearing through her false bravado. If he uncovered what she did, she could never face him again.

Chapter Forty-Nine

7:45 p.m.

After my family ate supper and Niko washed the dishes, Childs stayed with Noah and the kids to guard the house in case Kokkinos changed plans. As much as I yearned to protect my child, I needed to see this through. I couldn't remain a victim. How could I teach my son to stand on his own if I wasn't willing to do the same?

At 7:45 p.m., Niko and I pulled into the library parking lot. His plan was to catch Kokkinos on his way into the building. Ben and Frankie got caught at the red light. Because this was an ambush of sorts, Niko insisted they didn't use the lights or siren.

Within two minutes, Frankie pulled into the lot and parked alongside us, with Ben in the passenger seat. Per Niko's orders, she killed the headlights and remained in the vehicle.

Niko kissed the palm of my hand. "You sure you're up for this?"

"As long as you get him before he enters the building."

"Absolutely. Frankie has the copy of the DMV printout, too, so as soon as we spot him, we'll take him into custody."

"Wish me luck." In case things didn't go as planned, I kissed him goodbye. "Love you to the moon, 'round the world and back again."

He offered me a halfhearted smile. "You're not gettin' rid of me that easily." He squeezed me in his arms. "Love you more."

I strode into the library, where Patti was waiting for me.

"I can't tell you how thrilled I was to get your call," she said. "The group will be so excited to see you."

"Remember, I want to surprise them, so why don't you go ahead, and I'll meet you in the function room once everyone arrives."

Bouncing on her toes, she clapped her hands. "You're so fun! I can't wait to see the look on their faces." She waved over her head as she shuffled into the room.

I sat at the front table by the window with *Scarred* propped up in front of me, but low enough to not ruin my view. The plan was for Kokkinos to focus on me so he didn't notice the two Sheriff Department vehicles at the back of the lot.

Problem was, from this angle I couldn't tell who entered the building until they were inside the library. The glass door swung open, and my heart dropped to my feet. Two middle-aged women hugged my latest novel while they chatted among themselves—on their way into the function room, their stride in perfect unison.

I took a deep breath in and slowly released it.

The door swung open a second time. This time, three women strode straight for the book club meeting, never glancing in my direction.

One by one the remaining few women trickled in. The only member unaccounted for should be Kokkinos, but I had no way to know for sure. Patti could have approved new applicants. When we spoke earlier, I didn't think to ask about pending memberships.

A commotion outside the library drew my attention, and I hurried to the entrance. Spread-eagle on the snow, Frankie straddled a man, his arms wrenched behind his back. Hollering something intelligible, Niko bolted toward her.

Without thinking, I burst out the door. "Is it over?"

Niko flashed a flat hand. "Stay inside. You don't need to see this scumbag again."

Frankie hooked his cuffed arms and raised him to his feet, and I screamed, "That's not him! You've got the wrong guy!"

Deep lines creased Niko's forehead as he raised the suspect's chin to get a better look at him. "Why were you peeking through the window at my wife?"

Peeking through the window? He was watching me?

"She's my favorite author," he explained. "I was just trying to get her attention. I'd never do anything to harm her."

"Un-cuff him." My husband approached me on the stairs. "I'm sorry, babe. Kokkinos is a no-show. He must've figured out we were on to him."

"What do we do now? I've got a room full of readers who'll expect me to say a few words." Flames shot up my chest. "Honestly, Niko. How could you let her arrest the wrong guy?" Without waiting for a reply, I stormed back into the library.

He chased after me, hooked my arm, and spun me around. "Where're you goin'?"

I yanked my arm away. "To the ladies room."

"Oh. Sorry. Do you want me to tell Patti something came up?"

"No. I can't do that to her. Wait for me in the car. I'll be out in five minutes."

With both hands, I shoved open the ladies room door, heat assaulting every fiber of my being. Staring in the mirror, the deep bruising under my eyes seeped through the makeup. As much as I hated to admit, I wasn't angry with Niko. In the dark anyone could have mistaken that man for Dimitris Kokkinos. Same build. Same Greek complexion. Same knit hat like he wore to the book signing.

Once I got outside, I owed Frankie and Niko an apology.

When I zipped my jeans, someone knocked at the door, and I hollered, "Be right out."

After I washed my hands, I ran them under the air dryer. With a paper towel I twisted the doorknob. As if in slow motion I inhaled to scream, but before my voice released my terror, a white-cotton glove covered my mouth. The killer clown forced me back inside the bathroom.

Pinning me to the wall, he tilted his head to the left, then to the right—the same mask that haunted my nightmares, and probably Noah's too. The clown's mouth was splayed open, with razor-sharp teeth, blood dripping off the canines. Hunter-green diamonds outlined piercing-gold eyes, glowing under the florescent lights. The faux skin a grayish-white, the blood-red nose matched the lips, arched in a snarling grin.

"Hello, Mommy."

Stunned silent, time stopped.

"You've been inside my home."

Trying to break free, I thrashed from side to side.

"Why couldn't you just cooperate, Mommy? You're always meddling in my business."

This guy was clearly insane. With all my might, I chomped down on his fingers. He yelped and let go.

"You bitch." His tone dripped with hatred.

Both hands around my throat, he squeezed my airway, my body weakening under his power. I clawed at the mask, but he bobbed his head out of the way. Arms flailing, I had about a minute before I passed out. I could not let him win, so I closed my fist and backhanded the mirror. Glass shattered everywhere.

So many things coursed through my mind in a span of a few seconds. Memories flooded my brain like flipping through the *Book of Life*. The first day I met Niko, our courtship, how my heart skipped when he leaned in for that first kiss. The day I married my best friend; the attack in Boston when a serial killer cornered me in our living room; Colt and Ruger as puppies; Noah's birth; and the traumatic experience of losing him.

Adrenaline surged through my system as though angels were giving me one last chance for survival. Dizzy, oxygen-deprived, I felt around the sink. My fingers curled around a slice of broken mirror and I raised my fist above his head. Drove the makeshift blade into the side of his neck, and yanked it free so as not to form a plug.

Releasing me, his white gloves flew to the open gash, blood spurting on the walls, ceiling, and vanity as he stumbled around the bathroom, dousing me in death. The killer clown pitched toward me and I stuck him in the gut, jerked upward, and he crashed to the floor, striking his head off the vanity on his way down.

A low rattle gurgled in his throat.

With my hair and clothes drenched in blood, I emerged from the bathroom. Pressed my back against the door, trapping him inside, and slid down to the floor, my arms latched around bent knees.

Patti shrieked, her voice carrying through cathedral-high ceilings.

Breathless, I waved toward the exit. "Niko." My dry mouth barely formed words. "Outside."

Patti kicked off her heels and ran toward the front door. To allow a moment of repose, I closed my eyes. When my eyelids fluttered open Niko was charging straight at me, determination on his face.

Choking back tears, he squatted to my level. "Are you hurt? Is this your blood?" He fired off questions faster than I could comprehend.

"It's over."

His Adam's apple rose and fell. "I don't know what that means. Babe? Talk to me, honey."

The room whirled round and round. Niko's face grew more and more blurry.

"Babe?" He scooped me into his arms, my hands dangling by his waist, and sprinted for the exit. When he burst through the door, he shouted to Frankie, "Help me!"

With the last bit of energy I could muster, I stroked the side of his face. "He's dead." As my eyes rolled closed, I smirked a satisfied grin.

Chapter Fifty

Three months later... July 3rd, 2008 5:00 p.m.

The search of Dimitris Kokkinos' home revealed the demented man behind the clown mask. In the pile of newspapers Niko found a photograph of a young boy, beaten and bloody. His left hand had third-degree burns. Behind him, an angry woman scowled at the camera. We could only conclude that I'd been right about the abuse, but we had no way to substantiate my theory or to ID the woman in the photograph. The state had no record of abuse in the Kokkinos household. Didn't mean much. Kids get abused every day in this country, and many hide the family secret for years.

What bothered me most was, who took the picture? Shot at an upward trajectory, it might be a sibling. Also, I never discovered how I got ensnared in his crosshairs, except for our brief meeting at the library. Did he see his mother in me? Had he become so psychotic that when he read *Scarred* he related to John Doe? Or had he taken on his persona?

I wanted no part of going back to that rundown hellhole. For me and Noah, the nightmare ended the night I stole Kokkinos' life, and took back control of mine.

Niko flew Noah around the living room, his tiny arms extended like airplane wings. Ruger and I snuggled on the floor. The excitement triggered Colt's playful nature, and he ran circles around Niko's tuxedo-clad legs, chirping barks at his baby brother. Noah belly-laughed. Niko giggled too. Ruger gazed up at me, a wide grin spreading across his furry face. The darkness overshadowing our lives had turned to sunshine, and our family reaped the rewards. Blissful. Content. Pure joy.

I cupped my hands around my mouth. "Ground control to Captain Quintano. Do you copy?"

Mimicking a plane approaching the runway, Niko swooped Noah over our heads, and he belly-laughed. "Nicely done, Captain Quintano. Your landing gear's coming down." He buzzed him around the living room one last time, and Noah screamed with delight. Ruger buried his face in my lap, massive chocolate paws over his eyes.

"The guests will be here soon, babe. Shouldn't you get dressed?"

"Where's my maid of honor?"

Right on cue, Frankie slinked into the room wearing a fitted evening gown that hugged her curves. Slitted up the sides from mid-shin to thigh, her perfect breasts burst out the deep neckline. Chestnut locks cascaded past her shoulders, one side clipped away from her face by a baby's breath comb. She twirled from side to side. "Whaddaya think?"

"Stunning. I absolutely love that dress. You have to let me borrow it some night."

Still swaying, she leaned back and winked. "Course." A millisecond later, a fist flung to her thin hips. "Why are you still in sweats?"

A knock at the front door made me flinch, and I sprang to my feet. "Saved by the bell." When I answered the door our jolly mailman greeted me with a friendly smile. "Hey, George."

"Gotta package ya need to sign fer, Mrs. Quintano."

I signed his clipboard and passed it back, and he handed me a Priority Mail Sleeve. "Thank you, George."

He tipped his hat. "Ya have yerself a great day."

"You too." I brought the package to the coffee table, and a zing zipped up my arms. "Did you buy me a wedding gift, Mr. Quintano? You didn't have to do that, but I'm so glad you did."

Confusion rolled over Niko's face. "Yeah. It's upstairs."

I tore open the envelope. Inside was a card.

"Did Jess say couldn't make it, or something?"

"No," I said. "She's coming." With a letter opener I slit the inner envelope. The photograph on the front of the card depicted an ivory wedding cake with pink roses made from frosting. "Oh, this is pretty." When I flipped it open and read the sentiment inside, I dropped it like it'd burst into flames.

"Who's it from?" Spread-open on the carpet, Niko bent down to read it.

I'll see you soon, Sage Quintano.

xo,

John Doe

My stomach turned rock-hard. "When Kokkinos mentioned our mutual acquaintance, I assumed he'd found the information from my books, but now…oh my God, Niko. What if the hacker's behind this? He's still out there."

Niko smothered me in his arms. "Babe, we're renewing our vows today. Let's discuss this later."

"But—"

Eyes shifting toward Noah, he shushed me. "Later, in private, without little ears around."

Noah reached for the card, but Frankie beat him to it. "Little man, why don't you help your fairy godmother with the cake. If I'm not mistaken, there's some frosting on the edge. We should probably make sure it's perfect."

"Yay!" Prompting her to pick him up, Noah raised his arms above his head.

"Wow. You're getting heavy." In the archway between the living room and kitchen, Frankie glanced back at us. "Hey, love birds." She raised the side of her dress to show her garter holster. "If anyone dares to crash this party, they'll never know what hit 'em."

Niko framed my face in his hands. "She's right. For all we know, Kokkinos left this card for a friend to mail in the event of his death."

"Yeah. A friend like the hacker."

He pressed two fingers to my lips. "Don't let him steal another second from you." He patted my ass. "Now get dressed. I can't wait to remarry my best friend, and then we're off to sail around the Caribbean. C'mon, babe. Our new life awaits."

Upbeat, I said, "Can't wait." Inside, however, a foreboding dread seeped into my soul. What darkness awaited us? It might not be today, next week, next month, or even next year, but sometime in the not-so-distant future this nightmare would resume. No question.

ABOUT SUE COLETTA

Member of Mystery Writers of America, Sisters in Crime, and International Thriller Writers, Sue Coletta is a multi-published, award-winning author. Her work has appeared in numerous anthologies and collections, including a forensic article in InSinC Quarterly. In addition to her popular crime resource blog, Sue co-hosts the radio show "Partners In Crime" on Blog Talk Radio. She's also the communications manager for the Serial Killer Project and Forensic Science and founder of #ACrimeChat on Twitter, where she helps other crime writers' stories ring true.

She lives with her husband in a quaint country town in rural New Hampshire where she's surrounded by moose, deer, black bears, and the sultry songs of nature. Course, Sue would love to snuggle with the wildlife, but her husband frowns on the idea.

Get in touch with Sue:

Website
www.suecoletta.com

Facebook
www.facebook.com/SueColetta1
www.facebook.com/SuePhillipsColetta

Twitter
www.twitter.com/SueColetta1

Blog
www.crimewriterblog.com

Goodreads
www.goodreads.com/SueColetta

Google+
plus.google.com/u/0/+SusanColetta

StumbleUpon
www.stumbleupon.com/stumbler/SueColetta1

Pinterest
www.pinterest.com/suecoletta1

LinkedIn
www.linkedin.com/pub/sue-coletta/a0/1b9/161

Tirgearr Publishing
www.tirgearrpublishing.com/authors/Coletta_Sue

BOOKS BY SUE COLETTA

GRAFTON COUNTY SERIES

MARRED, book 1
Released: November 2015
ISBN: 9781311566508

When Sage Quintano barely escapes from a brutal serial killer, husband Niko, a homicide detective, insists they move to rural New Hampshire, where he accepts a position as sheriff. Sage buries secrets from that night—secrets she swears to take to her deathbed. Three years pass and Sage's twin sister goes missing. Is the killer trying to lure Sage into a deadly trap to end his reign of terror?